The Wid[illegible] e

Antonia Swinson

I should like to thank the following people who have helped me with this book. My husband, Alan Reid, and brother, Sheridan Swinson, for all the their help and patience. To Lindsey Good of Language Connection, William Jackson, and staff at the press office of the Finnish Embassy.

First Published in 1995
Gracewing
Fowler Wright Books
Southern Avenue, Leominster
Herefordshire HR6 0QF

Gracewing Books are distributed

In New Zealand by
Catholic Supplies Ltd
80 Adelaide Rd
Wellington
New Zealand

In Australia by
Chales Paine Pty
8 Ferris Street
North Parramatta
NSW 2151 Australia

In U.S.A. by
Morehouse Publishing
P.O. Box 1321
Harrisburg
PA 17105
U.S.A.

In Canada by
Meakin and Associates
Unit 17, 81 Auriga Drive
Nepean, Ontario, KZE 7Y5
Canada

Cover Design by Julie Giddens
Cover Picture by Dawn Sheermen-Chase
ISBN 0 85244 318 8

Typesetting by Action Typesetting Limited, Gloucester
Printed by The Cromwell Press, Melksham, Wiltshire

Chapter One

West London in June. Choking heat, choking tourists, and traffic going nowhere. Who on earth would choose to live in this crazy place apart from the mad, the bad and the super-rich?

Screech! The taxi rounded the corner as if on one wheel and skidded to a halt outside the yellow front door. Harriet, who had been peering through its grimy windows willing the driver to get from Shepherds Bush to Hammersmith in four minutes, waited for an eternity for the man to unlock the door. Come on, come on! Click. Stressed and mad applied to her, she thought as she leapt out onto the pavement. A mistake, the skirt of her suit was much too narrow. She ignored the ripping sound.

'Just wait here will you? I won't be long.'

Keys, keys, why did she always put the wrong one in? There! At last, she turned it in the lock and rushed inside her neglected little house. Automatically she stooped and picked up the junk mail, and threw it on the hall table, the answering machine flickered next to it. No time to worry about it. She leapt over the piles of ironing on the stairs and crashed into Laura's room.

From the landing window she could see the taxi down in the road, meter ticking, costing a fortune, purring in boiling heat. The driver was reading the *Sun*, his elbow sticking out of the window. Where? Where was the script in all this chaos?

Laura, of course, had howled hysterical pleas for help down a crackling line from Paddington, but hadn't bothered to tell her even what colour paper it was printed on. Was it pale yellow or pale blue, or white with the BBC logo splashed conveniently along the top? Laura hadn't even been sure where she had left it. By the mirror, she thought. Great. And which bloody mirror? There were books everywhere, in piles, or shoved in corners, clothes falling out of of the wardrobe, the bed half made, bank statements and the previous week's Sunday papers sliding off the crumpled quilt. On the carpet, old *Tatlers*, warred for space with apple cores, empty tights packets and crumpled balls of paper. A packet of condoms peeked cheekily out of the dressing table drawer. That was Laura, ever the optimist. Where had she left the script?

The taxi driver hooted. Then she heard him yelling through the letter box. 'You're pushing your luck luv, we'll get stuck on the West Way.' Wretched man. Wretched bloody script. Why was she even doing this? Laura could have got a later train, got another script from the production office? Even Tom had managed to remember his script, even when she'd had to do everything else for him. Tool of the trade. But then, Tom had learnt his lines days before, whereas Laura busked through every script like everything else she did. Eyes and teeth. Typical.

Harriet caught sight of herself in the dusty mirror, the long pale red hair plastered over her shiny face, crumpled silk blouse, what a sight! Her hair was too long, it was driving her mad, she kept saying she wanted it cut off, but never had time to ring the hairdresser's still less to turn up. She had what people called an expressive, interesting face, beautiful when she smiled, which wasn't often, some days. No make-up left, and was that a spot coming? Fantastic. 'Beep beep' came from the street below. 'Shut up!'

She found it at last, wedged under a fruit bowl which contained a rotting grapefruit and a dead wasp. Pale green this time. Laura's demented scrawl all over it. *Auctioneer*, just the title, and the writers' names, were enough for Harriet to know exactly what it would be like. Another Sunday-night drama serial, with spectacular scenery, designer clothes, wooden direction, this time set in a west-country auction house, but it could easily have been in a marina, or a country club. All the story lines, and the characters were interchangeable.

And, as usual, Laura, ('L-ow – as in wow, darling, not Law as in bore. Italian way, never heard of Petrarch's Muse?') would play the plump efficient secretary, with lines such as, 'Really! Your coffee's right in front of you Gerard!' Going on past form, her character would either turn out to be the other woman, or part of the office furniture, depending on how nice Laura was to the director and the writers before the second series. With empires to be built within the BBC drama department there usually was a second series – sadly for the general public. Though not for Laura's precarious finances, Harriet had to admit.

She just couldn't look at the room anymore, the smell of perfume and Laura was unmistakable. Harriet fled down the stairs, tripping over the ironing, and sending clothes spilling down onto the hall carpet. Was the rest of the house much better? Harriet thought, but didn't stop to pick them up. She only ever cleaned the house at night, in the five minutes between the evening news and crashing into oblivion, and the only reason the place was tidy, was because she was ruthless at throwing things out. Never enough time. 'Damn!' A piece of chewing gum had stuck onto Harriet's shoe, and then attached itself to a large birthday card. She flapped down the through the hall and out into her front garden, slamming the door behind her.

Heat shimmered in the street, distorting the shapes of the terraced houses in the taxi's window screen. As she came out, the driver looked pointedly at his watch,

'Sorry, got what I wanted. Paddington station as fast as possible please.'

'When's the train, love?'

'Four thirty.'

'On a Friday afternoon? Leave it out.'

He drew away in that extra slow way, Harriet thought all drivers must learn with the 'Knowledge', just for occasions when captive passengers were foaming at the mouth. Harriet was made of sterner stuff. She sat back, she wouldn't foam. If Laura's train had gone, it was Laura's problem, it was bloody nice of her to do this at the end of the week.

'Husband been dead long has he?'

Harriet was thinking of Laura. No wonder after a while all her men fled in the end, she frightened them off. Men were all little boys, they hated other people's left-overs in bed, only their own. If Laura ever had any publicity as the nineties' cool assertive woman, she would personally sell pictures of her room to the *News of the World*!

'Sorry? Wasn't listening.'

'Been a widow long then?'

Widow. How did he know? Fool, she'd said so on their cosy ton-up just now, down the Goldhawk Road, when he'd asked what her 'hubby' thought of England's lousy score. Why hadn't she just said he thought it was lousy too? She hadn't been very clever.

'Er five years.' She could see a harassed woman with three obviously sunburnt children crossing the road.

'You'll have to marry again. Nothing like it, married life. Second time around's better. I've got two stepdaughters as well. Life's more comfortable the second time you call.'

Oh no, he's not going to sing all the way there! Two step-daughters, ghastly prospect.

She unstuck the birthday card from her shoe. Laura's. Looked like Jeremy's writing, a good sign when agents knew you were still alive. 'Darling Laura, many more, love J.' Laura had been in a foul mood all last week, saying now that she was 40, she was in the dead zone, and would probably never work again. Tom had been a Gemini too. He would have been only 34 this month. Harriet found herself sighing. She thought of him so often at this time of year. The odd thing no-one ever seemed to understand, was that she didn't feel any less married, just because he wasn't around. Until death us do part, was rubbish. Though now she found it hard to picture him except in certain surroundings, like the pub round the corner.

She had once read about a mother whose children had been abducted to Pakistan by their father, who had trained herself not to go out shopping after school, or look at children in the street. She too had developed this selective vision, skimming round articles about bereavement and heart attacks. It made life more manageable. Features on single-parent families she could handle. That was not a category that seemed to apply to Billy and her. That was for unmarried mothers, divorced women, both of whom had had a measure of choice.

The man was still singing, and he kept turning round smiling at her. She wished he would keep his eye on the road. He had that look. Most men went a bit silly when they found out she was a widow. Good gracious a young widow, how was she managing the bills and what was she doing for sex? As if being a widow in your thirties put you somehow into a different category, in which your money worries were more acute, and your lack of sex more erotic. And what did other single women do? Muddled along and did without, that's what! Laura told her she was being paranoid, and to get out more, join something. But it was such an effort going out alone, and even worse having to be with someone else.

Tom, like most actors, had been a gossip, who had loved the latest news who had got which part, and better still who hadn't! He had told wonderfully funny stories too, when unemployment had not made him hell to live with.

Harriet sometimes wrote him long gossipy letters late at night, curled up in their bed, about Billy's life at boarding school, who his friends were, his fencing, his singing. How the business was doing, small triumphs like a new client, small hurts, staff problems, the latest details of their friends, his parents, her father. Gradually the number of people she had met since his death had grown, but she told him all about the new ones anyway, though all the time she was aware, that the these people saw her differently. She was no longer the carefree, seize-the-day, student Harriet she had once been, which was why perhaps she saw less of their old friends. But then she wasn't exactly twenty anymore, 35 was a horribly round number.

The letters often ran for pages. In the winter, a little girl again, she would screw them up and push them on the fire, hoping, just like the children's advertisement for a nanny in *Mary Poppins*, they would float up the chimney, and reach his cloud, where he would be sitting happily knocking back the booze, and planning which Monday morning would be best to slosh rain down on the car she'd just washed. The swine! Absurd, childish, yet this vision soothed her in a way no amount of kind words ever could.

From the depths of her handbag, came the intrusive whine of her mobile phone. 'Mrs Gosse, it's George Russell speaking. Your office told me to ring on this number for my lesson.'

Harriet snapped back into the present. She'd said she'd do the lesson instead of Mireille because she had had to go to the dentist! How could she have forgotten? The taxi, which had been crawling along Shepherd's Bush, suddenly tore into third gear at the Shepherd's Bush roundabout.

Flung forward almost to her knees, Harriet ruffled through her briefcase for Mr Russell's coursework. If + pluperfect = conditional. Laminated plastics. What was the French for laminated plastics? Her mind went a blank.

'Monsieur Russell?' She took a deep breath and in French, oozed Gallic charm concentrate down the line to Pinner. 'I had intended to ring you this afternoon. Mireille has had to go to the dentist, so we shall certainly have to arrange another lesson at a time convenient to you. But I thought, not to waste this opportunity, perhaps we could do the exercise on page one.'

Harriet knew that when Rome burned, she was a damned sight better than Laura at playing the cool nineties business-woman. Keep the man sweet, Harriet, she thought, we're talking school fees here.

'Par exemple, si vous aviez terminé votre travail, vous auriez pu aller au theatre. Mais oui. Alors numero deux.'

The driver eyes met Harriet's in his mirror. Harriet could see him thinking '*Très* sexy, French on the mobile, one of those dirty 0898 numbers are you?' The traffic came to a dignified stop on the Westway. 'Never make it now love', he said. Harriet ignored him. On the other end of the line, the client's accent was like sandpaper, how could Mireille bear to teach him? '*Oui très bien, ou peut-être, Monsieur, si vous etiez sorti, vous auriez rencontre Marçel.*'

She worked through her lesson notes, wondering if he would get a twenty-minute lesson, on the other hand if he did, then Laura's train would definitely have left.

The taxi lurched off the West Way, and temporarily the

line went dead as it went under the flyover. Mr George Russell deputy sales manager of Rushton Plastics (UK) plc sitting in Pinner, was feeling waggish. '*Où est vous Madame*, Piccadilly Circus?' He loved his phone lessons on a Friday, didn't feel a fool at all, more an international high-flyer, not just a cog in the sales force, third in line to any trips to la belle France. '*Je voudrai. . . .*'

But whatever it was he did *voudrai*, was cut off forever, when, finding its form at last, the taxi tore down the slope into Paddington station, shooting up in the air as it ran over the newly installed sleeping policemen. Harriet shoved the phone back into her handbag. She'd have to get him back later, somehow.

'What was all that about then?' The driver winked salaciously.

'Laminated plastics. Thank you, here you are!

By the time he'd put the money away, and thought of a witty reply, Harriet had disappeared.

The station was a sea of hot striped shirts, and fraying tempers. Like hungry penguins at the Zoo waiting for their fish, middle-aged men stood expectant, looking up at the announcement board, poised to dive the second their train flapped up. Nearby, as if to mock such hopes, the Western Region Brass Band played Chattanooga Choo Choo, whilst the voice on the tannoy announced yet another delay for the Bristol service. The announcer's apology on behalf of British Rail sounded triumphant, as if, Harriet thought, she only had to get to Perivale, when her shift was over, thank you very much.

Harriet stopped running. What a waste of time and money. Obviously Laura had already left.

'Harriet! Darling! Over here!'

Laura's husky contralto boomed across the concourse with the practice gained from more years demonstrating kitchen products at Debenhams, than she cared to admit. 'Over here! The train's late, thank God!'

Flap, flap, flap went the announcement board. Burnt-out executives swooped past Harriet. Every penguin for himself.

Harriet could see Laura waving, and she waved the script

pretending to slit her throat. From this distance, Laura looked quite petite, funny how the camera made people gain ten pounds, and she always looked plump on television, however much she starved. Bones were the thing, Tom had always said. Harriet began to worm her way through the crowd.

'Laura, I can't think of a printable adjective for your script. The cab cost a fortune. Don't ever do this again.' Harriet flopped down in the plastic seat next to her. She felt like kicking Laura's mock-Gucci luggage all over the concourse. 'Don't look so cool and boody collected.'

'I'm not cool and collected. I've been shitting myself for the last half-hour.' Laura was rifling through the script. 'Thanks Harriet – '

'You cannot imagine the traffic, and I had to give a lesson, to this plastics man in the cab. We were cut off mid-excercise. God knows what he thought. If I've lost that business, you're dead.'

'I'm so sorry Harriet. I just don't know why I left it behind. There's this one scene that's not sticking.'

'But your lines never stick.'

'It's just not as easy for me darling. Not like Tom, he used to learn them on the loo!'

'I know. We would all be hopping outside banging on the door!'

They laughed.

Harriet piled all her hair on her head hoping it would cool her down. It didn't.

'And now I've got to fight my way back to the office and placate Mrs Mac, which won't be easy, she was really pissed off when I rushed out. As for your room, I nearly threw up.'

'Awful isn't it?'

'A black hole.'

'Darling I already feel a heel, a rotten lodger, a rotten actress who can't learn her lines. I promise I'll come back laden with black bin liners and be hugely tidy.'

Laura lit a cigarette, always a sign of apology, and blew what was probably the finest smoked ring Paddington station had seen for months.

'You'd better, Marchant. I forgive you, just why are actors so hard to live with?'

'That's easy, we never, ever grow up. Good God, look at that. Where do people get the energy from, in this heat?'

In front of them, a few yards away to one side of the weighing machine, a couple were embracing with real passion, completely oblivious to their surroundings. At first, Harriet thought it was a young girl, she was so slim, and wore torn jeans and a cheap white T-shirt, but as she turned, Harriet could see she was older, in her thirties perhaps, something about her arms and her neck. But the man was much younger, tall and powerfully built, muscles bulging out of his white shirt, his navy blazer was neatly folded over the briefcase at his feet. It was an odd combination.

'Don't think they've got it quite right do you, H.? I think you need a bus stop and a line of disapproving old ladies really, for the full effect.'

'Stop looking, Laura, they might turn round.'

'Darling, they're hard at it. We're talking toyboy time. Now should I feel envious, or pity her for having to be so physical in this heat?' Laura put her head on one side to copy the angle of the woman's head. 'He is rather scrummy, though that thick neck makes one suspect that he might be two cogs short of a Moulimix.'

'Wherever do you get these expressions?' Harriet laughed, watching the couple for a moment. They never stopped for a second, not even for the announcement of the departure of the 5.10 for Swindon.

'Where's his other hand gone? Naughty. Personally, I think he looks a bit too energetic. Couldn't cope with all that rampant testosterone. But that's what you could do with H. Good meaningless sex, and lots of it. Trust your auntie Laura.'

'No comment.'

'O.K., O.K.'

'Laura, that boy does seem familiar, and the woman does too. Who do you suppose they are? Do we know them?'

'Luvvies you mean? No I don't think so, unless they're rehearsing for a remake of *The Graduate*, no she's too young, and he looks too thick. I'm just wondering if he'll ever let her up for air. No, no, give the girl a break! Phew! Now that's not fair, how come she's still kept her lipstick on? Awful shade though.'

'The 4.30 train to Gloucester is now standing at Platform 5. We apologise for the delay, this was due to signal failure.'

'Hoo-bloody-ray.' Laura stood up, and stamped out her cigarette.

'I'll take this case.' Harriet picked it up, and started to walk towards the trains.

'Wait for me. Thanks again darling, for bringing the script, you're an angel. Think of me working on it tonight. You know, I've got to kiss David Forsyth on Thursday, you know, the hunk in the chocolate ad. What a drag'. She lied! They stopped at the barrier. Laura looked at Harriet, 'Look after yourself H., and take some time off when Billy comes home. You need cherishing! I'll babysit.'

'Liar, you'll be living at the beautician.'

'I hate you Harriet Goody-two-shoes Gosse, you know me so well. How depressing.'

'Hope the shoot goes well. Ring me.'

'I'm so nervous it's ridiculous. No I'm not. Big breasts. In! Out! Give my love to darling Billy. Oh and enjoy his Speech Day, I forgot about that. Take lots of pictures.'

Laura waved and rushed along the platform. A dark head in exuberant pink amid the sea of bobbing shirts. A crowd of young schoolchildren went through after her, noisy, chattering, their teachers looking hot and desperate. Harriet turned and headed for the Underground, she looked around for the couple, but they had disappeared, as if they had been just a ghostly taunt. Fumbling for her rail pass, she was unexpectedly blinded by tears. Why they were there, she was much too exhausted to determine.

* * *

It was after seven when Harriet finally stepped off the tube. So weary, her briefcase, seemed to weigh like bricks. What a pay-off the devil had had from her good deed for the-day! She had got back to office to meet three last-minute crises, teachers throwing tantrums, and endless niggles, clients ringing up to grouch, suppliers ringing up to whinge. Let me out! Walking out of the station Harriet saw the rush-hour traffic still grinding its way into Chiswick, and suddenly wished she had leapt onto the train with Laura. A nice west-country location, only a few lines to learn, the luxury of it. Actors did not know they were born.

From the tube, the green of the Ravenscourt Park always burst in upon the eye after Hammersmith station, and tonight in the heat, there were still people lying on the grass grabbing the urban sun. Walking through the streets towards her house, there were all the familiar sights of a West London summer, people smoking on their doorsteps, windows open, all along the streets, and front doors too, in spite of the security risk.

Sounds of music, West Indian, jazz, classical. Cooking smells, delicious and pungent. All hit her as she passed by the small packed-together houses. More inner-city than Chiswick, less iffy than Shepherds Bush. Her own little patch of the London jungle, Brackenbury Village, as it now seemed to be called by every upwardly mobile resident under fifty, had its own familiar feel. Claustrophobic or cosy, moving up, clinging on, or giving up, its own particular street-life was never dull. A large Rolls Royce sneaked past, the chauffeur was obviously trying to cut out of one traffic hold-up only to crash into another. In the back, a middle-aged man, was reading a newspaper and smoking a cigar, but his windows were firmly closed, safe from such a mixed area.

'Coo-ee! Harriet! Araminta, stay on the pavement, a car could come round any minute. Florian, whatever it is you're doing, stop it!'

Two joggers came panting out of the off-licence clutching bottles of chilled Frascati, and Georgiana Gaskell, Harriet's next-door neighbour and uncrowned Queen of Brackenbury Village, was standing on the pavement, as Harriet trudged round the corner. She was wearing beige shorts, which showed off her rather knobbly knees, and was carrying a bottle of Evian water and a bag of frozen *mange tout*. There was no escape.

'Hello Georgiana.' By the time Harriet had reached the last syllable of her name, she had succeeded in injecting some semblance of friendly enthusiasm. But Georgiana was not fooled. 'You look so hot Harriet, thoroughly miserable. Poor dear. It must be such hell teaching French on the phone all day.'

'I don't. My staff do it now mostly.' Harriet tried hard not to grit her teeth.

'Now listen, Florian, walk in front properly, and stop picking your nose! How much a term? Harriet, Robert and I were wondering if you'd donate some food, and those sweet little kitchen chairs of yours to the street party. It's going to be next Saturday, before everyone goes away.'

'But that will mean Billy will miss it.'

'Well yes, but it can't be helped I'm afraid.'

'Oh. I'll have to leave it to you to contact everyone. Including the Browns and the Patels', said Harriet pointedly, knowing Georgiana was nothing if not politically incorrect.

'Er, yes. Must. Poor Harriet. Such a tired girl. At least you never have to worry about decorators. Mine broke the floral lavatory bowl this morning. Robert is going to go absolutely spare!' Harriet thought Georgiana's martyred tones were a joke, as if everyone in the entire road didn't know that she had lived with the same decorators in great harmony for years.

Harriet had often wondered why Georgiana had not decamped long ago, to Wiltshire or the New Forest. Then one day, she had suddenly realised that she and Georgiana actually moved into two different places. While she and Tom had moved to Hammersmith, in the early eighties, scruffy, cheap, unloved and inner city, where rasta music filled the skies, and the odd mattress decorated the doorsteps, Georgiana and many others who had moved in later, had come not to Hammersmith, but to bijou Brackenbury Village, an area of chic, terraced cottages and small, stucco houses, where no window was without its full quota of Viennese blinds, and calico swags, tastefully sandwiched between Hammersmith Broadway and the Goldhawk Road with dear, wonderful Queen Charlotte's Hospital.

Shops appeared, the owners also certain that they were in Brackenbury Village, wine bars too, and trendy, little restaurants with celebrated chefs doing their thing. The delicatessens, and the corner shops then started selling avocados, radicchio and the *Spectator*. By the time the peak of the property boom was reached in 1988, simple pretty cottages built for artisans and humble clerks ninety years before, had been pushed into the £175,000 bracket. The clerks were replaced by architects, lawyers and advertising executives on huge joint mortgages. And Harriet found she had succeeded in moving districts without leaving home.

Even now, though the nineties' recession had bitten deep into any middle-class sense of order and fair play, and made the locals nostalgic about the once ubiquitous skips, Georgiana and her friends still lived in Brackenbury Village, come hell or repossession. Though now they had to cope with the arrival of noisy tenants brought in by the hated local Housing Association, who were now buying up property for a song; and pretend not to hear the loud music which rent hot summer evenings, which was certainly not Bach or Vivaldi, not even the Nigel Kennedy version. Yet the Brackenbury Village Society continued to thrive with its social calendar. There was even talk of starting up a branch of the W.I.

Harriet always felt a rush of pleasure when she saw her own little house down the street in all its brave shabbiness. Wisteria looped over the white-painted brickwork, Home, a haven for Billy, Laura and her. Even if she could not boast a German kitchen, a supine male meal ticket or a loft conversion, there was always the satisfaction of knowing that she passed with the Village Mafia because her unswagged curtains were, at least, lined! She had once caught Georgiana mouthing the words 'unlined curtains' to a fellow member of the National Childbirth Trust, when describing the new Irish family at 45. An absurd vision had struck that day of ripping out the lining in her own front curtains, and dancing with them naked in the street.

They parted at Harriet's gate. Georgiana looked charitably at the cracked paving stones in her tiny front garden, 'When does Billy come home from school? We really must have him over to play.'

'Two weeks' time. I can't wait.' Harriet felt it better not to commit Billy. Florian and Araminta were his *bêtes noires*.

'Mark and I have decided we can't bear to part with Florian till he's thirteen. He can try for Eton then. Boarding's such a wrench at eight isn't it? You're so brave!' Georgiana patted Harriet's arm, and then shepherded her brood up her own carefully tiled path. 'As for the fees, I don't know how people manage at all. Not that you'd get him into a good day school now I'm afraid, you've left it far too late. Bye!'

'Thank you Georgiana', Harriet thought as she let herself in for the second time that day. 'Just remember she doesn't mean to be an insensitive, snobbish intractable old cow, she was just bred that way, to marry a bore who is probably juggling his debts on his gold cards as I speak!' Her tortoiseshell kitten came purring round her ankles. Thank God for the sanity of cats.

No Billy, no Laura. Just bills and a note from 'The Willows' announcing changes in visiting hours. They'd be banning visitors altogether next, on the basis that so few of their elderly residents ever got any, it would be better not to arouse jealousy.

She put the radio on in the kitchen, the CD player on in the living room, the clock radio in her bedroom, but drew the line at the musical box in Billy's bedroom. The radio in the bathroom was always kept on Radio 4, and she filled the bath with lavender water and bubbles then lay back, still aware of the real silence behind the false companionship.

Yet this should be, what psychologists call, the flashpoint of the day. Children demanding baths, supper and attention from tired mothers, husbands coming through the door demanding meals and attention from tired wives. Juggling, washing machine on, fishfingers and whisky at the ready. Yet here she was at 35, on a Friday night, soaking up the bubbles and thinking about painting her toe nails instead of cleaning the loo. Her life had other flashpoints.

Through the open bathroom door, she could see family photographs nailed up all over the landing wall. Her rogues gallery. Her mother, frail and pretty in a mini skirt, Tom and her on their wedding day, they looked so young! Not to mention penniless. Penniless actor meets penniless Edinburgh graduate language teacher at Edinburgh fringe. Hot kisses on Carlton Hill almost leading to hypothermia, followed by nuptials in an even more frozen church in W6. Never would she forget the surprise when her father offered to buy them the house. Unbelievable. The even greater surprise came, when the cheque hadn't bounced. Dressed like George Melly on a good day, and a tramp on a bad, she'd never thought he had any money at all.

Jester Dunne, artist impossible, whose oils had flowed in and out of fashion like a slick, always said money came along when you needed it, and painting like an avenging angel, in the Auerbach style, it usually did. He had dragged her along through France and Italy, leaving her to grub about with the local kids in whichever village took his fancy. She had grown up a trilingual gypsy full of disjointed learning, the object of fitful fatherly affection. They had belonged together. A pair of vagabonds. Yet while she had poured on him a little girl's devotion, she had always known somehow, that he didn't need it. That he reserved his real passion for the colourful women on his canvas and his couch, rather than for the flesh and blood creation of his loins.

Later wooed by American matrons, Jester had descended on Martha's Vineyard each summer lecturing, and doing none too complimentary portraits with irascible charm. The stroke had screwed up his hands and his perception of depth, and to his fury, had made him stop painting. Though he had once announced during Sunday lunch at the Willies as he called it, that the place was far too full of scraggy tits to make him get his paints out – or his pants down come to that. Luckily only Harriet had been able to make out what he was saying, and the residents had continued to be enchanted.

The phone rang.

'Mum, it's Billy.'

'Darling, how are you? Are you O.K? I'm really looking forward to Speech Day.' Harriet had learnt the hard way not to overdo it.

She really wanted to say that without you, I feel I have a leg missing, that you can't possibly know what it is to be without your child. What the guilt is like to live with. But she didn't. He was getting a marvellous education, and lots of male company, and he would never be a latchkey only child as she had been, heating up cold pasta on the stove, doing her homework alone in the cold house at the kitchen table, waiting, waiting all the time, often late into the night, for her father to come back from his studio.

'I'm singing the *Sanctus* in the service, though you probably won't be able to see me.'

'How exciting. Will they record it?'

'Shouldn't think so. Too mouldy.'

'Oh what a shame. Listen Billy, are you eating? Are you drinking that extra milk I'm paying for through the nose?'

'Yes Mum, do stop fussing. By the way, Matron's just got hitched to Rogers, and Crouch has gone ballistic. It's been going on for months in her flat, but he's only just got wind of it.'

'Matron, but she's in her thirties?'

'Yes, really ancient, but still pretty tasty.'

'Watch it! But he is a bit young for her.'

'Not according to her! Must go. Bye, Mum.'

'Yes, bye darling.' The line was already dead.

Of course! The couple at the station, they would have been getting the train back to School. *Nom de nom de nom*. A new twist, a RICH toy boy. Clever, not-so-old Matron! Harriet went downstairs to open the wine. What was she going to wear? It would have to be the pink dress she'd bought last year, with her one and only Philip Somerville hat. Now rather past its sell-by date, but still classy. She smiled as she remembered how Tom had brought it home with a flourish with his first cheque from Sampson House, then got as drunk as a tick. They were really going to be in the money, he had told her with a sozzled smile, before crashing out asleep on the sitting room floor. Two musketeers.

Later getting into bed, she thought how angry he would have been about Billy going to boarding school. Yet how could she have built up the business unless he had gone? Or had there been an alternative that she had simply not had the wit to see? Widowed parenting was an eternally one-sided conversation.

Without thinking, she picked up a small smooth block of wood off the bedside table.

'Mum, I kept planing it to get it straight, and every time I got one side straight, the other got wonky. Now, that's all that's left. The other boys have made magazine racks, but I couldn't do it.'

Eight-year-old Billy, still the new boy in his overlarge uniform and crumpled little face, had stood there in the Woodwork Department on Parents' Day fighting back the tears, and holding the small piece of wood out towards her. Aware she was breaking a hundred unwritten codes, she had knelt down and folded him in her arms.

She had told him how, at one school in Brighton, she had been told in Domestic Science to make a nightie. Not likely, since she didn't even know how to thread the sewing machine. At the end-of-term fashion show, there were girls mincing up on stage, who had made whole wardrobes of coats and dresses; while her own effort had been banished, a ragged tube of turquoise nylon, with two holes where the sleeves should have been, and a zip hanging precariously down one side. When Jester had seen it afterwards, he had opened champagne, and he and his friends had made her dance in it on the kitchen table, toasting all Domestic Science teachers to perdition. How she and Billy had howled with laughter among the perfect lampstands and tie holders. There is always something rather comforting about inherited incompetence.

Chapter Two

An angel passing over the roof of Number 43 Sandringham Square that hot, Saturday morning, would have been struck by its expensive perfection. Verdi's *Rigoletto* streamed out of the gleaming white French windows, over the black railings of the first-floor balcony and out into the square, to tease two roadsweepers, who decided it was probably Pavagrotty. Bacon smells from the basement, wafted onto the pavement, while the flowers in the window boxes wilted seductively.

Inside all was cool, and unharmonious. In the hall a Max Friedman glass sculpture retched at a tiger skin, Victorian holidaymakers at Southend-on-Sea looked in sepia incomprehension at the Tizia lamp on the Linley desk in the drawing room. Up and down the stairs fought a dozen unhappy marriages. A Steven Conroy urban brawl leered at a lifesize papier mâché Nubian slaveboy, bought on a whim from Harrods' decorative furniture department. The ladder-backed Mackintosh chairs in the dining room froze in presbyterian disgust at the generous proportions of the Santiago School steel phallus, on which someone had stuck a New York City car sticker 'Get Even With Your Children – Spend Their Inheritance'. 'What inheritance Dickhead?' had been added in felt-tip pen on a freezer label.

Upstairs, on the second-floor bathroom, a Saks silk dressing gown was sliding off a pile of Christie's catalogues, and Placido Domingo's La Donna È Mobile was now a duet, as Richard Longbridge lay in his deep circular jacuzzi belting out a reasonable baritone to his battery-operated rubber duck, on the perfidy of women. The tabloid newspaper he was reading was suspended above the bubbles on a reading frame, though the corners of the pages were wet, as the scented water moved.

He had dark, thick curly hair, large hands with manicured nails, and long legs which seemed to make the bath seem small. A generous fleshy, boyish face, which though still handsome, was now tipping expensively into early middle-age.

MILLIONAIRE'S SON WEDS MATRON AT TOP PUBLIC SCHOOL. Eton again, or was it Millfield's turn? He stopped turning the pages.

'Bloody fool, you're not supposed actually to marry them', Richard Longbridge observed aloud, while considering whether the big toe on his left foot was rheumatic, or just suffering from M.E. like the rest of him.

Undecided, he went back to his paper, unaccountably groaning with pleasure.

'Schooldays are the best according to millionaire son Boyd Rogers, 19, who yesterday skived off lessons at his posh £11,000 a year public school to wed school Matron Michelle 16 years his senior.'

'Posh public school my foot!' He carried on reading.

As headboy Boyd, son of a multi-millionaire Texan businessman recovered from flu in the School San, romance blossomed at the exclusive St Anthony's, Netbury, Wilts. 'I couldn't resist him even with a red nose and a temperature of 102!' says Kirsty Munro, 36, who admits her mum and dad live in a Paisley council flat.'

'Well I wouldn't have admitted that for a start.'

The coy lovers revealed that they:

* *Enjoyed midnight trysts at the school's 85-acre lake.*

'Damp,' said Richard.

* *Had sex romps in the San*

'Those springs must have made a racket.'

* *And following their secret wedding at a Swindon registry office, now plan to have a baby as soon as possible.'*

Richard Longbridge stretched, and put the paper on the floor. 'Another wee Mary who's upwardly mob-i-le. Talking of whom. . . .'

Suddenly a girl, with short dripping hair emerged from

the water. Breathing hard, she removed the peg from her nose and smiled at him.

'What a star! Victoria, you're wearing one of those ball-breaking smiles you've got to wear or else you lose points. I know the rules you know. How long were you under this time?'

'Two minutes 48 seconds.'

'Felt like longer. Australia's answer to Esther Williams with sex appeal. Which, as we all know, she didn't have. Come here.' He pulled her towards him and kissed her, sending a wave of water pouring onto the French lacquered tiles. 'You synchronised Sydney girls are really quite amazing.' He kissed her again. 'And I intend to work through the whole Olympic team! I'll dive into the middle of one of those flower shapes you all make with your legs. Wham! Underwater sex for hours and hours and hours.'

'You couldn't keep up with us Richard.'

She put the peg on his nose, and got out of the bath, the waves reducing the now soaking paper to mush. Richard threw the frame on the floor, and gave her bare buttocks a slap.

'Ouch! These things hurt, how can you stand wearing them. What cheek. I may be pushing it, but no-one can say I'm losing my stomach muscles then? Look at that!'

Contented, he disappeared beneath the bubbles.

* * *

'Hello, who is it?' Harriet managed to grab the phone with her eyes shut, but the flex had coiled itself round her alarm clock on the bedside table, and sent a glass of water spilling onto the carpet. Very clever.

'Harriet, wake up, it's eight o'clock.'

'Laura, I was awake, though it is Saturday monring.'

'Are you whingeing H.? No? Then try asking how are you my dear Laura, and how did you manage when the train broke down and you had to be transferred by bus to some god-forsaken branch line? And got in at nine o'clock.'

'Well how are you then? What a disaster!'

'I've been up since six. Landlady thought I'd like a fry

up at five thirty, can you imagine?'

'Poor old thing. What are the cast like?'

'Oh not bad. Marjorie's here. Good sort. Do you remember, we saw her in *Ladies In Retirement* in Bromley? Nightmare! David of course, looking all smouldering, and Fenella Frost. Knickers round her ankles as usual. And Derek you know, played the caretaker in *Sampson*?'

'Oh him, give him my love.'

'Asked after you. Were you still alive, that sort of thing.'

'Nice of him.'

'Old bore. Now what are you wearing this morning, wish I could do your slap, you never put on enough blusher.'

'The blue hat, pink dress, and what do you think? Hair up or down?'

'Down, none of the other mums will be able to sit on theirs.'

'Wish you could come?'

'I know, never even seen this school either. Looks frightfully posh in the photographs.'

'Expensive.'

'Still, he'll be able to do all the public-school boys' parts when he's older.'

'Billy is not, repeat not, going into the Business.'

'Yes I know, my son the cost accountant.'

'Banker!'

'Bye H. Enjoy the French master.'

Laura rang off. Incorrigible! Her mind ran on a single track. Harriet put back the phone, got up and and opened her bedroom window. Another beautiful day, thankfully. Next-door, Georgiana had already opened her French windows onto the terrace – woe betide anyone who said patio, social hari kiri! Ella Fitzgerald was Taking Manhattan this morning.

'Getting daring, Georgiana', Harriet thought, and then she thought about the day ahead, seeing Billy, the first time for four whole weeks. Since the last *exeat* in fact, when he had come home for Sunday lunch, flopped on the floor, and stayed there watching old films, until it was time to take him back, weighed down with enough home-made muesli and biscuits for a year. He hadn't even had the energy to go out for a walk. She went downstairs, a pile of ironing met her gaze. Not a chance.

'What an exciting life I lead, Moll', she said, but the cat seemed unconvinced.

* * *

The fact that St Anthony's had been described in the *Daily Blare* as a 'posh public school', as opposed to a threadbare operation, now packing in eight-to-thirteen- year-olds as well as senior boys, and selling off its art collection to break even, should, have started the day rather well. But for Henry Crouch MA the idea of sex romps in the san made him ill. And then there were the Governors, and the people at the Headmasters' Conference, who would undoubtedly have a go, and the parents AND the prospective parents who would dislike the publicity. It was bad enough spending all one's time marketing, the new educational madness, but now he would have to spend the summer embarrassed, and advertising for a new Matron — preferably post-menopausal!

The Headmaster charged up the path from his house towards the Main School. He didn't take in the beauty of the grounds, the peacocks, nor the perfection of the Decimus Burton stonework. His gown billowed out behind him as he walked briskly past the boys emerging from the East Wing after breakfast. 'Morning Sir, Morning Headmaster.' Respectful enough, though he could detect the odd smirk.

Ahead of him, he saw some boys had started carrying notices down to the car park, and other smaller boys were bringing chairs into the main hall. There were sounds of violins from the music room, shouts from the Chapel. His shoulders came down from his ears. Speech Day, a great day for the school every year, and no smutty rag was going to spoil it. With renewed enthusiasm, he swung open the first of the double doors leading to his office and smashed into the brick wall.

It took fifteen minutes before they could locate Jones the handyman, by which time the blood had oozed onto his white collar. The only person who didn't seem to be outraged was Hodges that design technology halfwit he'd been talked into taking on from the comprehensive. He was wittering on about first rate brickwork indeed! No he did not need Matron!

He remembered that he had the keys for the office French windows on this key ring, and walked round holding his nose with a Kleenex, only to meet the Chaplain, normally, the brand of Anglican so laid back as to be horizontal, now apparently about to have a heart attack in front of him.

'Headmaster I'm afraid the boys have played a disgraceful practical joke, monstrous! I cannot conceive how no-one heard them.'

'Mr Farrell, Jones is knocking the wall down now.'

'It'll take the fourth form as well as the fifth. Will there be time to remedy the situation? I doubt it. So little time!'

'I've just said, Mr Farrell, Jones is knocking it down, it doesn't take fifty boys.'

'The pews Headmaster.'

'Pews? So you're not talking about my office being bricked up.'

'No indeed Headmaster. Some boys must have got into the Chapel last night and turned them all facing the wrong way. All eighty! They'll all have to be taken out and put back in. I cannot believe it!'

Henry Crouch's head throbbed. The phone rang inside the office just as Jones kicked through the first brick, and the nine o'clock bell rang. Too loud.

* * *

The room had been designed in the eighteenth century as an upstairs drawing room for the lady of the house, but now the fleshy cherubim, on the ceiling of Frobisher Dorm, (recently restored with an English Heritage Grant), had to contemplate nine beds, regulation lockers and teddy bears in varying stages of putrefaction. Their friendly gaze was met in turn by the boys, who, when lying in bed in the early morning, would take considerable time to estimate which had the smallest willy.

The Summer Term's trading period usually ended on Speech Day, when the boys called in debts and offloaded incriminating stock before the Headmaster's Inspection. The school's internal black economy was based on two commodities, pornography and cigarettes. An 8% profit on a packet of Benson and Hedges, and 20% on a three-month-old copy of Penthouse at 50p per picture, was generally thought a healthy return by the braver, more entrepreneurial boys. There were of course unavoidable overheads such as the two fags and the centrefold usually demanded by the Dorm Captain but Jamie Longbridge and Billy Gosse were still quite pleased with their turnover.

'That all Jamie?' Billy finished adding it up on the calculator, and rubbed his eyes. He was pale and tired looking, as if he hadn't eaten meat for a term.

'Yeh. Mohammed took the Miss April in the end for two quid, tried to beat me down because of a tear but I told him to use his imagination!' Jamie Longbridge the taller of the two, stopped counting and lolled back on the pillows, his arms and feet sprouting out of the ends of his school uniform. 'Hurry up Billy, Johnson will be along in a minute.'

'OK. I've finished except for this.' Billy shut the accounts book, disguised by a dustcover of *Charlie & The Chocolate Factory*, and began to divide the money. 'Look Wilson, I've got you down here 50p for those two fags and a four-inch pic. Here it is May the 9th, it's now July. We want the money today, OK?'

'OK. But do you two ever think about anything but money? It's obscene.'

Billy Gosse and Jamie Longbridge did not deign to reply. Making money was the only thing that made life at school bearable. That and the promise of power of life and death over ten boys, which was what becoming Dorm Captain would mean next year.

To all the boys in the dorm, Speech Day meant less about glory and more about kit inspection, and disinfectant, pints of it, swashed about in large quantities to impress the parents, who of course you all prayed wouldn't embarrass you by turning up too pissed, or groping someone else's wife. Next door an appalling whistle came from the Senegalese twins 'on the bogs'. 'Piss off both you M'Bows, stop that noise, and polish the taps, stop dabbing at them.'

'Do you know, Johnson, your lot are even more useless than mine.' The Dorm Captains, magnificent at eleven, swaggered into the room. 'Don't you know how to make hospital corners yet, Longbridge? Pathetic. Get off your arse and do them again properly.'

Jamie didn't exactly rush. Just wait till next term!

'By the way boys, if you still have any fags or pics, off load them. Neame's just been nabbed with fags in his washbag, the cretin. A grade A nerd, in fact. Not a chance of being Dorm Captain next year, and damp fags too. Wilson, no books on top of the locker, you know that.'

The door swung behind them.

'I make that £32.47p after expenses', announced Billy. 'I think I'll take my mother out to tea at Simpsons.'

'You could buy her a car, the one she's got can't have cost more than a fiver.'

'Naff off Wilson. At least she doesn't have an electric blue Roller.' Jamie hated the bullying Billy got. It wasn't his fault his people didn't have money.

'I can't imagine what we're doing letting in one-parent families in here do you boys? Gossie, are you sure she pays full fees?'

'Shut it!' Billy sat quite still.

'Sure she doesn't give Crouch satisfaction in the hols?'

Several hospital corners were ruined in the fight, but the cherubim, who knew their priorities, never took their eyes off the cash.

* * *

'Come on boys quickly, we should be rehearsing!' The Chaplain was yelling. Inside the Chapel, the heating system was locked in its own Victorian time warp, and the Madonna, nicknamed Hypothermia, was normally the only person in the place not shivering. But now the air was thick with sweat and curses, as the boys heaved forty-foot-long pews made of solid oak out onto the lawn. In the searing heat, carved graffiti of the bored old boys already lay bare to the world.

* * *

'Bloody Aston Martins! Think they own the motorway. Look did you see that? Madeleine don't you think you've had enough. Look, it's not even ten o'clock in the morning, for God's sake!'

Several miles away from St Anthony's, in the fast lane

of the M4, a dark blue top-of-the-range BMW, containing Treasury Minister Eric Humble MP and his wife Lady Madeleine was cruising comfortably at eighty miles an hour.

'Stop being so suburban and boring, Eric. Even the Queen Mother enjoys a nip in the morning. Given your well publicised stance as an arse-licking Royalist I thought you'd have known that. You are a dying breed by the way, I'm turning republican. Vive la République d'anglaise!' She had reached the happy stage of her day, when she really didn't care a fig what he thought.

'If you could hear yourself, really hear yourself. Where the hell is this bloody school, which turning? Why did I agree to do this?'

'You agreed to do it, because everyone makes the most enormous fuss of you, and you are nowhere near your ghastly constituents. But mainly you do it because you always think these Speech Days will magically rub some of the public-school ooffle dust off onto you. Though the truth is you can take the boy out of the small town, but you can't take the small town out of the boy. Or the secondary modern in your case.' She tapped his knee, the Minister squirmed. 'I always wondered why you never joined the Labour Party? It's that turn-off by the way.'

Flashing lights began to appear in his mirror. It was not the moment to pledge undying love for the residents of Limpthorpe North, or the Conservative Party. Nor was there time to point out that he'd been to the grammar school from sixteen. Actually. The Aston Martin moved smartly into the inside lane and turned off. Missed it.

* * *

Driving through the grounds following the signs to the car park, it struck Harriet as curious that since last year, the mothers had grown younger, and the fathers had aged, as if they had traded in the older mothers for younger models, and then exhausted themselves in the process. Poor little boys, flyblown WASPS, expense-account tummies spoiling the profile of their Brooks Brothers blazers. Yet she could always tell which men, in which cars would be coming to the school even from the turn-off on the M4, they had a sort of expectant look at them, as if to say aren't we clever? Tom would have taken them off so well, he could have cornered the market in well heeled character parts. If.

Harriet found these school events difficult. Not that Billy would have ever boarded if Tom had lived, he would have loathed the idea. Institutionalised child abuse he called it. She missed him all the time, even for the things that used to drive her mad. An ache, constant, even though these days she had almost forgotten what he looked like. Old photographs did not help, only the old videos, which she could not bring herself to watch.

In front, a well preserved Morris Minor protested bumping over the muddy tracks. The woman was putting her hat straight, she looked nervous. Harriet pushed her thoughts back to parent categories.

Yes, she preferred the jaloppy brigade who rolled up usually late in sensible shoes, and lots of dogs panting in the back. Oddly, it was usually the ones in the expensive cars whose sons were quietly removed from school because Daddy couldn't make the fees. Lloyds, don't you know, expressive whispers were usually followed by a but-for-the-grace-of-God shrug of the shoulders, even when it was more likely to be divorce, drugs or redundancy. The jaloppies meanwhile, gamely took in lodgers, and bed-and-breakfasters, and tried not to think about their lack of a pension.

The sun beat down on the car bonnet, the wind pushing the small clouds away over the top of the trees. The parking arrangements seemed better organised than last year, better signs, and she eased her Renault Five down the narrow lane toward the car park. Suddenly there seemed to be trouble. Raised voices, high-pitched screams. 'I'd back up quickly if I were you.' A tall man just getting out of a red expensive-looking sort of car was calling out to her. Too late. A Volvo came round the corner. She opened the door. Mud, everywhere. How odd, the heat of the last few days had not even begun to dry it out?

'I gather we've been the victim of yet another Anthonian Speech Day practical joke. This is actually a bog.'

The man who had shouted at her had bent down. She took in the dark curly hair, the handsome face, even teeth, and green eyes. Who had an expensive dentist and tinted contact lenses? She smiled back.

'Well, it can't be worse than last year when they collapsed the marquee. Would you be kind enough to get my gum boots from the back.'

Harriet handed him the keys. In front of her a red-faced and overweight middle-aged man, was attempting to carry his wife up the lane, her lacy tights were already smeared with green. But the satin shoes were still immaculate, just. Not that one could laugh knowing what a pair of Blahniks cost, even second-hand. A woman in the bright blue Rolls convertible was standing up simply screaming at the poor chauffeur to do something. Anything! The boys must hate us very much, Harriet thought.

'One pair of boots.' She took the boots and stood up in the squelching mud. White lacy tights, pale silk dress – Jean Muir second-hand, but who was to know? Oh dear, he was looking at her. What should she do? Would he like a press release? Health good, dress size 12, well 10 if she starved, long hair, wrinkles – not bad considering constant money worries. One previous owner.

'Thank goodness, a girl who doesn't have green wellies. He looked down at her, smiling, and held out his hand. 'Richard Longbridge.'

Straight out of Mills and Boon, Harriet thought. He'll be offering to carry me away from all this next.

'Thank God you've got gumboots, I couldn't have carried you, I've got a bad back. I was laughing so much about this Matron business I slipped getting out of the bath this morning.'

'Harriet Gosse, How do you do. Don't worry, be prepared you see. I was a good boy scout.'

Harriet looked up at him, smiling. He's terribly tall, she thought, too handsome, obvious. How old, verging on the distinguished, forty maybe. He clearly assumed that she would find him attractive.

'Yes my son Billy told me about Matron and the Headboy last night. Apparently she's really ancient so he tells me. Thirty six! Which made my evening.'

'Children are horrible aren't they? Ah but have you read

the *Blare* this morning. Did you know of the romps in the San, and the midnight trysts at the lake? No, I can see you have better things to do on a Saturday morning, quite right.'

'Ironing actually.'

'Yuk never do it. Our sons should do it for pocket money. Is your husband coming later?'

'No. I'm . . .'

Here we go, Harriet thought.

'A widow.'

He took her elbow as they continued up the track. One of the school peacocks screeched out in the distance, but then again, it could have been a muddy ex-mistress.

* * *

Billy couldn't believe it. What was his mother doing? How embarrassing! Mum, he telegraphed with frantic eyes, get out. You shouldn't be sitting in the front row. Go back. GO BACK! Oh, no, here come the Governors. He couldn't look, and slid down below the eyeline of the pew in front.

Harriet couldn't see the small face among rows of small faces. Frustrating, because it was nice to be in the front row. Last year she had barely been inside the building. But how had this Richard Longbridge character found someone to look after her gumboots at the back, and then, while she was putting on her shoes, somehow commissioned a Prefect to sweep them into the front row?

From the corner of her eye, arched necks behind her made her sense some broken hierarchy, and yet this man seemed to be perfectly at ease. She felt Tom was still around, perhaps perched up on the pulpit, making faces at her.

'Richard, er, good to see you. Thank you for you help with the er, er.' The Chairman of the Governors ushered a well-dressed couple to seats next to her. What help? Wasn't he a Government minister, Humble someone? Phaw! Harriet could smell his wife's breath. But then she thought marriage to a politician had to be up there with actors and artists. And forgave her.

A distant trumpet sounded. No-one had come to turn them out. More trumpets. Richard Longbridge turned and smiled at her mischievously, as the Headmaster led in the procession. So what did he do for a living which made him so secure in the world? Brain surgeon? City financier? Her father always said the best Englishmen were pirates.

'Who's that gorgeous governor sitting next to the lush in the front?' A stage whisper back in the baritones reached Billy as he stood up to sing the first hymn. He slid his eyes along the floor to the congregation, and saw his mother's white shoes. She hadn't been turned out then, or got caught, down by the bog. Smart. He raised his eyes a bit further. What a dress! Must have cost a fortune, could she afford it? Although he knew there would be trouble, he was pleased she would be able to see everything this year. Who was she with? Looked a bit too pleased with himself.

Henry Crouch, the bridge of his nose now a rich purple, stood up to list the School's benefactors starting with Edward II. The boys dozed, while fathers dreamt of lakeside bonks with Matron. The rest of the boys survived by picking the longest words in the hymn sheet and wrote down as many words they could make. Resurrection – rest, erection, nit, cost, rot, tin, set, cut, con, eon, ten, sure, sent, tire, net, not, sore, rise, runt.

Other boys, with parents abroad, sat calculating their Air Miles. The smallest boys looked out for their parents, desperate to see them putting on a show, even if they did not speak the rest of the year.

'Whoso beset him round, with DISMAL stories.' In the next hymn, fourth-formers were belting out just one word per verse, while the Upper Fifth compiled a league table of sisters and girlfriends. Which was a ten? Whose had the most zits, and the biggest tits?

Billy's clear treble cut through the cold tedium. The *Sanctus*, sung in Latin, soared up to the roof and down to the cold congregation. Suddenly Harriet felt intensely proud. Her son. Hers! Private feelings masked by a hat. What being a widow is all about. Tears pricked at the back of her eyes, dispelled by a ladylike burp from her neighbour.

* * *

Afterwards they spilled out into the sunshine. Frightfully good fun! Fathers eyed up each others' wives, mothers priced each other's dress and ruined shoes. Their eyes glazed with long practice over the cheap hand-me-downs of the masters' wives, who were always drafted in reluctantly on a three-line whip, their dowdiness more cruelly exposed than usual in the sun's glare.

'Lovely to see you again, Headmaster.' Tinkly laughter. A hundred networks formed and re-formed in the heat, whilst waistcoated prefects oozing *bonhomie*, guided them down to the lake, for champagne. The little boys circled, looking for their parents.

'Er Richard, just how did you get us into the first row?'

'Well, I felt you needed a good view. Stop worrying! They were hardly going to kick us out. Anyway I'm helping to flog the pictures they were left with the house. I'm surprised the boys look so well fed, this place is an accountant's nightmare. Ah there's the boy with the champagne. I say!'

'Mum!' Billy darted through, followed by Jamie.

'Billy! You sang beautifully. Well done!' Harriet knew it wasn't the form to be over the top, so she gave him a quick hug, and smiled at his friend. 'Hello are you Jamie? It's so nice to meet you, at last. Longbridge, yes I've finally clicked, your father here helped me squelch out of the car park. He also got us the best seats in the place. Don't ask me how!'

Jamie, his dark hair falling over one eye, looked at her appraisingly.

'Mum, I was so worried you were going to be turned out in front of everyone!'

'Billy, so was I! Darling you look so thin, I can't wait to get you home to feed you!'

'Tell me you two, where are the Headboy and Matron? There'll be a few fixed smiles from his family today. Have you seen the morning paper?' Richard was looking around, apparently sizing up the women, or so it seemed to Harriet.

'No I haven't. The Headboy's over there, Sir, he's talking to Lord Stanton, I can't see Matron. Mum, the Lower sixth switched the signs round for the car park, and they turned the pews round in the Chapel and bricked up Crouch's study!' Billy suddenly kissed Harriet on the forehead. 'You look nice.'

'Thanks darling. But why do the tricks have to be so anti-parents?' Harriet knew she was sounding old. 'Those poor women have had their shoes ruined, we don't all carry gumboots. Talking of which, I'd better get them from the Chapel.'

'We've got to go now Billy, we're serving the veg.' Jamie tugged at his sleeve. He smiled shyly at Harriet, 'See you after lunch Mrs Gosse.'

They disappeared. Harriet noticed that Jamie had barely spoken one word to his father, who was being so utterly charming.

'Forget about the boots, no one's going to nick them. Now, champagne for the lady,' Richard Longbridge guided her down to the lake.

How odd that last year, she had felt so on the edge of events, and now suddenly this man was introducing her to people like an old friend? Through the heat, and the crowds, Richard Longbridge smiled at her, like a magician flourishing an unexpectedly cute white rabbit out of his top hat. But did she want to be a theatrical prop for this smoothie, thank you very much?

* * *

'Most girls would pay!'

'There's just no God, dear.'

Later, two masters' wives, clutching Coronation chicken, with white wine suspended on the edge of the plate in a plastic clip, looked across at Boyd Rogers who was pouring out the wine. Matron was chatting a bit too animatedly to some parents of the Junior boys about ten yards away. Her 'bit of rough' all right! His blazer could not conceal the body beneath, although the women at St Anthony's had long suspected that the cool stare from those blue eyes came more from a lack of comprehension than any mysterious depths. Not that that diminished his allure. Clever men were so dull.

'The Minister's wife is knocking it back rather.'

'Perhaps one of the boys should make sure she gets some pud.'

* * *

'I was horrified by what that reporter wrote, he made it up. Billy's such a lovely boy Mrs Gosse! And he's settled so well. So nice about the engagement. Not like some of them, Though I'd expected it. Have you seen the ring, its a diamond solitaire, Boydie calls it a rock!'

Shrieking with laughter, her hair tumbling very un-Matron-like, down her back, Kirsty Munro was proving more bubbly than the champagne.

'Congratulations Matron, I'm sure you'll be very happy.' What was one supposed to say? Harriet thought. Good for you for marrying up, get pregnant pronto? Or watch out, your mum-in-law has the sort of face-lift which looks as if she's swallowed a cobra down on the ranch. Anyway that Glaswegian accent would no doubt go down a bundle in Houston.

'You run a language school don't you, Mrs Gosse?'

'Er yes.' Harriet was embarrassed, she kept seeing the woman on the station.

'You see, Boydie's got to start working for his father in the Paris office. Now he's got to keep me in style. He won't be going to University in the States now of course. Would you be able to give me lessons when we're in London before we go?'

'Certainly, here's my card give me a ring.' However much she liked Matron, and however small his chances had ever been of getting into an Ivy League college, Boyd Rogers was paying a high price for a bit of adolescent sex. Although you could argue that as almost all men remained little boys in need of a Matron, (yes even Jamie's father, old smoothiepants over there), so perhaps you could say Boydie had gone for a professional.

* * *

The word 'bonk' seemed to have trailed after him like Banquo's ghost all day, two people from the *Blare* had been flung out by the First Eleven, but Henry Crouch was at last grabbing a bit of chicken. A heavy ring-laden hand clasped him on the shoulder. 'I gave you the pool, remember, and what you've given me is an ageing hustler to support, who's put out to the press, and who's going to screw up my boy's life?'

It was soft, hardly indignant even, yet the Texan drawl made Crouch freeze. Hector Rogers, Boyd's father, did not look prepossessing in this heat. Henry Crouch swallowed hard. 'I suggest that we have a word in my study.'

Well-bred murmurs rippled out of the lake, yet the surface of the day remained undisturbed.

* * *

These boys did not know they were bloody born. Up on the platform, standing behind a table decorated with a heavy white tablecloth, and some wilting flowers from the Headmaster's garden, the Minister was praising the Headboy who had been so charming to him and his wife since their arrival. The sort of all rounder St Anthony produced. The sound system hissed, and he wondered why that raised such a laugh.

Boyd Rogers smiled too. Harriet remembered again the scene on Paddington station. Steaming, rampant testosterone.

Henry Crouch thanked the Minster, and announced that Lady Humble had kindly agreed to present the prizes, after which there would be tea and sandwiches on the East Lawn. Wilting parents muttered 'Thank God for that!'

So much was everyone on automatic pilot, it was only the Head Boy, high in the triumph of his father's disapproval, who noticed that Lady H. was far from well.

'Headmaster,' he hissed along the platform, 'Headmaster, I don't think she should.'

'Shut up Rogers, I've had your father ranting at me in my study for half an hour. Now sit down!' Crouch switched the microphone back on, wincing at the feedback. 'Ladies & Gentlemen, we start with the Junior House awards for academic excellence.'

Apart from the recipients and their beaming parents, the rest of the audience was hardly listening. They were transfixed by the tall figure in the purple patterned Bill Blass dress, who swayed hypnotically like a snake after a double gin. 'Hello darling, what a little poppet!' They saw her kiss the first boy enthusiastically. Mothers looked at each other puzzled, she hadn't sounded like that on *Woman's Hour*.

'This sort of thing always has a fatal fascination hasn't it, just like when they lose their notes on the *Nine o'clock News*', Richard whispered in her ear. And it was true, there was a horrible embarrassing inevitability, Harriet just sat there, frozen.

'Do you know old Madeleine?'

'Yes, she's. . . .'

'Look at that! Now she'll be mixing up the prizes, the old darling!'

This Richard Longbridge, was now clearly taking this poor woman's humiliation as as a comedy turn laid on for his amusement. Her husband looked apoplectic. But what sort of husband must he be, to make her drink like that?

Soon all order was lost on the prize table. Billy, up for the Prep School Award for English was offered a hug and the *Victor Ludorum*. He'd been expecting a book token rather than this heavy silver cup, but took it anyway. Harriet clapped and clapped.

'You've got a lovely son Harriet', Richard Longbridge said in her ear.

Other boys who could not string a sentence together, took debating prizes, whilst the most knock-kneed boy in the school scooped the Rugby Cup. The atmosphere was becoming really rather jolly.

Finally, there remained just the St Anthony's Cup for Overall Achievement, donated by a grateful Iraqi, whose son had scraped into Oxford against all odds. Made in Lebanese silver, embossed with sapphires, it flaunted unenglish exuberance. To one side, a thin pale Prefect waited, eyes narrowed. A consolation prize for not being made Headboy. He'd already made Crouch suffer.

Lady Humble, still swaying, steadied herself, gripping the ornate handles of the cup. Looking at it almost longingly.

'And now the Award for the Prefect who has consistently made the most outstanding contribution to school life, the winner is. . . .'

Mr Crouch's words were drowned in the applause. Hurrah! Relieved parents could almost taste the Darjeeling, and as the boy began to ascend the platform, Lady Madeleine Humble, dimly anxious not to make a mess on the damask tablecloth, vomited into the nearest receptacle.

Chapter Three

She must have done it on Saturday afternoon and got the last post. Harriet couldn't help laughing, Laura was so good at these funny little sketches, a natural cartoonist. The postcard showed Laura with a feather boa and a tall lanky man, perhaps this David Forsyth she had been raving about, striking the pose of Kirsty and Boyd on Paddington Station. Very Brief Encounter, well perhaps not. Next to the two figures, the notice read 'You can find more than bears at Paddington Station.' And the bubble coming out of Laura's head said, 'And For This I'm Being Paid?' Harriet smiled and stuck the postcard into her diary, and continued her walk up the hill into Portobello Road.

It was a street with a hangover. Shops were still boarded up from the weekend. The market stalls were deserted but already packed with oranges, and the reflection from their shiny skins blinded passers-by in the early morning sun. Gradually, Portobello Road shook itself into action. Or tried to. Half past eight on Monday morning, it was hard to come alive even on a summer's day. The artists, actors, writers, gallery owners and dropouts, and the few locals who had not been bought out by greedy landlords, communed, pouring themselves into cappuccinos, tea and bacon butties in the caffs and coffee shops. The smell of coffee lingered in the middle of the road, as the stall holders produced stout thermos flasks, and shrugged with indifference, at a straggle of Italian tourists who came up, disappointed to find no antiques, just the cheapest grapefruit in London.

Harriet always had to stop herself from shopping first

thing in the morning. She loved the walk up Kensington Park Gardens, past pale, gleaming stuccoed houses dazzling in residential splendour and then the descent into the bustle of the market. But she mustn't stop. If she did, she would spend half an hour chatting to the stall holders, pressing the flesh of rival avocados, comparing prices and losing the momentum of the day. Losing momentum, the greatest enemy of the self-employed.

To work. Think of the school fees! £3,460 by September 11th. A mantra for the mad, or the bankrupt middle classes. Next to her bank, two workmen perched high up on scaffolding whistled at her. 'Mornin' darlin', give us a smile then.' Smiling back, Harriet decided that thirty-five was probably the age when you stopped walking by with your nose in the air, and started to feel grateful. A serious thought which made her laugh out loud.

When she reached her office, Mrs Mac had not yet arrived, which was good. Harriet always needed a few minutes to collect her thoughts before the phone started ringing. She opened the window, and threw the flowers which had died at the weekend into the bin. One advantage of working by a flower stall meant a constant supply. She hung up her coat, and noticed the note Marcus had stuck on the computer. Only a few people on the planet could decipher his huge scrawly writing, lucky she was one of them, Harriet thought. 'H., I've been in since seven, what a star! Man called Easton rang after you'd left on Fri, apparently Ulrike missed his lesson. Want to come out to the View at Lesley Waddington's tonight?' Harriet thought she probably wouldn't.

Bloody Ulrike! She needed to keep this horrible little man Easton and his people happy. Not least because Haldane Foods paid within 30 days. Then there was the piece in the money pages on Saturday, about their new contract in Japan, which would mean they would be needing Japanese soon. Which meant a really good mark-up if they did not now go somewhere else. Harriet sighed, how was she going to keep Ulrike teaching him, and Easton happy enough to give her some more business? The girls were soon coming in for their money. She would have to think of something.

Her language business had started when Billy was seven

weeks old, Tom had been out of work for four months, and she was getting tired of boiling chicken bones for soup. When a friend in Bristol had asked her to give him some French conversation by phone at 6.30 a.m. she had jumped at the chance. It had been quite funny, both in their pyjamas, at either end of the country, Billy and Tom snoring next door.

To Harriet's surprise, what had begun as a favour to a friend, soon began to take on a life of its own. She discovered that she had a real talent teaching by phone, and her friend could reproduce a mental tape recording in his mind over the day. It worked he said, far better than all those grammar books and tapes in the car he had tried for years. Soon she had a three or four friends of friends learning French and Italian.

The idea of learning languages by phone was so new and it seemed unimaginable that it could work. But as the reality of working in the EC became closer, people had to talk over the phone, to sell or simply to say 'I'm putting you through now Sir', with none of the benefit of facial expression or gesture. No-one had time these days to go to evening classes, and if they did, they were too tired by the end of the day to do the work. Harriet's workload grew, within six months she had seven regular clients, friends of friends of friends. And the beauty of it was there were no big phone bills or office to pay for, no fares or fancy suits, and the clients paid up-front and then rang her!

In the early days, it had been fun devising the course work, tailoring each class to the specific business of the client. French for a man from a tobacco company heading out to Algeria, Italian for a film editor. She would spend the day carting Billy around in his buggy round libraries for course material, and learnt to present a businesslike front on the phone, when all around were piles of ironing, and bin bags of dirty nappies. After years of teaching in evening classes and coping with spoilt parents in private schools it was bliss to teach this way – no office, no wardrobe other than sloppy jeans.

Life became more complicated, when she reached twelve clients, and they began requesting lunchtime and weekend lessons. Life working from home with a small child is never easy. In the early days, she had undercharged hopelessly, and Tom was no help, he pretended to be interested, but he didn't take it seriously.

She vividly remembered the day when she had been teaching from home for about a year, Tom was away filming, a solicitor was about to phone for his lesson and the au pair – an oversexed Danish cliché – had been out all night, and had still not arrived back. Praying he would not cry, she had strapped Billy into his buggy, dummy in mouth, in front of an Ivor the Engine video. That day he had gurgled patiently as she had taken the lesson on the upstairs extension.

But on other occasions when the childcare failed to materialise, his screams would rip through the grammar like a knife, making rigid knots of tension in her shoulders. 'Mr Cousins, my notes on the pluperfect are downstairs I'll be two seconds. That noise you can hear is just the opera singer next door, she's just been given a small part at the Garden and she's rehearsing non stop!' Until she had discovered that sacking the au pair, promoting the cleaner and giving Billy a lemon to suck equalled peace.

Then eighteen months later, Tom had landed the part of Howard Sampson in *Sampson House* and had started to earn regular money topped up with large fees for personal appearances, but though Harriet had been pleased by this new-found wealth, she found she couldn't stop. It was not just that he did not have a contract, and never knew when he would be written out, it went deeper than that, and soon every moment of every day seemed to be spent on the phone, before she turned into a pumpkin at 3.15 to pick Billy up from primary school.

And then Tom died, and the world stopped for several weeks. Then she had continued, working in even more chaos, and fighting the depression which had engulfed her.

It was her father's agent Marcus Whitehead, who had taken her in hand and taught her how to run a business, how to cost out her time, do a cash flow forecast, compile accounts. It was Marcus also, who had later talked her into taking the two rooms on the first floor above his new gallery in the Portobello Road, told her to go out and buy a suit and a couple of blouses and turn herself into Harriet Gosse Business Language School.

By then Harriet had started to do some research, and had found that there were one or two schools in London offering telephone tuition, and had sent off for their brochures. She added their sales pitch to hers – that the Japanese and French had been using this teaching method for years, that it was a more intensive cost-effective form of study. By pure luck she caught the tide of Euro-fervour as firms realised that doing business with Europe was the future and that after years of comprehensive education most of their employees did not possess the language skills their parents had been given.

Now, in spite of Britain being in recession, her company had forty corporate or individual clients and a team of self-employed teachers highly trained by herself, who when they weren't marrying or going slow like Ulrike, were said to be the best in London.

'Morning Harriet, did you see the newspaper? Your Billy's Matron marrying the Headboy. Shocking, I thought of you on Saturday, I told Bill, dreadful what these schools get up to, and so expensive!'

Mrs Mac burst into the little office, and thumped her basket on the desk. She had been buying fruit in the market, and now stuck more flowers into the vase Harriet had just emptied. Mrs Mac was plump, full of gossip, and immensely energetic. Marcus, who had a waspish streak, had once called her Kilmarnock's answer to *Carry On Camping*, but she had overheard him, and said she was a good Christian Presbyterian, who knew all about Sodom and Gomorrah, thank you very much. They now held an uneasy truce, circling round their precious Harriet, making sure neither took too much advantage.

The first day Eleanor Mac had come into the office, she hadn't burst in at all, she had been quite unsure of herself in fact. She had inched inside the tiny office, to find her new boss sitting on the floor stuffing brochures into envelopes because the second-hand desks had not arrived from the auction house. Promptly Mrs Mac had taken charge, and had told Mrs Gosse that she would sort everything out. She had somehow borrowed an apron from the woman at the flower stall, and a bucket and mop from somewhere else, and had scrubbed the office walls herself singing 'Donald Where's Your Troosers', while Harriet had looked on bemused. Then she had made Harriet a good strong cup of tea, produced shortbread out of her handbag, and had stood on the landing with her hands on her hips, making sure the two delivery men who were trying to bring the desks up the narrow stairs, did not bash the paint-work. After this, she had given them a piece of her mind for being late.

The next day she had turned up with a small vacuum cleaner, two wastepaper-bins and a brother-in-law who was throwing out an old filing cabinet. Within a week she had set up the office, and the books, and from then on, she had bussed in from Kilburn every day, and there had never been a late invoice or a bad debt. The lady at the flower stall gave her flowers for the office half-price and treated her with the greatest respect.

'So what do you think?' From her huge handbag Mrs Mac produced a crumpled cutting.

'Oh is this it? One of the parents told me about it.'

Harriet looked at it, and thought back to Jamie's father. All Lobb shoes and stripey Jermyn Street shirts. Like a City banker, and yet apparently not. Billy had told her later that Jamie and his father did not get on. Shame, there was so little time to get to know your own children before they went off with their own life. Did he realise what he was missing? There they were, the Paddington couple as she privately called them, in the photograph, Kirsty got away with being so much older because she was slight, much shorter than Boyd. Obviously she had brought out the protective streak.

'So how was Billy, did he sing well? '

'Beautifully. I can't wait to get him back home though.'

'You'll spoil him rotten, you and Laura, I know. Quite right. O.K. Where's the wages book, I need to finish off Keiko's money before she gets in.'

'By the way you'll get to meet Billy's naughty matron

soon, she wants to learn French, they're going to live in Paris apparently.'

'Not bad from a Paisley tenement, she did alright.'

Harriet had often wondered why Scots were always so critical of other Scots. No wonder so many left the country.

'Look what Marcus says in his note, could you get Easton on the phone, I'll have to grovel before I sort Ulrike out. The trouble is she's got me over a barrel and she knows it. We just don't have enough German teachers at the moment, with Liesl on honeymoon, and Brigitte away.'

Mrs Mac handed her the phone, and began to take off her coat.

'My father always used to say the Huns were either at your feet or at your throat.'

'Mrs Mac! We're all in Europe now!'

'Doesn't change them though.'

Harriet didn't answer, she was not going to debate the pros and cons of joining the EC on a Monday morning.

'Oh hello, may I speak to Philip Easton please, thank you. I'll wait.'

Occasionally as Harriet caught sight of herself in the glass and saw this confident woman in the check suit, she had to pinch herself to prove that she really was out there dealing with Training Managers, and in smaller companies with Managing Directors themselves. The worry and responsibility of keeping this expanding circus on the road, sometimes robbed her of the supposed glamour of being her own boss, yet even so, it was still exhilarating. Sometimes even fun.

These days she thought in terms of good PR, loss leaders, and sprats to catch mackerel. Like this oily little sprat who was about to blow her head off. Yet it was all still quite astonishing.

'Mr Easton, Harriet Gosse.' Harriet put on what she called her honey voice. Once at their Christmas party a client had drunk far too much, had once confided, in very serious tones, that he had always had an erection when he listened to her voice. She had blushed, and it had been quite embarrassing, but it had stuck in the back of her mind. Not that she assumed this particular humourless man ever had anything of the sort.

'Mr Easton, I want to apologise about Friday's lesson. Yes I appreciate this is not good enough, Ulrike is coming in this morning and I will be talking to her about it. I can only think that she misunderstood the time of the lesson. Yes, I'll be in touch later today with new arrangements. May I say how much I value your business Mr Easton. Please give us the opportunity to make amends. Yes. Goodbye. Phew!'

'Didn't sound as if he was in a forgiving mood', Mrs Mac came in with the tea.

'I think we've won a stay of execution, not a pardon, if I can get Ulrike to do it, there's no one else at the moment. We'll have to advertise. I don't think Liesl will want to come back now she's married.'

'I don't think so either. Not now she's got him. Did you know he's bought her a wee Porsche, and she's only twenty-three. Talk about getting your act together.'

Harriet began to go through the post, chucking the junk mail in the bin, and passing over the bills to Mrs Mac. She was pleased to find a nice letter thanking her for the brochure and asking her to ring in September. These days half her time was spent chasing up new business.

'I just hope that poor man from Warburgs knows what he's let himself in for. Liesl will have that terrifying mother of hers in their spare room before you can say annual report. The head of the Munich's mothers' mafia! The question is, how can I get Ulrike to teach him, so that we can pitch for the Japanese tuition? He even mentioned they would need Greek for the telephonists when we spoke last week.'

'I'm sorry Harriet but that's the trouble with hiring girls who don't need the money, and who aren't settled here. They just don't have the sticking power.'

Harriet did not rise to the bait. You could not work with a West-Coast Scot without being obliged on a daily basis to feed their need to be proved right. She put Ulrike's money on one side.

Ulrike was a sulky, blonde with an honours degree, a perfect figure and a Daddy who owned a large BMW garage outside Worms. In four months she had had some of the richest bachelors in London hanging on her every umlaut. But then all Harriet's staff were qualified teachers, graduates, often with business experience, articulate, young and frequently beautiful. The French, the Spanish, the Portuguese, they came and went with varying degrees of charm and commitment. And the Italians who smiled pure sunlight down the line and Guccied their way into Virginia Water.

Sometimes, Harriet thought she was just like a high-class madam, or the head of a dating agency – choose your six-figure salaried wheeler dealer here. Oh the passion of a tough exercise in the subjunctive: 'If I had a thousand pounds, I would take you to Paris!' Who could account for the mysterious alchemy of a telephone flirtation? Who could resist a twentieth-century Thisbe, whispering sweet grammar through a wall of distance to pin-striped Pyramus sitting in front of his flickering screen in Canary Wharf? Willing pupils, used to controlling every area of their lives, would revert to being little boys again, eager to please; until, in time, yearning to know what their teachers looked like, they would ask them out to dinner at the Ritz. To discuss the Course. Of course.

Harriet had given up buying new outfits for all the weddings she attended. She would sit on the bride's side of the church resigned to losing yet another well trained teacher, while across the aisle, mothers with fixed smiles saw their sons – hugely expensive products of Eton, Fontainbleu, INSEAD or the Harvard Business School turned to greet brides found on the phone teaching business French, German or Italian at £20 for twenty minutes. Plus VAT.

A fly buzzed impatiently round the room, and Mrs Mac got up to to swat it. They could hear the noises of the market outside. 'Ripe tomat-ers Three pounds for a pound. Ripe Tomat-ers. Come on darling!'

'Harriet, good morning.' A delicious concoction of suede, and blonde streaks slinked into the room. Harriet had forgotten, if she had ever known, just how much arrogance you could get away with at 25. Full marks to Matron.

'Sit down Ulrike. Mrs Mac, would you give us a minute?'

Harriet hated scenes like this, and she still didn't know quite how to handle them. Staff relations had always been so good, and she had never had a problem because the girls were well paid, well looked after and enjoyed themselves. Once a month, they all went out together for a meal. The whole feeling was women against the world. Except that is, for Jean Baptiste, the token male, who suffered them all.

'Ulrike, I've been talking to Mr Easton, you didn't take your lesson with him on Friday. He is extremely annoyed at being mucked around, and frankly I'm not exactly pleased.'

Ulrike sat down and looked full at Harriet with clear blue eyes. Direct, unapologetic.

'Harriet, 7 o'clock, it is too late on a Friday evening, I really do not wish to teach at that time. When I remembered and rang, he had left for the theatre.'

'Ulrike', Harriet reminded herself to keep the mood one of more sorrow than anger. 'When I took you on, it was understood there would be some 7 p.m. lessons, and you're paid extra for them. You're a very good teacher, you're normally very reliable. And I don't want to replace you.'

Ulrike shrugged. Harriet realised Mrs Mac was right. They needed staff who were married or settled here in London and needed the money. Yet the immediate problem remained. There was no one else. What was the girl's price? If she lost that business, after what it had taken to get it! The sun bursting through the office window hurt her eyes, and showed up the weekend dust on the filing cabinets, and the faultless finish of the girl's long nails. She got up to lower the blinds.

'Harriet, I'm sorry for you that I missed the lesson, but I don't want to teach him. He is very boring, and has no humour.'

Harriet remembered that when she had been a student, someone without a sense of humour was considered unfit to live. In those days, everything had been a scream, just so funny, hilarious.

'Ulrike, I can quite understand how you feel. Honestly I can. We've all taught people whose jobs are uninteresting, or they are. Can I just ask you one question. Why did you come to England?'

The girl seemed surprised at the change of tack, but Harriet knew she had to feel her way in the dark, to get behind the girl's mask of self sufficiency.

'To get away from my stepmother, my family. I wanted to improve my English.' Ulrike wriggled, a sulky teenager again.

'And what would you like to do in London? What would give you a real thrill when you got up in the morning?'

'Paint walls.' It was not what Harriet had expected. Not with those nails.

'I want to learn these decorative methods you do in England. Marbling and dragging. Paint pretend walnut woods, and oak woods. I want to learn it, and then go back to Germany and run my own business. Like you.' Ulrike's chin tilted up in challenge, and her face suddenly lit up, breaking through the sulky set of the mouth.

'Oh, fake finishes? I remember my father used to enjoy faking rose aurora marble in our house in Brighton, when I was a child.' Harriet smiled at the memory. 'But these days it's terribly old hat, Ulrike, in the nineties, it's going to be all New England clapper board, and bare white walls. I read it last week somewhere, recession means minimalism.'

'Not in Germany now. There are many old houses that will need to be restored with the Wall down. But a course to learn all this would cost a thousand pounds even two. And my father will not pay for it, he thinks his daughter to be a house painter, it would be socially embarrassing.'

Suddenly Harriet knew how much it was going to cost her. This was the price, a course against the £15,000 Haldane looked ready to sign for this year, as well as keeping Ulrike on for the other clients in the pipeline. Cheap, if it didn't screw up the cash flow.

'Ulrike, I am keen for you stay with us.' Harriet leaned towards her, confidentially, 'You are a first-class teacher. So. I will undertake to pay for a course in decorative techniques up to a cost of £1500, which you will work off at an agreed rate over the next six months. I will pay for the course in instalments, so that if you let me down again, the course will cease.'

Harriet knew Mrs Mac would kill her, but there was

too much at stake, Billy's school fees for one. If Easton took the Japanese for all his employees she could bill half immediately, which would be £4,000 plus VAT. Though all this still left the small matter of finding four more Japanese staff. But she'd worry about that another time.

'I agree.'

Ulrike's expression betrayed a mixture of shock and mistrust. Yet there was a spark behind it all, a touch of real life there after all. Unexpectedly, Harriet found herself feeling really sorry for the girl. How much personal interest had anyone ever really taken in her, for all those family deutschmarks?

Harriet handed her her pay cheque. 'I'm sure you could create a very successful business Ulrike, it is very popular in France and the States, so why not Germany, particularly with all those East German Schlosses crying out for restoration?'

This girl could do anything she wanted, if she did but know it! Trouble is, Harriet thought, you were usually hemmed in, and into your thirties, before you realised what you could have achieved at twenty five.

Harriet got up briskly, 'I will find out about courses today. Marcus will know. Then once we've discussed it, we'll sign you up. Now, I want you to ring Philip Easton up, tell him you misunderstood, and say how delighted you are to be teaching him over the next three months. *Verstehen*?' The girl nodded. Thank God for that. Harriet thought of Laura's card, 'And For This I'm Being Paid?'

She went into the library, making a mental note to advertise for more German teachers. She must never be in this position again. Please God the others wouldn't find out, or she would be held to ransom for beauty courses, modelling courses, you name it. Good. Ulrike had got through. Why does English always sound so sexy when spoken with a foreign accent? Yet when the English speak German, they always sound as if they are filing their teeth with an an emery board.

The library was a rather grand name for what had once been a storeroom. Harriet, Laura and Billy had painted it themselves one weekend. Laura had painted 'Biblioteca' in gold lettering, which Marcus had called hopelessly vulgar. 'Which I am', Laura had replied.

It was small, with just one large window. It was arranged floor to ceiling with course books and information. The different languages occupied separate shelves, subdivided into subjects. The German shelf bulged with material on accountancy, building, and chartered surveying all the way up to viniculture. Japanese took up half a shelf, concentrating on social conversation, few British businessmen had progressed beyond the pleasantries of the restaurant meal. Italian had the biggest sections on the film business, museums and fashion, Portuguese featured international law and merchant banking, while French took up two shelves, from brewing to zoos.

Harriet was proud of this collection, brought together with so much blood and toil over the years. The girls accepted it as a matter of course, many worked for other schools, and brought in tales of whole rooms devoted to a single language. But then they had never had to hulk a buggy with a heavy baby all over a public library for a man from a toy company about to take on Geneva, with half-forgotten O level French.

'Good morning girls.' Keiko and Mireille, Harriet's mainstay in Japanese and French stopped giggling over the coffee machine. Mireille was chic. Keiko small, razor-sharp, and dressed like a relic from Carnaby Street in the sixties. Theirs was a world of *Time Out*, Wembley concerts of groups Harriet had never heard of, restaurants and clubs which ceased to be trendy the moment people like her walked past the bouncers. Not that she ever did.

The girls loved popping into Portobello, it had street cred, although many clients were surprised by the address. But Harriet needed this fusion of the business-like and the bohemian, she could not disown her past. She revelled in its colour, and the fact it was not some soulless and expensive business centre. Her office was a necessary home from home, with Marcus underneath and his protégé Danny upstairs lashing his canvas with paint.

'Coffee, Harriet? '

'No thanks, Mireille, I've just had tea. Let's see, Keiko,

you have twenty lessons in total this week, sorry it's not more, but I'm presenting to Dawsons the publishers later today, they want small groups for their reception staff in Japanese. Fingers crossed. Mireille, you're starting with Mrs Collins on Tuesday. And possibly a new girl Kirsty Rogers soon, though she might have to go to Jean Baptiste, if you're too busy. Could you get back to Mr Russell, I had to take his lesson on the mobile and got cut off. Long story. Your money's ready.'

The girls picked up their books, and still giggling at some unknown joke, left the room. Telephone training had such a narrow margin for error, lost lessons and wasted time. It was like running a military operation, ringing up the clients the day before and then ten minutes before to remind them to ring at the right time. The teachers having to be ready to burst onto the lesson and force the pupils on.

Harriet found herself far too prone to judge the girls by their attitude to Billy. She knew this was wrong, and unprofessional. Yet love me and my school, love my child. What fun it all was for him in the holidays. Spoilt rotten he would 'swap' foreign swear words for extra tuck, or so he said, though Harriet suspected it was often of a nicotine variety which he could sell on. She could only hope he did not smoke. She could still hear his clear high voice that day in the library, when he thought she was still out at a client. 'Rosella, *stronso* got me two Galaxy bars, but what does it mean?' How she had choked back the laughter and the disapproval on the stairs.

Now he was ten, and old enough to help Mrs Mac around the office, and he loved it. All fierce loyalty, he would draw dinosaurs all over the brochures of her competitors. Handouts with titles like 'We Help You Make The Most Of Your Language Training Budget', dissolved into pterodactyls in red wax crayon. He had a streak of toughness, and often put her wise to the teachers who would leave.

The morning wore on. The shouts from the market below began to die down. The smells of spaghetti from the restaurant next door, reminded Harriet about lunch. Mrs Mac brought out her blue tupperware sandwich box and switched on *World At One*. 'That's me until after

The Archers, whoever rings', she said, switching on the answering machine.

Harriet picked up her handbag and went downstairs.

'Marcus I'm going out for a sandwich, and some shopping, do you want anything?' She found Marcus fussing round a canvas as usual. Marcus Whitehead was 75, but looked a young sixty. He had spent the best part of fifty years successfully fussing round canvases, and now said he could not stop. He was always beautifully dressed, with his trademark, the most embroidered waistcoats in London. Marcus had a rich almost theatrical voice which boomed above the noise of his wonderful parties. Yet in a world of surfaces, he had been a real second father to Harriet, when Jester had been off limits. Always concerned for her well-being. Harriet had never known much about his private life, not even where he and his friend Ian lived. Yet it had never seemed to matter, the gallery was his stage and his whole world, and it was there that Harriet always thought of him, never fussing around his house or doing his garden, if he had one. Even when Ian had died, Marcus had never once let down the drawbridge.

'Well if you're buying fruit I'll choose it for you, you always buy everything over-ripe, and then wonder why it goes off. I'm the one with the eye for quality. Now my dear, what do you think of this?'

He stood back to admire a canvas five-feet-square which seemed sludge on sludge, with a red gash spurting down the left-hand corner, and a figure hurrying past with a dog. Harriet stood looking at it for a moment. Her tummy rumbled unaesthetically. Yet even though she could not have lived with such a painting for two minutes, she could see the passion with which the artist had blasted on the paint, and the energy. She was always been reluctant to dismiss anything creative out of hand.

'The dog's marvellous, and it's got terrific life, Marcus. Is it Danny's?'

'No. Alasdair Maston. Helensburgh. Twenty-nine, terrific.' Harriet could see Marcus had made a new discovery. He needed them on average at least every couple of months, or else he would become moody and introspective, and worry that he had lost his touch since he had sold his

Mayfair gallery. Though why he still felt he had to work so hard after making so much money was a mystery to her.

'Already exhibited in Prague and Berlin. We're giving him a show next week.'

'Is it sold?'

'Nearly. You'll come to the View won't you Harriet? You're such a good judge.'

'You mean because I am complimentary in front of your customers.'

'Partly, but then darling Harriet, you're now almost a business woman. Almost. And you know that if the gallery didn't pay its way, I'd have to push up the rent. Besides, you've inherited Jester's inner eye, and you ought to come for your own pleasure.'

Even in the summer heat, when tourists tramped past raising dust, and the blind accordionist laid on the schmaltz, the Whitehead Gallery was always cool. Marcus however, was continually mopping his brow with a Paisley handkerchief. On meeting him for the first time, one might have thought his taste would have been for overblown Victorian oils rather than the contemporary restless spirits who expressed themselves over the wide white walls.

'Oh, Marcus, I forgot. Do you know anything about courses in *faux* finishes, you know marbling, dragging and ragging that sort of thing? I've got one of my teachers wanting to do it.'

'Not really, darling. By the way which teacher is it, not the frightful Keiko?'

'She's not as terrifying as she looks, you know. No, Ulrike.'

'Not surprised. *Faux* finishes, now I think of it, I noticed last week that the Europa Gallery in Cork Street had a team of young people in marbling their fireplace. Silly really, as if that would help sell those tacky Tachists, but you could ask them where they sprang from.'

'Thanks, I'm up in Mayfair this afternoon, I'll pop in.

The door opened and a well-dressed man stepped in, obviously American. Harriet smiled and slipped out to let him do his stuff. Good old Marcus, still at it.

'Alasdair Maston, yes an exciting talent. Great integrity. Clive Sawston wrote a nice piece about him last week, last issue of *Modern Painters*. I've got it somewhere, if you're interested.'

* * *

'And that's why we were given Cyprus of course. Remarkable man Disraeli.' Mr Armitage started writing their history prep on the board, and the boys wrote it down in their books. Why did every master always think theirs was the only prep which mattered, and gave far too much? Billy was thinking how long it would be until the holidays. How many days? Nine weekdays, eleven including the weekend till he saw his mother again, nine days before he could laze in bed till ten if he wanted, or go into the office and see the girls, or go out with Danny, or perhaps even visit Laura at the studio.

'Gosse are you listening?'

'Sorry, Sir.'

'I want decent writing, I'm tired of reading work apparently completed by demented spiders. Understand?'

The master's parting shot was greeted with general laughter. The bell went, and the boys pushed their heavy satchels onto their backs and clattered out of the classroom. The smell of chalk and sweat and floor polish. Always the same smell that hit you, wham, after the holidays. Billy jostled his way out into the corridor. Games next. He groaned. Why couldn't he be like Jamie, who never seemed to bother and could just, do, cricket, rugger, soccer, anything? Roll on, Saturday week, and his mum, his home. Still, perhaps better not to think about it yet.

* * *

Cork Street W1. Harriet sat back, having just finished her presentation. She did not think she had done badly. They had listened, and she felt she had made reasonable sense. Dawsons Ltd were never going to be the most exciting clients in the world, technical publishers never were, but if they just signed up, and paid-up more to the point, that would be more bread and butter work to keep the show on the road. She looked down the table, eight men, except for the middle-aged secretary, who had obviously been bullied for years, and would certainly not be getting any French lessons.

They were now all looking at the figures, and clearing their throats. Harriet knew the importance of silence in these situations. Why were there flies everywhere she went this afternoon? This one, a bluebottle in fact, kamikazied against the dusty office blinds until put out of its misery by the Personnel Director, a Scot called Paterson, who vented his aggression with her glossy brochure. The afternoon heat was unmerciful. She found herself thinking longingly of cool Autumn days, and wondered if she dared slip her shoes off under the board-room table. Just for a minute. Oh the relief. She kept them close just in case she was asked to leap to her feet, she had no wish to play an embarrassing game of footsie to find them.

'Mrs Gosse, thank you for your presentation. Perhaps you would kind enough to give us your initial assessment of our language needs, having completed your language audit?' J.G. Lossard, Deputy Chairman, was talking to her. His tone was challenging. Harriet noticed that his arms were crossed defensively. Mrs Gosse, not Harriet, she thought, still a lot of work to be done then. She looked around the table, and smiled. All these men, walking residues of forgotten 'O' levels in French and German. Scratch underneath and you'd find they still felt that if the natives don't understand, all you have to do is shout louder. Besides who wanted to talk to the bloody French and Germans anyway, unless the bottom line forced them to. Depressing really.

'Gentlemen, thank you for asking to me to come this afternoon, I have enjoyed our meeting. For your sales team I would suggest a specially tailored French programme of 30 lessons, then we could reassess.'

'Mm which would be £600 + VAT per person. Is this open to negotiation?'

'The price includes all teaching materials, monthly assessments, and a report sent to you at the end of the course. The price of the course is fixed at a competitive rate, but there are discounts for clients who sign up for several courses at one time.' Harriet smiled sweetly, inwardly thinking how nice it would be just for once, to find a client who understood about cash flow in small businesses who paid up in full on time, without expecting pints of lifesblood, thrown in for free.

An hour later, Harriet hurried along Cork Street, calculating how much Dawsons was in for now that they had agreed to the French for the six salesmen. £3,600 plus VAT, not bad for starters. She'd have to try harder to get the Japanese. Across the road the Europa Gallery gleamed, daring the street dust from the taxis to eddy into its doorway. Her eye was drawn to the black lettering in the gallery's window 'The Arena of the Canvas: Tachisme of 1950'. Tachisme, from tache for blot. What had her father once said? Art for rich American blottos painted by lazy French ones who can't draw.

An ice-cool blonde, the sort bred specially for West End commercial galleries, guaranteed to freeze the pants off anyone coming in with less than ten-thousand pounds to spend, looked up from her magazine and eyed Harriet indifferently. 'Can I help you?' She clearly doubted it, and gave Harriet's now crumpled second-hand Chanel suit nought out of ten.

'I wonder if you could help me? I believe you recently had the fireplace marbled, and I am trying to find out where one can do courses of *faux* finishes?'

The girl continued to look at Harriet with distaste. She's a Stepford wife, thought Harriet, suddenly. Any minute the whistle will go and she'll have to take a pill.

'Were they students from a school, or perhaps you could give me a name?'

Suddenly weary, from doing battle with London, Harriet put down her briefcase. Her feet ached, her nose was clearly now as shiny as the gallery's front step, and all she wanted in the whole world was a cup of tea, and Billy, for a hug.

'As far as I know they were from the Cecil School of Specialist Decoration, Chelsea. They'll be in the book,' said the girl, in a voice which implied that she was now certain Harriet couldn't read.

'Thank you. Next time I'll come in to enjoy the paintings.' Remnants of a smile, Harriet hobbled out.

girl's face, as the proprietor suddenly burst, shoeless, out of his office, and slid across the polished floor to crash out into the street after her. Sadly, life's ironies usually happen when our backs are turned.

Chapter Four

The woman had just finished her French lesson. As he'd rung off, Jean-Baptiste had made her laugh, praising her use of the future tense, and promising to post her homework back to her by first class post. Then she had told him that she had bought herself a fax, just for her French! He had sounded so impressed. Not that she'd worked out how to work it yet. Maybe the housekeeper's son would know. These days, six-year-olds usually did. Poor Jean Baptiste. *Le pauvre*. Teaching in such heat! It threatened to overcome the room in spite of the fan and the open windows. The distant traffic going over the Vauxhall Bridge ebbed and roared in the distance.

Sitting in her lyre-back chair, she rocked back putting her feet on the highly polished desk, ignoring her own good advice on how one should treat really good furniture. A man who listened, really listened. The sheer pleasure of it. Someone who cared, and didn't raise his voice to drown hers. Why was she always so much wittier with him, than anyone else? Fun seemed to bubble out of her, she felt eighteen again. So alive, and young, and giggly! Her fingers reached inside her. Shamelessly. Who's a wet girl?

Hearing his voice still in her mind, she pressed the white phone against her soft, wet flesh, it moulded into her warmth, and the edges of the numbers rubbing against her, satisfying. Whoever would have thought the invention of the telephone could have brought such results. Yes! There again, was that familiar mixture of triumph. Completeness, secret guilt. Long years being the well-preserved provider of dinner parties. Who would have thought that her body would still remember? She looked at the receiver now wet and sticky. Oh dear. Smiling to herself, she wiped it with a Kleenex. Then she started to laugh. From the sublime to the meticulous!

'My wife is a European these days', her husband would say, surprised at this new ability to crack jokes in French over dinner. It was his way of acknowledging she was not just the invisible woman he usually grunted at between courses. She tried to get up, yet the afterglow forced her to sit down. 'Get sticky knickers, and you'll go blind', old Sister Mary would say at the school. So many years ago now. Who'd be a convent girl? Here we go again! For the first time she realised why they were called multiple orgasms. She could just hear her daughter's voice. Oh MUMMY!

At last, gingerly, at first she walked naked through the bedroom into the bathroom. Feeling the juice run down her legs, trying to reach the bath in time before the Aubusson was ruined. She tried not to laugh, that would only make matters worse. How indescribably precious. Never to be judged, or suffer jokes about being traded in for a younger model. Not that her husband could afford it. Where had she read that in a recession a faithful wife is more valuable than a Rolls Royce?

Good old Jean-Baptiste with his Yves Montand voice. He would never know that after four children her breasts sagged, and her stomach was more Titian than tight. She would never have to suffer pain if his eye wandered, or his breath smelt.

She ran the bath water right up to the top, and poured in a whole bottle of expensive bubbles from Harrods. What the hell. Then, she lay back in the bath, remembering his voice. It thrilled her every time. *Bonjour Madame*. Who cared that he was probably twenty years younger, an out-of-work actor who lived in Acton. Probably some ghastly bed-sit with a gas ring. But on her telephone they were both eternally young, good looking, in perfect harmony, in their own universe.

She thanked God for the day she came across the Harriet Gosse Language School. Three twenty-minute sessions a week at £20 a go. The perfect way to have a romance. 100% above reproach. Educational, scandal-free and cheaper than HRT! Yet wasn't this verbal but unspoken romance as real as the orgasm, which now satiated her body and soul? She splashed Caleche all over her breasts and hair, and then splashed it into the bath too. Asses' milk next time!

The Catholic in her admitted that strictly speaking, she was of course committing adultery in the eyes of God. But on this hot Pimlico afternoon she felt he was infinitely patient and understanding. As she slid beneath the perfumed water, it suddenly occurred to her that behind that stern warning, Sister Mary had obviously known all about sticky knickers. And Mary Magdalene too, no doubt.

* * *

'Harriet! I say, Harriet, do stop!' The voice, with its expensive edge, echoed along the street, breaking into Harriet's thoughts.

It took a second before she realised that the elegant man running towards her was Richard Longbridge.

'Oh, hello.' Harriet felt suddenly quite annoyed to be meeting him.

Yet he seemed so pleased to see her. Odd for London, where people one spent hours with at dinner parties or school Speech Days come to that, then cut you dead in the street the next day.

'Good afternoon Richard.' He drew level with her, shaking hands, and panting. Excusable, as it was 90 degrees.

'You run the Europa, I didn't realize.' A gallery owner she thought, hence the pirate confidence. Of course! Harriet felt that now she was on track to understanding the man. What other business needed quite such bare-faced cheek? Even Marcus admitted that!

'When you said you were a dealer, I thought you were one of those people with a flat in Little Venice and a little black book of rich clients.'

As she said this, she began to take him in, and realized that he was wearing rather fetching yellow silk socks on his feet, but no shoes. Oh, how she wished she could kick her shoes off too.

'Harriet, you do walk fast. No, I would be richer that way, but I have a hugely expensive gallery to run instead. More fool me. I was working at my desk when I saw you in the monitor.' He paused, wiping his face with a Paisley handkerchief, and then looked at her and smiled. A look which she would have said perhaps to Laura, was impish, but it seemed a rather low-ticket adjective for someone so tall, and so very expensively turned out.

'What brings you here? I seem to remember during our fascinating conversation over that cheap plonk the school see fit to call champagne, you said you live in darkest Hammersmith? A case of shop till you drop is it?'

'Actually I've been working, Richard. Nothing would get me to darkest Mayfair in this heat otherwise.'

'Oh come, Harriet.'

'Which monitor did you see me in?'

'In the office. We have one for security. It's wonderful to see you, Speech Day was such fun with you this year. Normally it's bloody agony. Jamie in a foul mood. Me feeling guilty. Hell really. Wonder why one does it half the time. Look do come in and have some tea.'

Harriet looked at her watch, ten to four, she'd need to be back at the office before Mrs Mac left.

'I'm afraid it will have to be a very fast cup of tea, I've got to get back.'

'Understood. I have an extra-fast kettle.'

She laughed, and began to walk back with him. 'Thanks,' she said as he took her brief case. 'So tell me, why do you feel guilty? Jamie's been so nice to Billy. I think they're hoping to see a lot of each other this holiday, so be warned.'

'Well that'll be good for him. The thing is Jamie thinks both his parents are the pits. Can't blame him, I would if I were in his shoes, we are both appallingly selfish people. But I live this side of the Pond, so I come in for more disapproval. Here we are, welcome to the cutting edge of London art scene.' Richard Longbridge stood back to let her into the gallery, looking at her, like an interesting picture whose price had yet to be fixed.

'You know, I've still got a mental picture of you in that marvellous pink dress and the gumboots. Saturday you were a Bonnard. All pink and ethereal, floating through those over-dressed women. Now today terribly Edward Hopper, pale, urban and frightfully businesslike!'

'Believe me I need to be businesslike. Have you seen what the fees are going up to next term?'

'Don't! I sometimes wonder if we're all mad doing this, why don't we just fling the little buggers into the local sinbin, and keep the money for their psychotherapy sessions in later life, when they can spend hours and hours saying what bastards their parents were. Think of the saving! That was not a criticism, calling you businesslike by the way, said he with bare feet. I just envy your energy. London is hell in the summer.'

Harriet thought it was turning into one of those odd days, it was like a dream, the yellow socks, the way he was talking. It was so peculiar, when he barely knew her.

Richard beckoned over to the girl who had been so dismissive, 'Er, Chantal this is Mrs Harriet Gosse. Chantal does all our publicity and marketing.'

'Good afternoon Mrs Gosse.' 100 watts' worth of toothy charm was now directed at her. Harriet thought that on balance she had preferred the scornful apathy.

'You look terribly hot. My mother has that red-headed colouring. Always goes like a lobster.'

Although her head was bent, Harriet could tell the girl was smirking. 'Well this lobster, as you so charmingly put it, would love some extremely fast tea.'

'Two teas Chantal, the fast teapot, the one we use for creditors not clients! Right let's go into the office. Tell me what you think of these?'

Harriet had a sudden vivid mental image of the stallholder in Portobello Road, who wore a red woollen scarf in all weathers and an earring in his ear. Every day he would shout out to the tourists, successfully flogging pictures of weeping children, and of improbably furry kittens. 'Come on darling, two for three quid, lovely for your lounge walls!' She could hear his voice. Richard, in overalls, unvarnished.

'Are you interested in the Tachistes? No perhaps not, I

see you more of an Impressionists sort of person.'

They were standing in front of two paintings whose brash colours burst out from the canvas, assaulting the eye.

'The thing about these pictures is that it really seems as if the canvas becomes an arena where the painting is unfolded, as if it's part of the artist's life. Jackson Pollock said that. Yes I do like some of them. Camille Bryen for instance. I saw a Georges Matthieu collage was sold at Christie's for £2,500 recently, though I expect you'd want at least £4,000 if you were selling it here.'

Not for the first time, Harriet thought it was just as well she had a photographic memory. Good old Marcus, piling up old catalogues in the office loo, with the price each lot fetched, neatly recorded in black ink.

She was pleased to see she had surprised him. The cutting edge of the art world looked uncomfortable, wriggling his shoulders, and looking as if he was reassessing her. Delicious! Probably thought she'd never even heard of Edward bloody Hopper!

What right had these commercial gallery people to be so snobby and exclusive and all-knowing as if the rest of the world had no eyes to see! Just because the rest of humanity could not, or would not pay their absurd prices. Marcus's old gallery was always full of all sorts of people, penniless art students to millionaires. Why had the eighties made art such a soulless business?

He led her round. 'We have about 2,000 square feet here, could do with more, but it gives us this space and the smaller exhibition area at the back. We have about eight in our stable at the moment. All Europeans. This is a Hester Brossadi. Do you know her work?'

'No, I've not heard of her before.'

'You surprise me. Well she's having a View here at the moment, her first outside Germany. Wonderful use of texture. This is a Puriddu, the Sicilian. The actor Alain Le Feuvre is having a show here at the end of the month.'

'Really? I didn't know he could paint? I used to love the Garçon Emil films, we used to see them when we lived in France.'

'Yes? Well I suppose he's a sort of Euro-Hollywood living

legend isn't he? Should attract a lot of old dears who lusted after him years ago who'll now have a chance of getting their hands on his body of work, if not his body. He's not bad actually, though of course he thinks he's a genius. Artists these days do, I find, irrespective of talent. Whatever happened to tortured uncertainty?'

Lovely job for Chantal, Harriet thought. French film stars one week, and Beau Longbridge spouting pretentious claptrap at all times.

'We deal mainly in contemporary work, but we feel our role is partly education, and we have two exhibitions a year of major Euorpean movements, our Italian Furturists show will be in October.'

'Who's we?'

'Well, me I suppose. And the staff, and my bank manager!'

Harriet suddenly felt she was beginning to lose her bearings. Vast white walls, dominated by large canvases. Lesser-known French painters of the fifties she had to admit she'd never heard of. And then the fireplace which seemed oddly domestic in such a stark setting. She stopped.

'Listed.' Richard said suppressing a groan. '*Faux* pink marble.'

Harriet could see Ulrike, cloth and brush in hand, and daubing away in some vast East German moated grange. Pushing those perfect blonde streaks out of her eyes. Action painting of a different sort.

'Actually Richard, the reason I came in was to ask for some information on the people who marbled your fireplace. One of my teachers wants to take a course.'

'Oh. The Cecil School sent a team along. Did it in Rose Aurora. Hot on ragging, dragging, and bragging. All thought they were bloody Michelangelo. Still they did a good job. Brochure's somewhere. If you hold on I've got their brochure somewhere. Come in.'

Richard beckoned Harriet into the office which turned out to be an antidote to the cool perfection of the gallery behind her. On a noticeboard, invitations to private views were stuck up, one on top of another, just looking at them made Harriet feel exhausted. The idea of going to them was quite beyond her. A dusty crate of champagne acted as a door stop, while the heavy desk was buried under heavy art books, and papers. Everywhere, canvases were piled high up to the ceiling, demanding attention. Not like Marcus's office, which was neatness personified, and manned by his dragon secretary. Manned being the right word in her case.

Then she thought of her own office, with paintings by Billy, family photographs and neat piles, bullied daily by Mrs Mac. Here was the public face of the public man, no indication that he had a child, or a wife. Chantal arrived with a tray of tea and chocolate Bath Olivers, oozing charm. 'Like a designer slug', Harriet suddenly thought, imagining her leaving silvery trails across the polished floor.

'Tea. That was quick. Now, one specialist decorative brochure coming up. Their courses cost a fortune. Full of bored Sloanes and pop stars' wives.'

'Thanks. I'll bear that in mind.'

'So. Sugar? No? Milk? What did you think about Saturday? What with old Crouch's purple nose, Madeleine Humble throwing up, and of course the bonking matron. England at its best I thought!'

Harriet felt so tired, she couldn't imagine how she was going to get out of the chair. 'Yes it was. I meant to ask you, what did you mean when you said in the service, that the school was thinking of selling its pictures. I thought one of the best selling points, was that the boys would grow up surrounded by art.'

'Well, I'm afraid the boys won't be surrounded by it for much longer, at the rate the Governors are going. No, I managed to sell a Corot and a small Stubbs for them for one-and-a-half million, but from what I've seen of the accounts, that will only be enough to pay the staff for the next six months, and stop the school from falling down completely.'

'This is awful. I did think the grounds weren't as well cared for as last year.'

'No. That's because the boys are doing it themselves. Stay tuned. The Governors are getting restless, the tom-toms are beating.'

'And there was I worrying that the publicity about the

Matron might damage the school's reputation.'

'Why should it? Quite an improvement to morale. At least the boy's doing the decent thing. Besides, most of the fathers there on Saturday, will have gone to bed with their matrons in their time. I did.'

'You didn't?'

'Of course. Dear Harriet, you clearly don't know boys' public schools! Clearly. Better than, how can I put it politely, a going-over by the headboy. He had halitosis and B.O., whereas Matron only had a moustache. Much better prospect. Biscuit?'

Harriet decided that it would be a miracle if Billy emerged from this culture in one piece. Was Georgiana right? Was she too late to try day schools?

'Poor girl', Richard was saying. She began to wonder how soon she could politely take her leave from this rather exhausting man. 'All bonk and no brain that boy. He'll bore her rigid in a year, even with all that dosh. If she's any sense, she'll get pregnant, have a boy, and divorce him.'

Harriet didn't like to remind herself that she had thought exactly the same. This man voiced the unspeakable in such a relaxed way, as if he really did not give a toss about anything much, or anyone. Late thirties, early forties perhaps, that was a two-thousand-pound suit he was wearing at the least, very together. *Molto, in gamba*, in leg, as Italians would say – long, lazy expensive legs in his case.

'Tell me, did Billy have to give back the *Victor Ludorum*? Poor little sod.'

'Oh yes, but I had his picture taken for posterity.'

'Bright kid. Good voice.'

'Thanks. He was teased quite a lot, at first, because his father was on TV before he died, but Jamie stepped into the breach and sorted them out I gather.'

'My son the good Samaritan? Doesn't sound in character to me. Your husband was in *Sampson House* wasn't he? You see I do communicate with Jamie occasionally, not that *Sampson House* is my idea of popular entertainment.'

'Unlike the *Daily Blare*?'

'*Touché*! No, it's just that everyone seems to be on the fiddle, or having a nervous breakdown. If they are not having children by their close relations.'

'Well, for someone who never watches, you seem to know the plot lines pretty well.'

'I'm an inveterate channel hopper, and it can be quite funny before the News. Which character did your husband play? '

'Howard Sampson. You won't remember him, he died five years ago. Now, I really will have to go I'm afraid.'

As she gathered up her things, Harriet felt disloyal. It cheapened Tom to encapsulate his whole life in that sentence, and then to hope people would NOT remember him. But that was how it was. When would time leave her any other perspective?

Pushing the Cecil School brochure into her briefcase, Harriet thought bitterly for the hundred-thousandth time what a great joke it had been. Sick. She suddenly pictured the night Tom had come back with the script, and told her the story line. Good old Howard Sampson in his black leathers, pushing thirty, oldest swinger in town would somehow eat a live snake for a bet down at the Log & Partridge. A scream! There would be all the build up, and a nice bank-holiday cliffhanger. The old tarts in Props were having hysterics. She had told him she thought it was utterly stupid, and they'd ended up having a row. Tom just couldn't see it was a problem, 'I'll play it for comedy', he had said. 'What do you know about it anyway?' 'Instinct', she had replied, 'I just know it will go sour. It's an awful idea.'

But Tom had told her to stop fussing, it would boost the ratings, and so it had proved. Howard Sampson and his snake-eating exploits had the nation in stitches, a supplement had run an in-depth studio report of the episode. It seemed unbelievably naff now looking back. But that was the eighties for you. And then the animal rights people had started. What a mistake to swallow a snake.

A huge debate began in the press, and continued in Parliament on the undesirable influence of soaps on the nation's youth. The tabloids led a witch hunt, and Tom's agent issued a statement, a stupid, unthinking, just-a-jobbing-actor-doing-his-job, sort of statement, which had made everything worse, because it laid the blame firmly at Tom's door. Soon, Tom's name was poison. Every day the hate mail came, through the letterbox and via the studio. One parcel from Harlesden contained a dead snake. And just as it seemed to be reaching a lull, Princess Diana was quoted at a charity lunch, saying the episode had made her feel sick. Kiss of death.

Journalists camped out at the door sleeping in their cars, and when they got bored, started going through the dustbins, and grilling their neighbours for quotes. The stress made it impossible to sleep, they were under siege. Rumours began to circulate Tom was to be written out, a scapegoat. Someone had to go. None of her clients could ring her, because she had had to take the phone of the hook. She would lie awake at night worrying about money, worrying about the effect that all this would have on Billy.

The doctors at the hospital told her the stress of the publicity could have contributed to Tom's heart attack. Caused it, they meant.

The terrible power of television, she could barely bring herself to watch it these days. For the poor bloody actors and their families in all the soaps now running right through the days and each evening, it just meant notoriety without redress. No-one ever said a word about the scriptwriter who'd thought up the stupid, stupid idea to boost the summer viewing figures.

'Not the chap who ate the snake! Good God I remember that, that must go down with 'Who Shot J.R.' as one of the biggest hypes in soap history. Was it a real one?'

'I must go.' Harriet knew the script backwards if she didn't interrupt it now. She hoped Richard's grin was not meant to be as cruel as it looked. 'My husband was a good actor. It was just his job. Like selling expensive pictures is yours.' She meant overpriced.

She got up. Through the window, she could see the back of an office block. A single figure hurried down the stairs, carrying books in his hand. A girl on another floor, filed her nails against the window, looking up at the sky. As if to gasp some air, as if she'd rather be anywhere else on earth than central London in ninety degrees.

'Listen, please don't go. I. . . .'

'No honestly I must get going, thanks for the tea.'

'Well let me walk with you to the tube. Which station do you need?'

'Any will do, though Green Park is the nearest.'

'Look I'm sorry, I didn't realise. Of course it must drive you mad people making stupid remarks about that silly series. What do you think of this? I've just acquired it for a private client.'

Like small boy trying to bring Nanny round. He unwrapped a bubble-packed picture and held it up. She looked at it, quite overwhelmed, it was an Alfred Wols.

'I paid one million dollars for it last month in New York. It's for a private client. What do you think?'

Was she supposed to be impressed by the price tag? Yes, she had been right about him. It could just as easily have been furry kittens and weeping children off the back of Ford Transit.

'I think it's very expensive and very good. I'm also thinking what's it doing on your desk, if its worth that sort of money?'

'It only arrived today, the client is coming in later he's terribly excited but too mean to pay for security. So often the case. Let me carry your briefcase, I'll just lock the office.'

'Poor old Wols. He hated galleries you know, he was never exhibited.'

'I never knew that, did you study History of Art?'

'No. I just used to hear people talking about him. The idea of his work fetching a million dollars at some high-society auction in New York would have struck him as obscene.'

'Do I get the feeling you think it's obscene too?'

'More a feeling of bad timing. He lived in great poverty in the South of France for years. And that's something I know about.'

A saccharin smile from Chantal, and then they were walking down the road, stopping every now and then to look in the windows of the galleries. Harriet noticed he looked somehow discomfited. It's odd that an English pirate doesn't like people talking about a lack of money, only an abundance of it.

'Harriet, you ought to come with me one night gallery-hopping. Soon.'

'I'm sorry. I don't go out during the holidays, except with Billy.' And suddenly Harriet didn't really want to talk about art to this dealer. However handsome. It was far too important.

'I'm ashamed to say I don't see as much as I should of Jamie. When he's here with me, I'm out four or five evenings a week. It's hard having a son. I rowed constantly with my own father. I suppose it's different for girls?'

'Not really. Though girls try harder to please.'

They stopped to look in a gallery window, at a large John Sloan etching which dominated one wall. A Washington street scene in a mud storm.

'My father always said buying an original work of art was like gaining a piece of immortality, a slice of the artist's soul. I suppose that's why he always thought his stuff was sold too cheaply. Grumbled like mad.'

'Did he paint? Professionally?'

'Yes, he's Jester Dunne. Of course he doesn't paint now.'

'Dunne. The St Anne's Tryptych? Well no wonder you know your Wols. You'd give Chantal a run for her money. She wouldn't know Lowry unless it had a label.'

She ignored the compliment, she was thinking of Jester. She sometimes lit a candle for him in her local church, hoping the Madonna who stood over the candle holders and the prayerbooks, would give him back the use of his hands. (10p per candle, the piece of paper said underneath, I believe, help me where my faith falls short.)

She saw her father walking up the aisle, looking at the large painting of the Transfiguration, everyone thought was by Honthorst and worth a million, until the day a snooty chap from Sotheby's had come and told them it was great fun, but actually third-rate fifteenth-century Tuscan. 'That's right, me old darling, tell us to go away and enjoy it. Sothebyspeak for piss off it's not worth fourpence.' Jester had growled, tweed cape flung over one shoulder, his Havana cigar spewing smoke over the pews. 'Was there any post this morning, Harriet? Commissions?

When will Marcus pull his finger out? No I will not take my hat off. The Almighty isn't a *petit bourgeois*, like this bloody idiot!'

'He's done some very fine work. I remember his retrospective at the Academy.'

Harriet jerked herself back to the present. What was he saying?

'He's still fetching good prices too, one sold for £24,000 at Bonhams last week. Do you have any of his work?'

'Three or four pieces.' This handsome, charming, spoilt man seemed to think everything had its price. And everyone?

On Piccadilly they were suddenly surrounded by a party of American students. They looked enormous to Harriet, over six foot five, some even taller.

'Huge this generation of Americans these days, it's very odd for me having to look up.'

'How tall are you?'

'Six three-ish. I think Jamie will be taller. Useful when he goes to Harvard.'

'Why do you want him to go to Harvard?'

'Anne my ex-wife is set on it. She's American and she doesn't rate Oxbridge. I'm not really bothered if he goes anywhere, as long as he's making some money doing something he's interested in.'

'Harvard's out for Billy, but I never think more than six months ahead. You really don't need to come all the way to the tube you know.'

'I want to. It's an excuse to get out. Such charming company after Chantal I can tell you! No that's unfair. So, how's business? You run your own school don't you? Language teaching?'

'That's right, it's hard work, but I suppose I can't complain.'

'But you teach it by phone, Jamie tells me. Extraordinary. I've never heard of that before. Does it work?'

'Very well. It's economical and flexible and much better for your average Englishman. Not seeing the person he is speaking to gets him over his embarrassment!'

'I'm sold. God, it's hot. Do you have to go into the bowels of the underworld. Sure I can't get you a cab?'

‘I’m afraid I can’t afford one Guv’nor.’ Laura called it her Liza Doolittle voice.

‘All money going out isn’t it? I’ve just done the Basel Art Fair, did quite well. Washed our faces, corporate collectors, and the Japanese have started buying contemporary stuff which is good news. Had their fingers too badly burned with the Impressionists. But there was such a fortune to pay out before we even got there.’

‘You ought to take Japanese lessons. I have a marvellous teacher. Just think how much easier it would be to swing a deal if you knew the right phrase to describe a painting.’

‘I’d probably get the wrong tone of voice and end up saying your mother’s knickers are in the fountain or something! Do you have a card? Portobello Road? How *outré*!’

‘That’s the beauty of teaching by phone, the office could be anywhere. Besides I like being *outré*!’

He laughed. ‘Look, let’s do dinner one night? Can’t do it till Thursday. I’m off to New York tomorrow, but what about Friday or Saturday?’

It came so naturally. Such a nice pirate, as pirates go. Just waiting for her to get out her diary, fix a date. A when and a where, a beginning.

‘That’s really nice of you, Richard but I’m teaching every night at the moment, and I’ve got several teachers to train before Billy comes home. One of the disadvantages of this business.’ She gave him a wry smile, the smile she had practised so often.

‘Lunch then? ’

‘Not at the moment I’m afraid.’

‘Another time.’

She shook hands with him, and disappeared down into the station. The puzzled look in his eyes, stayed with her as she headed down the escalator and the city came between them.

* * *

Weeds. Large dark-green ones needing two hands. Small ones which gave up without a struggle. Bindweed strangling the strawberries. A thin orange-coloured worm wriggled. No thank you. She smashed at it with the edge of her trowel.

Gardening was no answer this evening to her sense of

restlessness. Why had she turned him down like that? An intelligent, successful man asks her out to dinner. He does not look like a rapist or a wife batterer. He even apologised about the snake thing. And yet she ran away, like a gauche fourteen-year-old. And what on earth could he think?

'Oh God, he probably thinks I'm playing hard to get!'

Cheeks burning, she swept the weeds onto the compost heap. Maybe being a widow did mean part of you closed down. Went numb? Yes your brain, you cretin! Why hadn't she just built a pyre on the compost and thrown herself on it? *Suttee* in W6? It would have made nice follow-up headlines to the snake for the nationals!

The two young, police officers had been obviously in a hurry. Just the way they had parked their car, the front end jutting out into the road as if for a quick getaway.

'May we come in Mrs Gosse?' An ordinary, wet summer's day. She had spent the afternoon playing with Billy, going over his letters in his *Letterland* book. H is for hairy Hatman, A for Annie Apple, Q for Quarrelsome Queen. Billy said she was Golden Girl, very flattering. Daddy was Jumping Jim – suitable as he played Howard Sampson, the character who spent most of the time jumping about, usually into the married neighbours' beds!

She cleared a pile of old scripts off the settee, and the two officers sat forward on the very edge, on the cushions. Just in case they might be drawn into her world.

'I'm afraid we've got some bad news for you Mrs Gosse.'

On one level, she had known at once. But on another she could not take it in at all. Not for weeks. 'I'm afraid your husband suffered from a sudden heart attack an hour ago. He was taken immediately to hospital but it was too late. He was dead on arrival. I'm sorry.'

Looking back, she would often wondered just how sorry they really had been. The woman police officer had clearly felt more sorry than the man, she was very taken with Billy – who wouldn't be? But it was as if a film had been put over their reactions to other people's emotions. A professionalism she later came to envy, even tried to emulate. Taking refuge in a gay, unsentimental superficiality.

'Why did no one ring from the hospital?' Frozen, she could only deal with minutiae. 'Why are you here? Was he mugged?'

'No. Your husband was taken ill in Charlotte Street, one of our colleagues saw him and called the ambulance, but it was too late. The officer recognised your husband. I should say that there are already some reporters outside. This snake business won't help. It wasn't real was it?'

'They said it wasn't in the *TV Times*, John.' The policewoman looked at her, embarrassed. Men.

The practicalities of death. Could a neighbour help with her little boy? Billy came up immediately for a cuddle – how grey his eyes were. Should they contact her mother? No, she was dead. Where was the tea pot?

It became a slow-paced black and white film. Exaggerated expressions. People's faces peering at her, with captions of their words, feelings and assumptions imposed over her own.

It was the small details. Not knowing where she kept the sugar, where her front-door keys were. The flashing cameras as she arrived at the hospital. Tom's eyelashes, so long and dark and still. The shock. The feeling of having been jilted, of outrage that he had left her alone, without goodbyes. Leaving behind so much unfinished business. Leaving behind Billy. Where's my daddy, where's my daddy? Billy's voice in the night.

Logic fought this strange semi-reality. Twenty-nine-year-old actors do not fall down dead in Charlotte Street on the way to rehearsal. That's for soap operas like *Sampson House*. The sort of crumby trick script editors pull when someone asks for too much money. Or won't go quietly.

Later that night, before the sleeping tablets claimed her brain, she remembered feeling a terrible urgency, if she could only find the right nook or cranny in the house, she would be able to speak to him. That he was there just beyond the tips of her fingers, the sound of her voice.

All the press were there. *FANGS FOR THE MEMORY. SNAKE EATER SOAP STAR DIES* – worth a front page in the silly season. Lots of snakey puns – how he writhed in agony on the pavement. As if they had all been there. Famous for his hooded blue eyes. What a load of cobras! etc.

The funeral was even run on the Friday edition of the early evening news, with the cast, dressed up to the nines generously sharing their sorrow with the cameras. What a pro Thomas Gosse had been, a real trouper. Just one or two, like darling Laura, had felt enough grief to let the tears streak through the face powder, as the coffin passed them by. The worst moment. At the graveside Harriet noticed how the florists had left their logo on the wreaths along with the cards, free publicity. Snakes in the grass.

Her own role had been newsworthy enough to attract letters and flowers from hundreds of fans and weirdos. Her plight was used in articles in family money pages later that week, on the wisdom of taking out life assurance when you are young. Yet her role as single parent coping with debts and a mounting overdraft was ignored. More dead snakes arrived in the post. She had a row with the production office for not screening the post. Not their job now he's left the show they said. Bastards.

She began to sigh as she spoke. As if the air in her lungs did not have energy, nor the will to finish a sentence. Her language teaching became an ordeal of acting, fighting the fog which prevented her from functioning in any language. A new life where bills turned into debt, and loneliness to fear. She considered changing her name back to Dunne, to save her from the *Sampson House* curse. But people advised her not to, bad psychology for Billy they said.

The tiny amount of life assurance she had browbeaten Tom into buying, soon went. Child benefit, the widow's pension but mainly her teaching kept them afloat, just, from month to month. Laura came to live with them, renting out her house in Brighton to an American Express executive. Her rent and her humour helped, and odd cheques appeared for the sale of the programme to Turkey and the Philippines, which bought Billy shoes or paid some bills. Getting by. Every penny was saved and planned and worried over. When the programme was sold to a New York TV Station, Laura told her to splash out, buy some clothes, take a holiday, but the money was salted away against the next month's Armageddon.

Soon she was an economy junkie, buying second-hand clothes, large bottles of cheap shampoo, scouring out lipstick from the bottom of the base with a small brush, and posting up coupons offering 3p off on the kitchen noticeboard. She and Billy were two musketeers, all for one and one for all. He grew up, perhaps too fast, while she, though wary of putting too much on his small shoulders, sank into his company rather than anyone else's. She made a point of talking about Tom, keeping him part of their lives, though they never watched *Sampson House* once Laura was written out – running off with the piano tuner. And then the business took off, and Billy went to St Anthony's, best thing everyone said, even Billy. She began to buy more expensive makes of washing-up liquid, even the odd magazine.

Meanwhile fourteen million people a week continued to watch *Sampson House*, and their world moved on. Just occasionally in a pub quiz, the question came up, who played Howard Sampson, before Richard Clifford. Ah yes, the man who ate the snake. Whatisname. But Thomas Gosse offscreen became a near forgotten shade in the nation's consciousness. There's nothing quite so dead as a dead actor.

* * *

It was the vulgar streak in him his mother always said. Taking Concorde because it was there. Yet he could just see her adjusting all those large, vulgar rocks on her claw-like fingers as she said it. Very English rose, more Irish bog. Yes he took Concorde because it was there. Whether he could afford it was another question altogether. But it was there, so why not? Just as she continued to admire those absurd bright gold taps in all her bathrooms. Early Jeddah Renaissance he had called them, to her fury.

'More champagne, Mr Longbridge?' A circle of lip gloss spoke to him, Moet hovered.

'Yes please.'

Richard stretched his legs. A foolish move. No money on earth seemed to buy a seat on Concorde which didn't make you feel you'd spent the trip with your legs wrapped round your neck. It was the only time he envied the short Japanese. Probably been built with them in mind all along. Now, now he mustn't be xenophobic, he should be learning Japanese she had said.

New York. Astonishing how after all these years it still stirred the blood. The endless possibilities of the Manhattan skyline. When he had first met her, Anne had described his enthusiasm as 'cute'. The most leaden word of the well bred New Yorker who saw the city as certain streets, certain stores, certain restaurants, and only very certain people. And he had married her. Lesson number one to Jamie, never marry a woman without a sense of humour, however good her connections. Or her legs come to that.

Suddenly wriggly and impatient, he had to fight the urge to pull off the toupee on the man's head in front. (Now there's a syrup, his father would have said!) He thought of his lovely aquatic Victoria, and then of that uptight little widow who, well, it was pretty obvious what she needed poor darling! Harriet. Even her name was goody-two-shoes, sensible lace-ups. She had something quite special though.

Sighing, he forced himself into an article in *Art In America* on a woman who makes jewellery out of children's milk-teeth. Now what would his bloody mother make of that?

Chapter Five

'*What can I do to you, Sir*?' The receptionist gazed into the hotel guest's blue eyes. Pleasant desperation, then mirth and then finally embarrassment spread over her face. The guest corpsed.

'Cut! *For you*, love. The script says, *What can I do FOR you*?' The floor manager raised his eyes to the ceiling, as the young girl, blushed right up to her dubious blonde roots. 'Form a queue, I'm the producer and I'm first!' Craig Lockhart stepped onto the floor. 'Very nice Georgia darling, lovely new dialogue, but this is before the Watershed. Dammit.'

Oh God, please, let's get on with the scene, Laura thought. She was wearing what were probably the most uncomfortable shoes in the whole history of showbusiness, and lunch was a distant prospect. The sound man had already bitten her head off. Was it her fault her tummy had rumbled during her bit? Please get ON with it!

Camera rolling. Standing in a dark corner of the studio, Laura looked at her script. Unappetising, not to say unworkable. If they cut her part much more.... But it's work. Don't knock it. She tried to think what eating those gorgeous greasy canteen chips would do to her – give her a pot belly like that old studio carpenter, snooking off for a crafty fag. Lucky bugger. She looked round for a something to sit on, but there was nothing in sight. As usual.

Suddenly, she thought of Harriet rushing through the station. So serious and hidebound these days. And yet in those few seconds in Paddington she'd seen again the

Harriet she'd first known, wearing funny hats, rushing to collect Tom after a day's shoot. The most lusted-after woman at the cast party, cheekbones so high they seemed to reach up to the studio lights, thick reddish blonde hair whooshing in behind her, never fat, never on a diet, the cow. Not that she ever knew the effect she had on people, which was why you couldn't dislike her.

In front of her, the pathetic excuse for a scene intended to introduce Cosmo D'Arcy the Mr Big of the Georgian silver world, droned on. And ON. Cosmo D'Arcy, alias Derek Dixon. Poor old Derek. A crumbling money pit of a house falling down around his ears in Shepherd's Bush, and a boring geography teacher of a wife making his life hell. I just hope Wardrobe lets him buy the suit.

She thought of her tenant who now said he needed a new washing machine. What did he wash in it? Spare parts for his rowing machine? And to top it all, her father had rung up hoping that they might, perhaps, now meet. Dream on! Laura had never got on with her father. She considered him, on the rare occasions when she gave him any thought at all, as a nasty combination of Mr Murdstone in *Oliver Twist* and Squeers in *Nicholas Nickleby*. And she never mentioned him to anyone. They had parted by mutual consent when she was eighteen and off to RADA. It had taken a short marriage to a talented but alcoholic director, and several years of expensive therapy to able to talk to him, even on the phone. Yet he had his uses. Whenever she had to play anger, she just thought of him, and to quote her therapist, she rediscovered her inner child. Had she, or had she not been a seriously snarling Wicked Witch in the Watford panto last year?

'Right people. Next scene. Office set. Now then, we want Annabella, Sergeant Miles, Cosmo D'Arcy and Oliver Richards.' Laura wondered why production assistants treat actors as if they have a mental age of five and a half. Annabella – God preserve us. Laura, feet aching, walked onto the set. Derek smiled.

'Hello darling, now what are you going to do to me today? Dry?'

'Fuck off Derek. Your nose is shining.'

* * *

Anne Osborn – Anne with an E, Osborn without – had developed the technique of pushing an organic endive salad around a plate into a new performance art. But then if she knew one thing, she knew about Performance Art. Her new lover Guy Rossini was *Art In America*'s latest discovery. Richard groaned inwardly and felt hungry. Anne's three broiled bay scallops lingered unloved and calorific at the side of her plate, and Richard wished briefly, he was back in St Ant's, where you either nicked each other's food, or starved, which was what was happening to him right now. Any chance of a bread roll? And butter? He knew what she would say. Married life was always so predictable, even when you didn't live it any more.

Anne let the endive off for good behaviour, sipped her mineral water, and lit one of her low-tar cigarettes. She was still a lovely woman, of the never-too-rich, or too- thin variety. Her eyes always reminded Richard of a David Hockney swimming pool – deep blue and deeply commercial. He suddenly had an image of Harriet in the gum boots, peering at him out on the hot street. Lunchtime on East 76th between 5th and Madison. Busy, busy, busy. Women! Richard felt disgruntled.

In New York, you know you are at the right restaurant when Paul Newman is at the next table. You know you have the right table because Paul L'Étranger of the Gutfreund Museum is waving at you, whilst peering past you to the window to see who Diana D. Brooks of Sotheby's New York is talking to. At Les Sylphides, Anne being high profile and old family, always got a great table.

'Richard, you must be careful. Otto's always so generous with his portions, Richard you're putting on weight. You need to shed twenty pounds. At once.'

Their marriage ended, unofficially, on the first day of the Andy Warhol Sale, April 1988. It was one of those special days, at the very height of the eighties' art boom, when to be in the art world, and to be in Manhattan was to have the top table at the *zeitgeist* ball. So someone had said. Stretch limos stretching down York Avenue at 72nd, cabs clawed for space at the sidewalk. It was the sale of the decade, and what a decade. Farewell to a genius. Andy would have *loved* it! High tension, and millions of dollars cascaded down the phone lines as the bidding sizzled. Fortunes were paid for cookie jars, as the beautiful people of New York City, and the less beautiful, but equally aspirational out-of-towners, fought for a little piece of Warhol's soul.

It was in the crush of the saleroom, that Richard Longbridge came to the conclusion that he did not love his wife. In fact not only that he did not love her, but he was actually beginning to dislike her. It was one of those definitive moments when life-changing decisions are made. And not long afterwards, a grateful Anne, had slipped back to New York permanently, giving the tenants of her brownstone notice, and mortgaging it to buy a partnership at the Lapham Gallery on East 79th. The Warhol Sale made over 24 million dollars, while Sotheby's worldwide sales topped 2 billion that year. And for once old Maggie Thatcher's trickle-down theory had certainly trickled down to Cork Street and Madison Avenue. Yes it had been the very best time to be in the art business. It had also been just the time to be newly single.

'It's such a pity you're not here this weekend, Guy and I are off to the Hamptons. We're staying with the Van Hoorns. They would have loved to have seen you.'

It was the sort of rhetorical remark, which had no basis in reality. But then Richard had long ago discovered that well-bred New Yorkers always spoke on two levels. The real and the polite. She would have been truly horrified if he had stayed and taken up her invitation.

'I think Jamie should come out to me for three weeks on July 30th, is that convenient with you? The house in Amagensett will be ready by then.'

'Yes that's fine, Anne.' Richard's tummy rumbled as the waiter slipped two black coffees onto the table. He reached for the sugar. Anne and the waiter looked at him disapprovingly.

* * *

What a difference four yards makes. It wasn't that Hector and Maxi Rogers had not spent a fortune on their clothes. It was just that it was the wrong fortune on the wrong clothes, and so they had been seated at the wrong table. Some yards from where the right clothes had been bought, probably on Gold Cards, but who cared?

Hector, who had asked for steak, was hot and already exhausted by the City heat. His body needed fuel, fast. He broke his hand-ground cholla with determination, and spread it with real butter.

'I don't pretend to understand it. I don't mean to understand. And Maxi, I never, repeat never want to go to such a thing. It's a waste of my life.'

'Alright dear. It was only that Justine thought it would introduce us to the inner feelings of New York.'

'The only inner feelings I am interested in right now are those in my stomach.'

Maxi sighed. What a mistake it had been, to follow her decorator's advice and drag Hector to a Performance Art show. What made it worse, was the knowledge that secretly she agreed with him. The man with the blue paint and the lizards had been totally weird! And she couldn't see what connection it had all got with the New York's homeless, the lizards had little cages to go in after all. It was so different from Houston. She looked around the room, her eye caught by the woman in beige talking to the tall handsome man. He looked vaguely familiar, probably a chat show host. Now that was the table to get she thought, enviously. Not too near the door. Near the window, where you could see everyone in the room and they couldn't see you.

'Hector!' Her voice squeaked. 'That's Paul Newman. Paul Newman there in the corner!'

It took a great deal of character for her not to go up and ask him for his autograph. But no, she had to be cool, she was now mistress of a New York duplex apartment.

Maxi was a great reader, a magazine was never out of her hand. And over the years it had been reading the English *Tatler* Magazine, that had given her the idea to send Boydie to a real English boarding school to prepare him for Europe in time for the company's expansion there, she had told Hector, not mentioning all the London shopping trips it would mean. He'd be so near France. He would get real

English manners and could go to College anywhere. Hector had agreed not least because he wanted to impress his friends at the Country Club.

Then Boyd had married Michelle, the school nurse on the sly. Maxi thought she would never get over her disappointment. A faxed copy of the *Daily Blare* had gone to Martha Peston straightaway, from her daughter living in London, and it became easier to speed up their plans to move to New York. Business is business as Hector always said. And the first rule of married life, was what Hector said was right.

It was said that when the recession hit Houston in the mid eighties, billionaires had overnight become millionaires, and millionaires had started collecting the garbage. Hector Rogers on the other hand, had collected garbage from the start, and had become a multi-millionaire. Almost a billionaire. The RGR Corporation – short for Rogers Garbage Recycling had opened plants all over the U.S., and now Mexico and Brazil. He had franchised the operation and his empire had spread all over the Far East. The Green thing had caught on, and Hector who had gone into business because he liked making money and hated waste (his mother Mary Jo never threw away a piece of string, and sold broken cookies door to door), had in time found himself to be both seriously rich and politically correct, though never fully accepted by the lawyers and the banker and the oil men of his home State in spite, or perhaps because of, his financial acumen.

But now all his plans for his son had let him down. Boyd had been groomed to take on the business, and Boyd, Maxi knew, had disappointed him. Bitterly. Marriage to a nobody just after his money. No time even to draw up a pre-nuptial agreement. Maxi sighed, as she watched him cutting into his steak.

'Mr and Mrs Rogers, how nice to see you here.'

The chat show host was coming towards them. How strange, he seemed to be English. Maxi was a sucker for an upper-class English accent. Hector half rose to meet him.

'No, please don't get up, you may not remember me, I'm Richard Longbridge, our sons are at St Anthony's. This is my dear ex-wife, Anne Osborn.'

'Oh yes, how nice to see you.' Hector and Maxi looked discomfited.

'Mr and Mrs Rogers were at the Speech Day, Anne. Boyd has been a good Head Boy. Very nice to the little squirts in the Junior House.'

Maxi flushed with pleasure. Who were the squirts?

'Are you in New York long?' Richard liked what he called real Americans, he always thought New York was an exciting aberration.

'No, just a week. We've come to do some shopping and see how our new apartment is shaping up.' Maxi couldn't help but be flattered by his interest. Not just two out-of-towners, but people with something in common with people who got the best tables. 'We've just bought an apartment in the Stein Building.' And she just couldn't keep the pride out of her voice. They had made the grade with the residents' selection committee.

Anne smiled sweetly, and gazed at the couple in front of her. New apartment. In the Stein, there was none under two million dollars, even now. Bare walls. *Nouveau riches* with plenty of riches, judging by the emerald on the woman's hand. 'I have always admired the Stein building, you are so fortunate. What is your field Mr Rogers?' Southern ole boy accent, and how! Oil? No couldn't be, they were all broke these days.

Hector was wiping the steak juice off his chin.

'Garbage recycling. Ma'am. My husband is the CEO of Rogers Garbage Recycling Corporation.' Maxi suddenly felt overdressed, and huge, this woman couldn't be more than a size 6.

'How interesting. It's very nice to meet you Mr and Mrs Rogers. Jamie has said how very kind your son has been to him.'

'Oh er, good.'

Anne's eyes shone like a little girl who had just seen Santa Claus. 'Well we mustn't keep you from your meal.'

'Hector and Maxi please.'

'It's been so nice to meet you both. 'She tried not to shudder at the steak juice which was on the man's chin. 'If you're in the City this week, maybe you might like to come to the new Show at my Gallery. Gertrude Ledermeyer, a marvellous sculptress we've just signed, from New Mexico. Very important work.'

Anne produced her card, mentally making a note to check him out when she got back to the office. 'We American St Anthony parents must stick together!'

'Oh yes! Goodbye Mrs er, Miss Osbut.' Maxi tried to read it, her contact lenses had greased up. But she knew a class act when she saw one.

'Goodbye.'

Richard and Anne went out into the street. Richard exploded with laughter.

'Holy shit, garbage recyclers at the Lapham Gallery! Times have changed!'

'Don't be so vulgar Richard they seemed good people.' The moral high ground had always been Anne's natural habitat.

Surprised, he realised she was going to walk. He had expected her automatically to hail a cab, although the gallery was just a few blocks away.

'You're walking!'

'Richard, stop snorting in that awful way. I have two legs and a lot of debt. These days I walk. Now are you going to come on the right side of me?'

'Walk' said the lights, and they walked, in the searing New York heat, Richard like a gentleman, on the outside of the sidewalk to keep his sword hand free.

* * *

It was a picture of a villa in Kuusisaari, Helsinki's Belgravia. 'Dear' Jaakko had sent it to her last Christmas. It showed his precious collection of New Houston School canvases on display in Scandinavian splendour, all light woods and white carpet. That $22,000,000 he had paid her in 1988 seemed a long time ago. The Dentons, Hestonvilles and Greenbachers would, he had assured her, change the way emerging Finnish artists would see mixed-media work. She, who didn't give a damn about Finnish artists, emerging or newly hatched, had nodded encouragingly, banked the cheque, and seen her partnership announced in the *New York Times* the following week. Happy days at the Lapham

Gallery. Now the picture of those pale Finnish walls made her want to scream.

'He's going to dump it. The catalogue's already printed. Butes mailed me a copy. It's a fire sale. The estimates are a suicide note. And he doesn't care what it fetches. He wants out. I told him it was a long-term investment. It would have to mature, but no he just has to sell it.'

Anne was upset. Now safe from the gaze of the diners at Les Sylphides, she bit the sides of her red nails and lit another cigarette. These days, her office was all Shaker-style furniture painted greens and blues, their idea of the colours of Heaven, Richard remembered. Bloody uncomfortable. He put the picture down. He couldn't help but feel a little bit amused, 'dear Jaakko,' that larger than life industrialist – he of the textiles, the industrial plant, and the phallic office buildings, Hell-stinki's answer to Donald Trump, had been a talisman throughout their divorce. The symbol of her success as a gallery manager, of her belief in Southern Art, which, as Richard had always told her, was crap.

'So what will happen if he sells the lot? It's not your problem, You were paid upfront, there were no bank loans.' Anne had always got too uptight he thought. Even in bed, Especially in bed. Never relaxed for a second.

'Don't be so fucking obtuse, Richard. The Lapham Gallery made the market with this group. We set the price. We created the New Houston School.' Anne leant over the desk, keeping her voice down in case the staff heard. Whispers overheard were worth a fortune in New York. Richard noticed the fine lines now webbing her fine porcelain skin. She was growing old. The tautness of the skin over the high-cheek bones made her seem vulnerable.

'The forty pictures at Butes' North American sale next month will fetch two million sterling. Tops. Most of London will be on vacation. So where's the interest? Except the press, they are always around when you need them least.' Her tone was bitter.

'Well you never know, most of New York will be on vacation in London, so someone might take to a Greenbacher or two.'

'But where will we be with such volume being dumped?

At once! We have no control over this. Our Greenbacher show in the Fall, with his new work, will be a joke. Even though it is over in London, for which small concession I thank the Gods, but even so, news travels. So, just as we are starting discussions about rescheduling the loans, the banks are going to smell blood and will press for payment of the whole lot, yesterday. I'll probably lose my home. Prices here are already 40% down in the saleroom. In London who cares about American Art except spare-me-a-dime Hampstead critics? We're talking decimation. These are difficult times. And I have just two weeks to get him to withdraw the sale. Quietly.'

'I just don't understand how he could go broke so quickly. Why would he be prepared to get such a bad price?'

'Do you think I haven't asked him that?' Anne hissed, wishing that for once, Richard would try to understand, and not imply, as he always had, that she was merely overreacting.

'These people are very different. They're mentally, if not physically in the Arctic Circle, most of the time.' She lit another cigarette.

Richard felt himself tensing up just looking at her.

'I read that Finland's in recession, like the rest of us, unemployment, insolvencies. So what's new? Can't you just talk to him, and ask him to let you buy it back? Say you have an interested customer.'

Anne was prowling round the room. Like a cat on a hot tin roof, or a tin pot gallery, thought Richard. I wish she would sit down. I need a pee.

'It's revenge, Richard! He wants to expose what he calls the hypocrisy of the New York art scene. It's not true, I know for a fact the Tate in London has bought three of the Greenbacher's in the last year.'

'Things are as bad as that are they? I had no idea. That's no guarantee of anything. Except of enraging the coach parties.'

'Don't be flippant. Jaakko apparently invested heavily in real estate in the London Docklands district, which is now standing empty. Now, apparently, the Russians are saying they will start currency-based trading, at the end of this year. So instead of bartering their gas and oil for Jaakko's precious textiles and plant, they will give him roubles, which he needs like a hole in the head. The banks want their money, Jaakko's down to his last Renoir, and he seems to think it's all our fault, and won't be happy till he takes us down with him.'

'Poor man. But I still think you just need to get someone to pose as an interested customer and go to him direct, talk him into withdrawing the lots and selling privately. For cash. His anger will be overcome by his business instincts.'

'Agreed. That's our only chance. But we just don't have the money to give a fake customer. The only other thing would be to have two plants at the sale to get some heat in the bidding. But the banks won't lend us the money. I'd need to sell my house, which I am not going to be able to do in this market. Galleries are bad news these days, Richard. We don't all have rich mommies to bail us out.'

'Don't make me laugh. Besides, your old ma isn't short of a bob or two as I recall.'

'No, even if she had it, it wouldn't help. We're talking millions to bring him round, or keep the price consistent with the rest of the market.' She fixed him with those blue eyes, that had once sent him reeling across the Guggenheim. Long ago. 'Richard, I need you to help me.'

'I'll try, Anne. But honestly no-one in Britain is going to spend that sort of money on your Greenbachers and your Dentons in Virginia Water. For one thing you couldn't live with them for five minutes. And there's no way I can help you. I'm completely fucked. My overdraft is enormous.'

'Best of all, short of him not selling, is to find a real person with real money, who'd want them. All.' Anne sounded almost tearful.

'Yes I can see that one rich sucker might save your bacon. But let's face it, it isn't going to be easy. Not in new markets with an investment angle. How did anyone know how to price Manet, or Van Gogh. They didn't? It was only what someone would pay, which wasn't much. And no one thought about the pictures as an investment, only whether they liked them or not.'

'I don't need a lecture on art values Richard, I need your

help. There's a percentage for you, if you pull it off.'

'Well, I'll do my best. After all I did introduce you to the Rogers just now. O.K., they're tasteless I agree, but loaded. Their son just ran off and married the Matron so they're not happy bunnies. He needs cheering up. With a happy little Greenbacher. Anne, where is your loo? I'm bursting.'

Anne sighed and reached for her packet of cigarettes. Empty. She remembered the first time she had met Richard's father. Old Ernie Longbridge, into freeway restaurants, caffs he called them, bomb-damaged land, up to anything for a fast buck. She had trodden on his foot going up the steps into the Ritz. 'Oi! Bloody 'ell gel, watch it!'

'Bloody 'ell' said Anne with feeling.

The hot summer evenings were her favourite time. Especially Tuesday evenings. She had brought up a cold bottle of wine to her room, and put on her pale pink silk negligee. Her husband had bought it for her after a trip to Oslo when he had taken his mistress instead of her.

'C'est Jean Baptiste, bonsoir Madame.'

She couldn't help but cross her legs, what if he knew! Laughing, she plunged into the future tense . . .

Dear Richard,

I hope you are well. I am well. Thank you very much for coming to Speech Day.'

Jamie lied. and bit the end of his pencil. His father wasn't the least bit interested.

'I have had a good term, and hope to be Dorm Captain next term. I shall find out next week. Please can I have a mountain bike? Please can I have the money for some more computer games?'

Given I'm an only child from a broken home. It's the least you can do!'

Tuesday night was Letters Home night. Yawn! Several pencils had been chewed for inspiration, but even so, few parents were going to get any letter worth reading. Phipps, reading the paper in the corner had already told them off twice for talking, and Mr Crouch had come in once with a pair of prospective parents. Fat and oiky. Must be scraping the barrel. The boys, well drilled, tried to look well-fed, happy and motivated, until the door had shut, and they slumped back into the early evening stupor.

I hope to see Billy in the holidays, they live in Hammersmith and there is a tube there straight from Knightsbridge. Could we go to lunch on Saturday with him and his Mum? I think she is nice. I don't want to go to New York this holidays, could Mummy come here?

Jamie hated his mother's flat with its freezing-cold air conditioning. He also loathed Guy Rossini. He didn't understand a word he said. Worse than Edward Morgan, his mother's previous 'partner' who folded his clothes ever so neatly, and said Jamie ought to go to Law School. No more school of any sort after this one, Jamie had vowed already.

Please may I go and stay with Granny Mary in the holidays?

Jamie rubbed his eyes, and thought of his Granny, of her cuddles, and treats. Billy would like her, and it would make the old sod happy. He never took him out once. Never! Except to see horrible messy pictures in horrible galleries, where there was nowhere to sit, and everyone drank salty fizzy water.

Goodbye.

Jamie.

He wouldn't put love, why should he?

His father maddened him, while his mother, a distant beacon of perfection, had nothing to do with real life. Jamie licked the envelope and stuck on the stamp. 'Parents!' Nods around the room. It was perhaps as well for their mental equilibrium, that St Anthony's mummies and daddies were not due for any end-of-year reports from their offspring.

* * *

'No picka de nose. You're disgusting. Get off my desk.' Harriet pushed Danny off.

'I'm not, I've got paint up my nostril, I've been spraying today. Its great. Eat your heart out Bratby!' Danny Messenger was blue with inspiration. And red, and green. And sludge. He was a Puck of many colours, who'd put a girdle round the earth from a semi in Pinner to Portobello, via St Martin's and the Royal Academy School. His coming downstairs normally signed off both his working day and her own. And was Harriet glad to see him....

'Promises, promises I've closed the doors, and brought you hardworking young people a drink.' Marcus, magnificent in a red bow tie, came through the door of the office with a bottle of red wine and three glasses. He opened the fire-escape door, and let in the evening heat.

'I've sold two pictures today. Cheap art for first timers. Both under five hundred quid, but that's the future. I have now covered my phone bill, and can pay the cleaner for another two weeks.'

'Stop pleading poverty Marcus, we all know you've got your mattress stuffed with tenners Now will you two be quiet – I've got to finish this report.'

Danny read it over her shoulder on the computer screen.

'Much progress has been made with the use of the subjunctive, and conditional tense.' What are they when they're at home?

'If I WERE sensible I WOULD brain you with this claret bottle.'

'Alright. I'm only asking. – However, Mr Quick needs to concentrate on building up his vocabulary, and improve his knowledge and use of idiomatic expressions. – His whatee whatee? Our Mr Quick seems a bit of dickhead.'

Harriet groaned. 'He is, Danny. But, every twenty hours of tuition, I have to do a report to his Chairman, and in it, I have to strike a nice balance of making them see the progress he has made (if any), while intimating that another twenty hours could just do the trick. Goodbye Mr Quick. I hate to say it, but it's usually a waste of time teaching beginners over 50.'

'Now that is charming. And I brought you in the wine.'

Harriet filed, exited, and switched off.

'You needn't be like that Marcus, it does get too difficult to start a language from scratch. But I've taught everyone else on the Board of Grenvilles. And I'm after repeat business. Much better than spending your time cold calling. Anyway, whatever, it's all bloody hard work. Where is that drink?'

'Do you deserve it, I ask myself? Not that I have any desire to learn Portuguese or whatever language the poor man is endeavouring to learn, but even so, I resent being put on a linguistic scrapheap.'

Marcus who spoke only one language, the one you find on a cheque, had dealt with every nationality in his life. In the sixties, seventies and eighties his gallery in Bruton Street had been a byword for cosmopolitan art and glamour. Slumming it these days of course, but he earned a crust, and if the touristicos who came slouching down Portobello and into his gallery didn't understand about conceptual art, he simply said it had been reserved.

Harriet felt the alcohol course down the back of her shoulders.

'Did I tell you Marcus I went to the Europa the other day, saw the fireplace you told me about. The Cecil School did it, in Chelsea. Ulrike's starting there on Monday. I hope to God that will keep her happy – and the clients, more to the point.'

'I thought you were mad to agree to that, Harriet, much as I love Ulrike, and that sulky act of hers. How was the Europa? Now that's one gallery still living in another age. Lovely big round prices darling. Don't know how he does it.'

'Richard Longbridge? He has a son at St Anthony's, I met him on Saturday.'

'Oh we are going up in the world. Cork Street.'

'Shut up Danny. He asked me out actually.'

'Well I hope you said no', said Marcus, 'because, mark my words, that gallery will be the next one to go under, you can bet on that. Unless, that is, old Ma Longbridge, who let me tell you, is the fattest Philistine in Fitzrovia, gives her little boy some cash.'

'He is very attractive, but no, in case you're interested Danny, I did say no.'

'How much is he worth then, this Longbridge man?'

'Danny! And they say women gossip.'

It was often said that Marcus Whitehead knew everyone, or knew someone who did. He'd been around forever and before that, Marcus poured himself another drink, and lit a cigar. 'His old man, Ernie Longbridge, was into everything in the fifties and sixties – boxing, scrap metal, tearing down Nash terraces for ghastly office blocks. You name it, he didn't care a fig, as long as he made money. By the seventies he had turned respectable and was into classic cars, and property development. Used to come into the gallery from time to time. Tried to get me to take on that son of his. I wasn't interested, so he dragged him round everywhere else, until eventually he paid Hugh Geisler to train him up. Arrogant, public school, Oxbridge. Knew bugger all, even after two years trying to learn to paint in Paris. Unsuccessfully, I need hardly add.'

Marcus took a slurp. Nothing like a captured audience.

'Worshipped that gorgeous Annunziata Tarrant, and slept with both the Ostler sisters before he married some tight-arsed, well-connected American, and probably after. Billed by Dempster as the Wedding of the year, which was scraping the barrel somewhat, but then the Royals weren't obliging. Anyway, I gather it was all Anglo-American harmony and light, until the wedding cake fell over. Big bits of hard white icing all over the carpet. Rather like stucco from one of Ernie's demolition jobs, someone said at the time. Rather amusing. Contract went out on the baker they said. Rubbish of course.

'How awful!'

'Not really Harriet, if you ask me anyone who has to have five tiers when they're one generation out of the Commercial Road, is simply baiting the gods. Anyway when Ernie died two years ago, they found he'd already done a deal with the Inland Revenue, who promptly took over the stud farm. He left millions in trust for his only son and heir on his wife's death. But of course, as she loves spending and intends to live until she's a hundred, and as he loves mounting exhibitions of pisspoor European painters, and so I've heard pisspoor European actors. Alain Le Feuvre next month. Can hardly wait. And so the banks just go on waiting, and waiting. Drink up.'

* * *

There is never a wrong time for a bacon sandwich. Richard woke up at three o'clock in the morning in his suite in the

Carlton Hotel, and decided, like Winnie the Pooh, that it was time for 'a little something'. He phoned room service. 'Two rounds of bacon, no ham, sandwiches, a pot of Earl Grey please. No I would not want coriander in it.' What a bloody awful idea. He doubted they would have H.P. Sauce in the Carlton. He never remembered to bring his own.

Something was bothering him. It had for the last two days, and now in the small hours, he realised what it was. He was thoroughly pissed off that Mrs Harriet, holier than thou Gosse, she of the achingly beautiful hair, and the horribly practical manners, had turned down his dinner invitation. He didn't consider himself a vain man, but frankly he was not used to women ever saying no.

Richard's stretched his long legs down to the bottom of the bed, soothing his hurt vanity. Where do they get these marvellous sheets? He suddenly had an image of Harriet lying on a bed, in black satin sheets. Richard! Richard! His erection started to harden. Black satin, very Lawrence Harvey, you're showing your age, boy. But just what did she do for sex? Any young widow, come to that. Five years too. She'd rushed down the steps at Green Park station like a frightened rabbit. Frightened of it probably. The thought of Harriet, throbbing with pent-up sexual frustration, was rather engaging. No, he was not going to give up that easily! These thoughts were interrupted by the knock at the door. 'Room service.'

Hell! There's timing for you. He padded to the door. How can Americans always sound so fucking cheerful at three o'clock in the morning?

* * *

'What do you mean, you're calling from New York?'

Eight thirty a.m. in the village of Chadlington in Oxfordshire, Roger Descartes-Jones was in a bad mood. The post had just brought notice of school fee rises for all three children, last night the nanny had written off one of the cars, and this morning his wife had refused to give him, well anything at all. Didn't even pretend to have headache these days. And now this house she had insisted on them buying, turned out to have 15,000 quids' worth of dry rot.

None of what Richard was saying made any sense. 'You want to pretend to be me so you can have Italian lessons on the phone? I don't understand Richard. Whoever heard of lessons on the phone, other than those 0898 numbers. What do I have to do? Fax you the homework. Homework! You! Is this a joke? Because I have to tell you I am not in the mood. What time is it there?'

One of his children vroomed in, knocking his coffee over the French kitchen tiles. 'Giles, you wretched child! Tell nanny to bring me a cloth. I know her name's Tracey, now just piss off and get her, can't you see I'm on the phone. No, sorry Richard, its Giles. Well, you can use my name, and we'll fax you anything that comes through, but my price is two tickets to the Tyler Jones fight next month. No negotiation.'

He put down the phone. *Chercher la femme*, lucky old bugger, he thought His wife stumped past the Aga on the way out to feed the dogs. Now *French* lessons might be an idea.

Chapter Six

Her fingers were trembling so much she could barely dial the number. What a bastard he'd been, so unreasonable, how much longer could she stand it? How much more did she have to take? Children were practically grown up. She could get a job, women did, even at her age. She had French, a London guide for instance? Why wasn't he answering?

'Jean Baptiste?'

'*C'est moi* Madame. Are you O.K.?'

'No. Not really. But I've done the homework you set.'

'*Tres bien. Alors*, I ask, *Vous aimez Paris*?'

The woman sighed, trying to think of the right answer. Half the time she couldn't think straight, these lessons were the only oases of sanity in the week.

'*Oui beaucoup. Mais j'aime aussi voyager. La semaine prochaine, je vais passer quelque jours en Provence.*'

'*Vraiment*?'

'*Vraiment*. I wish I could go to France, Jean Baptiste. You cannot imagine how simply ghastly it is being married sometimes.'

* * *

'Tables over there, chairs over on the pavement! No, Mrs Marsh, let's put the table cloths on before the food! Looks so much prettier with them don't you think?' Georgiana Gaskell was trying not to bawl like a Billingsgate fishwife, as her mother would have said, but really! She was standing in the street wearing a rather fetching orange sun dress which she had picked up in the sales at Peter Jones, issuing commands, in the way she rather imagined Daddy would have organised the troops in India. Leadership was such a rare quality.

Saturday lunchtime, and the Bathurst Road Street Party was beginning to take shape, despite a temperature of 95 degrees in the shade. The police had lent bollards, and neighbours who never spoke to each other normally, sweated in unity as they put up the bunting together. A large banner stretched from number 45 to number 52, with the words 'Street Party' written on it colourfully, in some child's felt-tip pen collection. Very wartime spirit, Georgiana thought, but then, hadn't the recession made everyone feel as if they had their backs to the wall?

Bathurst Road, was in many ways, a typical London street. Inside its carefully planned, rather pretty terraced houses, with their small-paned windows, and stuccoed detail over each front door, all levels of society co-existed within yards of each other, and in varying degrees of stress and solvency. There were barristers and old barrow boys, chartered accountants, and turf accountants, the employed, the self-employed and the unemployed, living in identical houses – give or take a loft conversion or a conservatory – who had bought at different times, and for radically different prices. It meant of course, that the more upwardly mobile one aspired to be, the less mobile one actually was, thanks to negative equity. And yet the more one felt forced to spend to create an illusion of sophisticated city living from housing stock originally intended for the lower-middle classes.

So the professionals who had bought into Brackenbury Village in 1988 at top prices, led a struggling martyred existence hemmed in by mortgage repayments, expensive childcare and school fees, slowly sinking into debt and their nightly bottles of Sainsbury's plonk. While in contrast, luckier neighbours who had bought earlier and would have said if asked, that they lived in Hammersmith, had net curtains, stonecladding, two foreign holidays a year and meals out every weekend.

Harriet, who did not fit particularly well into either category was sitting on her kitchen floor going through the morning post. Her kitchen chairs (according to Georgiana's precise written instructions), were already lining the road with no-one sitting in them. Harriet wondered whose idea it had been to have the party so much earlier this year. In truth her heart wasn't in it, because Billy was still at school, and couldn't share the fun. The children always made the street party a wild success, whirling like dervishes to the energetic noises of the band – provided by the tree surgeon would-be Elvis, who lived at number 98.

The tuna-and-pasta salad was ready – all clingfilmed according to Major Gaskell's instructions. But this morning she could not really concentrate either on the party, or the bills she was opening. She was thinking instead of the man who had left a message on the answering machine asking for Italian lessons. Real cockney, nice change from all the smoothies. In sales, with a suspiciously inventive double barrelled name, Descartes-Jones.

The main problem was, she would have to teach him herself, because he wanted lessons so early. At 6 a.m. None of the staff would want to know, and frankly she needed every client she could get at the moment. Tourist Italian his Needs Assessment had said. Other languages, French. Usual abysmal British level no doubt.

Through her open windows, she could hear the stereo out on the street. Early Who. Oh dear, Georgiana certainly wouldn't approve. She got up, and went over to her brief case, and put the form away. She had tried to train herself not to think about the office at weekends, but she did not always succeed. Particularly when the bills arrived, and one of those little notes from the school giving notice of yet another costly little 'extra'.

The last letter in the pile was from her father. He was at least now able to write himself, which was progress, although the indecipherable scrawl which slithered along, page after page, was much harder to read than the neat almost childish writing of the day nurse who had previously written his letters for him. Just a question of working out each letter and joining them up. 'Dear Harriet, please send me some pints.' Pints of what? Milk? Blood? Paints. That's great!

'Can't stand being idle any longer. Will kill those stupid buggers if canvas and easel don't appear pronto. When are you next here?' Harriet sighed trying to think when she could next make the trip. So much to fit in every day. No time or energy for anything, or anyone.

'Harriet! Are you there? Give us a hand will you.'

'Laura! Is that you?'

'Who do you think? Now give us a hand while I attend to Irma la Douce outside. I swear she's got a dodgy meter, over sixteen quid from Paddington!'

Harriet was about to go out into the street, when a young and extremely handsome man came in with two heavy suitcases.

'Hello, are you Harriet?'

'Yes, how do you do?'

'Harriet, come here, give us a kiss. I'm sorry, I forgot it was the street party. Ancient Hammersmith ritual, David, welcome to insanityville. Look H., I hope you don't mind, I've brought David from the Show. Would you mind terribly if he slept on the sofa bed tonight?' Laura was on top form, exuberant lipstick, bright yellow trousers.

She had a nerve, Harriet thought, giving Laura a hard stare, how could she say anything, with the poor man standing there? Though he looked quite starry, in spite of the regulation designer slash in his jeans.

'David Forsyth, Harriet Gosse, I told you her husband was in the business.'

'Yes, I remember. Look Harriet, I hope you don't mind.

'No, not at all. The sofa bed is famously lumpy, but you're very welcome.'

'Harriet's method of making sure no-one stays more than one night.'

'Don't be so horrible, Laura. Anyway how's it going? '

'Don't ask.' Laura collapsed into a chair kicking off her shoes. Gucci loafers Harriet noticed, which desperately needed heeling. Laura never changed. Thank goodness.

'The scripts. Crap beyond crap. A child of five could write better, Bily could in his sleep. The director is a grade A cretin, and the schedules are Dickensian. Apart from that, the cast get on, the clothes are a dream to wear, and if we could just get Fenella bloody Frost off the set, we'd be laughing.'

'Methinks you doth protest too much, Laura.'

'So do I, Harriet. Laura, this is the first I've heard of all this.'

'Don't gang up on me you two. Of course I'm sensibly grateful to be in work. Not that our David here has to do this sort of rubbish for much longer. Just signed up for the National, the swine, and he's only twenty-five. Makes you sick.'

'Really? I'm honoured. Are you coming to the street party either of you, it should be quite fun?'

'Later Harriet, I'd love to later, but I've actually got to see my agent this morning.'

Harriet caught Laura mouthing 'Hollywood' behind his back, and she suddenly remembered, David Forsyth! Of course he was in *The Cassidy Line.* Quite a womaniser according to the Sunday tabloids, which of course she never read – except in the privacy of the corner shop. But if he was doing so well, couldn't he afford a hotel?

She decided to leave them to make coffee and join the party. Outside in the street, long tables were filling with food. Quiches, salads, cold chicken, tomatoes, jelly (jelly in this heat!), French bread, bath buns, fairy cakes with hundreds and thousands, pork satay, Greek dips, Marks & Spencer's American style cheesecake, bread-and-butter pudding. The flies were having a field day, but though no-one was eating, the wine was going rapidly, and the band hadn't even started.

Robert, Georgiana's husband wandered over to Harriet with a drink. A partner in a city law firm, he always found it difficult coming down to a human level. For today at least he was obviously trying his best. Off-duty casual with a large gin in hand, he smiled on Harriet with benign largesse. Though she had long suspected that this Olympian stance was a bit of a reinvention – she had once heard Georgiana berating him for being a jumped-up grammar-school boy.

The street apartheid had already taken shape. Lawyers, barristers, and interior designers in one group. Musicians, journalists, less successful architects and public relations people in another. Down the other end, older residents clubbed together over sweet sherry, wincing at the band tuning up. None of the black families had come. Feeling suddenly ashamed, Harriet ran up to the house of the nearest family, and knocked on the door.

A middle-aged black woman with a small baby in her arms opened the door.

'Mrs Smith are you coming?'

'No dear no. It's better not. Not with the baby and all.'

'Oh go on, come, there are plenty of kids having fun. You'd enjoy it, really'.

'Thank you for asking dear, but no. My daughter will be coming home soon.'

The door shut, and the street was left to the white middle classes.

The party was in full swing when the red Aston Martin veered round past the off licence and with in an impressive emergency stop, smashed into the Georgiana's neat line of bollards, which separated the party from the rest of the street. Laura was in the middle of describing how she learned her lines to the *Evening Standard* journalist at Number 12, when the noise made her turn round. 'Bloody hell! Who's that?'

A tall elegantly dressed man emerged from the leather and walnut interior, and stood looking at the tables full of food, the dancing half-hysterical children, and at the band who was Getting No Satisfaction, as if he had just landed on Mars. On cue, a half-eaten melted quiche slid off the table in front of him.

'Can I help you?'

Georgiana's normally pale, bony face was rather flushed, whether from the wine, the heat or a sudden lust for the man or his car, it was hard to determine. The man looked at her, and smiled with even white teeth. 'I'm so sorry, I just didn't see those damn bollards. I wonder if you could help me, I'm looking for Mrs Harriet Gosse's house. Do you know it?'

'Harriet! Oh, yes she's over there, Mr?'

'Longbridge. Richard Longbridge. How do you do. Tell me, is this how you normally spend Saturday afternoons? I've never been here before.'

'Oh no! This is our happy annual Street Party. Welcome to Brackenbury Village. I'm Georgiana Gaskell, Harriet's neighbour. I live over there.' She gestured vaguely towards her house. 'The one with the statue in the garden, NOT the other one! Please come this way. Do have a drink, there's lots of food left.

Bemused, Richard was led through a now merry group of neighbours, who were well on the way to an early hangover. 'Twist and shout!' The band were really going down memory lane now. 'Come on, come on baby!' They found Harriet talking to old Mrs Knole, the resident local eccentric. 'Harriet, your friend Richard is looking for you.' Georgiana gushed.

Harriet looked up astonished. Behind him she saw Laura advancing.

'Harriet, I'm sorry to burst in on you, but I just came to ask you, no not out to dinner, but you see, I got this letter from Jamie when I got back yesterday. He wondered if he and Billy could go out for a meal after we picked them up on Saturday.'

'I see' said Harriet, who didn't. She only knew she had the beginnings of a right royal headache. 'No I'm sorry Richard, but I did promise Billy we'd go out for lunch, You see we have a special place we always go to.'

'Well, I don't want to be a pain, but would it be O.K. if we joined you. My treat. You see I don't want to get it wrong again, Jamie is not pro me at the moment.'

'Then, yes. Of course I'm sure Billy would like it.'

Standing there in his candyfloss pink shirt and cream baggy linen trousers, and suede brogues Richard looked twenty cuts above the beer guts and the cheap cotton clothes around him. But he seemed to her also less pleased with himself than he had been the other day. Quite the concerned father and the sober citizen in fact, if it weren't for the way the car was half mounted on the pavement.

'Well that's settled.'

'Yes.' Harriet was already beginning to regret having agreed.

'I'll pick you up at ten.'

'No don't bother, the boys will have so much clobber, we can drive separately.'

'That would be making a meal of it. Look I'm bringing the

other car, not this, more room. Is that alright? Good.'

She caught the pleading note in his voice. A fleeting thought went throught her brain, that there could not have been many times that he had driven up in a £200,000 car to ask a favour from a woman dressed from the Hammersmith Oxfam shop? The thought, made her quite charitable, and she smiled her goodbyes, and watched him walk back to the car. Another thought then jostled for attention. Perhaps he had leant at an early age just how effective this little boy lost act could be, wheedling Matron into bed perhaps? And all those other women Marcus had mentioned?

As Richard roared off down the road, the set of his back seemed to say to Harriet, 'Beam me up Scottie.'

'Now that is what I call an attractive man', said Georgiana, who for once was not threatening to write to the Council for traffic-calming measures. 'Who is he? How did you meet him?'

'He's the father of one of Billy's friends at school. They live in Belgravia I think', said Harriet.

Laura, who was by now mixing cocktails, joined them on the road. 'You think! You, jammy beggar Harriet, kept him quiet. Who is he? What a car. Wouldn't like the repayments on that!'

'That sort of man would not, as you put it Laura, have repayments on that', Georgiana bristled. 'He's obviously from a good family.'

The band began to play 'Long Tall Sally', and Harriet, feeling that she had probably made a terrible mistake somewhere along the line, was allowed to melt back into the background.

* * *

Richard drove back to town feeling he'd done his duty by his son, and made his point to the lovely widow of W6. What a godawful part of London. Depressing. All bijou squalor. Tinpot houses built for the poor clerks, now oozing pretension. Anyone who bought one of those must be mad.

She had freckles. He had not noticed them before, but then she had been wearing make-up the other times they had met. He sighed, why was he getting into this? Roger had thought he was quite mad. Yet he was looking forward to starting the lessons, he had even gone into Dillons and bought a dictionary.

He wriggled with impatience as he waited for a woman with a buggy to walk across the crossing. Hurry up! Let me out of here. Shepherd's Bush, what a dump. The eighties had obviously completely past it by. Revolting. Come on lights!

Harriet. She was obviously a good mother. That cold little letter of Jamie's, which had greeted him on his return from New York, was a bit of a shocker. Where was he going wrong? Yet Ernie had been such a bastard until the last few years. Not much of a role model. Who'd be a parent?

Heading back into town, civilisation returned, as soon as he reached Holland Park Avenue. A scoot down Park Lane, and soon Richard was parking in Cork Street, though he couldn't help noticing how depressing it looked at the weekend with so many galleries closed down. Gaps in the line. He shivered, and walked up the steps to the door.

'Hello, Mr Longbridge?'

He turned round. Standing leaning against a parking meter was a short woman about forty-five, with attractive, rather frizzy red hair and the same look of disdain worn by policemen whenever they see a Porsche.

'Cremona Kent, *Sunday News* Magazine. We had an appointment for midday.'

'Miss Kent, forgive me. I hadn't forgotten, I was delayed by a corporate client. But I had a feeling I was going to be interviewed by a Miss Catherine somebody?'

'Yes the editor was due to do it, but she broke her leg last week. At Annabels. No use telling her she's fifty, not twenty-three!'

'Oh dear. Well we've all done it in our time. I'm so sorry, do come in. How long have you been waiting? I'd better stick the kettle on, whilst you look around.'

Cremona Kent never worked on Saturdays, unless that is her editor begged her to in tones which offered time off in lieu and the next swimming pool interview in L.A. Catherine had been livid. All set up to do the story herself too.

The Most Eligible Bachelors In London was a crap idea

anyway. Everyone knew they were only doing it, because Catherine wanted to get hitched again, and single men who were not gay and had a trust fund, were few and far between. And this Longbridge man? Public school wasn't he? Which is what Catherine pretended to be herself. Though you could hear the Essex vowel sounds when she was pissed, or angry with the advertising department for putting ads for anti-flatulence tablets on her pages. Cremona Kent looked uncomprehendingly at a picture, more like a fist fight under canvas. £2,500. Must be joking!

'Who are your customers, Mr Longbridge? Who could afford such amounts for a picture like this?'

'That's a Camille Rouen. He always sells. Marvellous artist. One of the great post-war French painters, from the Cevennes. Immense power and strength don't you think? Of course, his technique is very solid.'

'Oh is it? Wouldn't know I'm afraid. The price certainly is, though. How long have you been here?'

'I opened in 1982, my father bought this place on a 25-year lease, said it was cheap at the price to get me off his back! That was supposed to be a joke.' Cremona noted this down, unsmiling.

'We've 2000 square feet here, this main area, the second space which we use for specialist shows like those pre-war Sicilian paintings of Carese and Puriddu, and then there's my office which doubles as a meeting room.'

'How many artists do you represent?'

'Eight, all leading contemporary European painters, including Angus Hepplewhite, Brossadi, Hans Scherrer.'

'With nice mark-ups I suppose.'

'Well, every gallery has to get at least a 100% mark-up. I have to pay for three staff, as well as storage, framing, photographs, publicity, insurance, catalogues, wine for everyone who shows up at a View, and God help me if its cheap. If I'm arranging exhibitions of my stable in other galleries then I take a 16% handling fee, to cover transport etc.'

'So are you telling me that it is hard to make money even charging £2,500 per painting, which, with respect, my five-year-old nephew could do just as well.'

'Listen, there are a lot of expenses before I make a bean,

and if your nephew can truly paint as well as Rouen, I'm interested!' Like every gallery owner since the public began to think they knew about art, Richard had learned to fend off the it's-only-a-pile-of-bricks routine.

'So who do you sell to? Not many *Sunday News* readers, I bet.'

'You'd be surprised. Many people buy art simply because they like it. Some 25% of my business comes from private clients who come in and buy something they like the look of. Then there are Museums and University galleries – I've just sold two to the Tate this month, and one to the Arizona State University in Tampe. Recently I've been doing a lot more business with corporations, then we also sell to other dealers. And we do shows abroad – ARCO in Paris in February, Frankfurt in March, Basle in June, the biggie in Chicago in May.'

'And how much do all these foreign jaunts cost?'

'Miss Kent, I can assure you, they're not jaunts, they are bloody hard work. In general they take about five days. There's the stand – not much point in going for less than 1000 feet, shipping, insurance, promotions. Two staff, a telephone and so on, and cost roughly £25,000 each'

'Twenty five thousand! And do you make money, because you've still got all the expenses to cover here?'

'No, not always. But you're selling to new and existing collections, promoting the gallery in the media, and making contacts with new galleries who could exhibit your stable at some point. Anyway, what has all this got to do with being an eligible bachelor?'

'I should have told you Mr Longbridge', Cremona smiled, 'that I also write for *Business London*. And besides, it is all relevant for the piece.'

'I don't see how.'

'You've just told me what you have to pay out, upfront. I understand now why you have to charge so much, but there's hardly a Sold sticker in the place. And with prices going through the floor in the salerooms, and galleries going bust every week, I imagine, but for your father's money, you'd be reading articles about eligible spinsters who could bail you out!'

'If I may say so, you are being incredibly rude. Do you people think you can say anything?'

'No. But it's true, isn't it?'

Cremona realising that she had perhaps gone a little far, smiled at him.

'It's the devil's advocate act isn't it? Getting your subjects to defend themselves. Yes you're right, these are difficult times, but I'm doing O.K., though I'm working all the hours God sends. And that's got nothing to do with my father's money. Make sure you write that down!'

'Of course. I expect the banks are extra understanding to someone in your position.'

'I wouldn't push your luck, Miss Kent.'

Cremona noted the flushed cheeks under the tan, swished over a page in her notebook and smoothed into other areas.

She wanted to know about his life at St Anthony's, Arch, and Anth at Cambridge 'the degree for people who didn't want to do any work whatsoever!' Then painting in Paris, father buying him the lease. Eleven-year marriage ended three years ago, still good friends. What sort of women did he like?

Force of habit made Richard assess the woman in front of him. Short skirt, too short showing plump footballer's knees, fleshy calves. Big earrings, heavy choker, no wedding ring. Attractive in a near-the-edge sort of way, nice eyes, like an overripe peach about to fall splat on the ground. Very Matthew Smith.

'Will you be able to mention the Alain Le Feuvre exhibition? It's the first time he's ever had a show, exciting work, a lot of theatre in his style.'

'When is it?'

'Three weeks' time.'

'Should think so. When's his next film coming out?'

'*Les Aventures des Tantes*, it's opening at the Curzon at the same time. A fine film.'

'I'll mention it to our art correspondent.'

'Thank you. I hope you have enough.'

'Yes thank you. The picture desk will be ringing you on Monday to arrange a time for the photographer.' Cremona smiled at him, the red lipstick was edging into the little lines around her mouth. Richard suddenly felt scoured like a greasy pan inside and out. She would make him look like a complete dickhead. Oh Lord, he'd forgotten to make her some tea.

Bells ringing, hammering on the door. 'I can see you standing there, Richard Patrick, leaning against the door like a witch's broomstick. Let your old mother in.'

In the doorway they saw a small figure peering into the gallery, through the glass, a taxi chuntering behind her.

'Oh, it's my mother', Richard said lightly, thinking Oh God it's my mother.

Outside, dressed to the nines, in a large flowery hat, and enough gold jewellery to open a pawnbrokers, stood Mary Ellen Longbridge, Dublin's answer to the Queen Mum. A lady who would never give in to old age without a brawl.

Richard unlocked the door, and bent down to give his mother a kiss. 'Mother, come in, nice to see you. This is Miss, Miss Cremona Kent from the *Sunday News.*'

'Good afternoon, Mrs Longbridge. I'm just about to go.'

Cremona Kent took in the rouge, the powder, the high heels and the large rocks on the clawed hands. What a story she must have to tell. So Richard Longbridge was as got-on as Catherine. They'd be perfect together.

'Did you remember Richard, you're supposed to be taking your old mother out to lunch. Or had you forgotten?'

'No Mother I hadn't.'

'Liar. And why, may I ask, are you in the news now?'

'We're doing a series on London's most eligible bachelors Mrs Longbridge.'

Mary Ellen Longbridge snorted.

'Holy Mother, he can't hold a proper job down, let alone a wife. Still, it's just possible I suppose, that some fool woman would make an honest man of him, and give me another grandchild. Though', she added as she prodded him in the ribs, 'the amount he drinks, I doubt it.'

'Really? Your son tells me he doesn't have anyone special in his life, which gives hope to our readers.' Cremona twinkled at her. One normally got the best lines on the way out, and this looked promising. With a bit of luck, the old dear might produce pictures of him naked at two in the bath. Though twenty-two would be even better.

'Well actually there is someone special, but she doesn't know it yet.'

Richard was getting irritated by this unspoken alliance, and was determined to wrestle back some control. 'Very beautiful, knows about art, runs her own business. She turned down my offer of dinner. Which I was a bit miffed about, but I'm still working on it.'

Mary and Cremona looked at him. 'She turned you down for dinner?' Cremona started writing again.

'She did indeed, quite a blow to the *amour propre* but there you are.'

'Is she single?' said Cremona.

'Yes.'

'Is she a lezzie?' Mary Ellen never minced her words.

'No mother! I've no reason to think so.'

'And where does this special lady who has such good taste and common sense live?'

'Er, Hammersmith actually.'

The way Richard was standing blushing with his hands in his pockets, reminded both women of a small boy caught stealing from the sweetie jar. Obviously part of his charm, thought Cremona, who was always relieved when she knew just how to start her first paragraph.

* * *

Four o'clock in the morning. Harriet lay in bed looking at the lights of a car passing in the street, that danced upon the ceiling. She heard a car door open, voices, a car door slam, and the car drive off, more lights on the ceiling. Someone had been making a night of it. Besides herself! She was still quite shocked, even astonished at what she had done. And yet, as she wriggled down into the warm depths of the double bed, there were at the edge of this astonishment, twinges of self satisfaction. And pleasure, yes pleasure. Guilt too, the liberating variety – the sort she had had when she had broken a school rule and got away with it.

It had not been like riding a bicycle. After so long, one

did forget the finer points. She had remembered afterwards, how she would drum her fingers on the base of Tom's back when he came. But she had felt quite relaxed considering. David Forsyth stirred, and put his arm across her. You forget the hardness of men, she thought, the beauty of those long firm thighs. Their smell, their gentleness.

She suddenly realised that she had been awake for at least fifteen minutes and had not thought about money once. Not bills. Not about the taxman, nor the school fees. Mentally she had put them all into a black bin bag, and booted them over the garden fence into Georgiana's knot garden. Get knotted. She thought of the Aston Martin, streaking along the road, and felt, funnily enough quite chuffed.

David nuzzled into the nape of her neck and began to kiss her, his hands travelled down and he began to caress her. Then he slid on top of her.

'David,' she smoothed the dark hair out of his eyes. 'I'm not on the Pill you know.'

'Forgot.' David leant over and bit the packet with his teeth, and then tried to work out how to put the condom on

He caught Harriet's look and smiled sleepily. She smiled back. 'You know, you could play comedy?'

But David Forsyth, brown hair, blue eyes, six foot two, Central School, Perth Rep, three seasons at the Bristol Old Vic, The Cassidy Line, Spotlight Number 1945, and the next James Bond if his agent had anything to do with it, for once did not seem very interested in his career.

The weather had broken suddenly, just as she had been about to go inside and the party behind. The heavens had opened, reducing Georgiana's red Harrods paper table cloths to instant mush.

Screams from Georgiana, and the other women who had spent the previous day in the hairdressers. Crack as the thunder sliced through the skies above the Hammersmith Flyover. The band, no romance in their souls and fearing for their electrical instruments, had made a precipitous dash indoors, leaving soaking wet children dancing in the gutter. Doing a Gene Kelly, if they had but known it, until their mothers newly equipped with umbrellas and waxed jackets had hauled them inside. Harriet had allowed the rain to course down her face, and mix with sudden tears. She always seemed to be crying these days!

People had grabbed their share of the bottles and fled. Water had filled the bowls of half-eaten fruit salad, and sploshed into the quiches. No-one ever ate quiche so why did people persist in bringing it? Realising that the cushions on her kitchen chairs were now sodden, Harriet became suddenly practical and began to drag them indoors. Three trips, and she had closed her front door on the remains of the party. She had opened the kitchen door and, and gone out into her little garden, where the pots and tubs were chinking merrily in the rain. Crack! More thunder and this time lightning had lit up the sky catching a large jet who'd decided to make it to Heathrow after all.

'Harriet! I'm off.' Laura peered out at her from the kitchen door. 'Great party wasn't it? I'm going to the theatre now; I'll see you tomorrow. Thanks for putting David up. Byee.'

'Bye Laura. You're leaving early.'

'We're eating before the show. See you.'

Harriet switched on the outside lights and sat down next to the pond. She could barely see the fish, but she wondered what they made of the lightning and thunder, or were they tucked away in their secret green fishy world insulated from everything but fear of the cat's eyes.

'Richard Oxbridge I think he said. Awfully attractive,' Georgiana's voice had sounded muffled as she closed her kitchen window, though Harriet had heard the beginning of Robert's grunt from the bottom of his fourth or possibly even fifth G & T of the evening. Then she caught the chink of expensive china. Georgiana would be preparing another lethal dinner party, 'to make contacts'. Death by cholesterol. Still at least she wouldn't be Poor Harriet for at least two whole weeks until it was clear Richard Longbridge was not a fixture. Then it would be back to pitied widowhood.

In the darkness of the storm, it had taken several minutes before she had realised that the front door bell was ringing. David Forsyth had stood there dripping on the step.

'David! Laura's just left. Aren't you going to be late for the show?'

'I don't know where Laura's gone?' He had stepped into the hall. 'I was going to look up a couple of friends in Clapham, but I got caught in the rain. Anyway, I hate south London.'

Twenty five, just like Ulrike. Enjoy it while you've got it! Harriet had thought, followed by a feeling of annoyance. Bloody Laura leaving me to entertain her friend.

'I'm afraid there isn't much food in the house.' No, she thought, I'm not going to cook you a meal young man, however handsome you are.

'That's all right Harriet, I've brought you a bottle of wine as a thank you for letting me stay. It is really kind of you.' The smile. She had it now. It belonged to the Russian ballet dancer who threw the chocolates up to his lady in the box. Won an advertising award, and had started a whole series of articles in the press about how chivalry was not yet dead. All written by famously hardbitten female journalists. He'd got the lead in *Auctioneer* not long afterwards. No wonder Laura had brought him back like a prize bone.

Thinking back Harriet couldn't exactly remember how they had fallen into bed. One moment they had been staring up at the stars in the dripping garden and the next he was kissing her. Her stomach had turned to jelly, but she had been so surprised that she had responded. Suddenly engulfed in an unexpected, thoroughly unHarriet desire. She could not get her clothes off fast enough. Tore them off most of them, or he did. Rediscovering her body again, nipples, her beautiful pubic hair. He had been rough and tender, mocking, conciliatry, outrageous!

Her screams as she had had her first orgasm in six years, had coincided with the guests' arrival next door, and she imagined had probably done Georgiana's dinner party, no end of good.

He left the next morning. Lying there watching him dress, she knew by his haste that she would be just another scalp. She'd be one of the 2000 lovers he would brag about in the autobiography he would write at 60, settled in Malibu with his twenty-year-old fourth wife, and his late life toddler.

On went the leather jacket. He brushed the hair out of his eyes and looked down at her briefly. 'Bye bye, David. Best of luck. Don't forget about comedy.' He was too young to have the grace to kiss her, thank her, make a fuss of her, he was a young man in a hurry. But at least he wasn't in the least embarrassed, nor pretended he would call her. She wouldn't want that at all.

'Bye, Harriet. Laura said you were really nice.'

Thump thump thump down the stairs, slam and out. Harriet shook off the sheets, and looked at herself naked. No stretch marks. White skin. No, nothing to complain about. She walked stiffly into the bathroom. Sun shone through the mottled glass. She switched on the radio for *The Archers* Omnibus.

The door slammed. Was he back? No, it was Laura. Something about her walk, and the sound of a large handbag being plonked down in the hall, told Harriet that Laura had only just come in from her night at the theatre. Where had she been? Well, she wouldn't be the first to tell her. Why deprive her of her life's goal of getting Harriet laid! Very quietly, she shut the bathroom door, and slid the lock.

* * *

'*Bien sûr Jean Baptiste, je comprends. Au revoir.*'

'*Au revoir madame. A demain.*'

Sunday lessons too. The woman ignored the bells, and rolled on the bed, laughing. Fifi jumped onto the bed and licked her nose, yapping for a chococlate. 'Sunday lessons too my darling. How much Mummy needs to be loved.' She remembered that her husband would now be at the meeting in Brussells, definitely not 'getting by', in his terrible schoolboy French. Served him right for leaving her behind, and taking that slut instead. She switched on the radio for the Archers. She had wondered so often what they all looked like, just as she wondered about Jean Baptiste. 'Better not to know my darling we all need a little bit of mystery don't we?' she whispered, burying her head in the dog's fur.

Chapter Seven

He was standing over him, camel-hair coat, velvet collar, much older than the other fathers. His Cockney accent sounded so harsh, pinging off the school walls. 'Keep your voice down, Dad. PLEASE! All the parents can hear you.' The pink Rolls was parked at the front door of the school, mum in the back in her bunny fur having a nip, sniggers from the upper dorm windows.

'No I bloody well won't. Dick, if you're going to run a book, don't get caught. And you paid out too much. No idea have you. And what's all this about a Mini on the housemaster's roof? Bloody plonker you are. Right fruit and nut putting the car radio on and waking everyone up. Don't get found out! First rule of any business.'

Hot, blushing. Failure. 'Sorry dad. But don't shout, the other fathers can hear.' They have. Cold stares. Cold shame. Of his parents, not his misdeeds.

His father then seemed to turn into an old man, with a stick, looking into a dusty room, 'This do, Dick? Cork Street. Good address. 25 grand a year. O.K. But what have I always said? Impressions count. Look at me, George Bridge, nicked his old mum's name, and don't you think it didn't make a difference with those City buggers, 'cause it did. Ena Long, God rest her soul. She knew. Cut a dash she'd say. But listen, it took me twenty years to get those bloody banks off my back. Don't go near them, you'll never make money that way. Start small. Dick, are you listening. Dick?'

Richard woke up with a start as the alarm cut through his father's wasted warning. 5.45 a.m. Bloody hell. What day? Monday. Raining outside. Italian. Harriet Gosse. This was a really stupid idea.

Stumbling out of bed, Richard put on his dressing gown, sloshed cold water over his face and went downstairs to make coffee. In his study, he looked at the Gosse Lesson Plan which Roger's secretary had faxed through to him. Alphabet, must be learnt for spelling over the phone. Ancona, Bologna, Comno, Domodossola, Empoli (where the hell's that?), Firenze, Genova, etc. etc., Presentation excercises. Shouldn't he just come clean, particularly now he was going to see her on Saturday?

But the leprechaun in Richard's soul spurred him on, wanting to control, get her off guard, take revenge for the way she had beetled off down those stairs. After all, she hadn't been that bothered to see him on Saturday nor for that matter had seemed the slightest bit impressed with Doris. The car usually did the trick if nothing else did. Funny girl. He had never met anyone like her.

What's so special about her anyway, a small voice within him insisted. No background. No money. No spring chicken. Washed-up painter for a father. So why had he shelled out £200 plus VAT for ten lessons and insisted on a 6 a.m. slot so she'd have to teach him instead of the native speakers, which as she'd pointed out, would be so much better?

Personal analysis was not Richard's strong point at any time of day, so instead of carrying on with such introspection, he thought of his need to improve on his cappuccino Italian. 'The Futuristi Italiani needa to maka Riccardo de money', he announced to the anorexic Giacommetti sculpture by his desk. Something will have to soon, or else it's another trip to Mamma Mia and the Trustees.

'Roger Descartes Jones' felt less than his usual urbane self as he dialled the number.

* * *

Harriet had been up since 5.30. Dressed and made up, she was all ready to leave for the office. She always found that wearing pearls made her feel in control of things. Over a year now since she'd done any teaching, over a year. Italian at six o'clock was like old times, John Dill in Bristol, with Billy sleeping in his cot in the next room.

She looked at her lesson, in three parts, everything in context, the student in the centre of the lesson, the core of communicative teaching. Which she supposed was a fancy description of the way she'd originally learnt the language, running along with the local children in piazzas all over Italy until suddenly thrust into a Brighton girls' school at 15 and told to get some O levels. I have, I would have, I would have had. I did.

She'd just finished her tea, when the phone rang.

* * *

'Billy! Wake up!' Matron sat on his bed, all jeans and floppy sweater. First Bell had gone, and the other boys were slowly coming too. In the dorm there was the smell of bodies, and night-time breathing. No-one ever opened the window. It was always too cold for that.

'Matron.' Billy rubbed his eyes, and pulled on his school sweater over his pyjamas, for the dash over the icy lino to bog. 'What is it?'

'I'm leaving now Billy, after breakfast, to stay in London. Boyd and I are renting a flat for a while, while he works there. I just wanted to say goodbye, and also to ask for your Mum's office number. I lost her card she gave me.'

Billy wrote down the number on a piece of paper torn from his Latin prep, though he couldn't see why she would want it so early.

'Your mum said I could have French lessons with one of her teachers. Not that I was ever any good at school. We're going to live in Paris next year. Can you imagine it? How on earth will Boyd get the French to recycle their rubbish? Anyway I'm off now. Mrs Lunn, the new Matron arrived last night. She's quite nice so don't worry – old though. I don't think Crouch wants to take any more chances.'

She opened the curtain. Without make-up, she looked older and less self assured. Billy noticed the large stone of her engagement ring, glinting in the morning sunlight. He still thought it was odd her being married to Rogers. What would they talk about?

'Wish me luck Billy I'm dead-nervous.'
'Good luck Matron. Thank you.'
'What for?'
'For everything. And thanks for going to my Mum. She always needs new business.'
'Bye Billy, you're sweet, you know that? She's lucky to have you to look after her.'

* * *

'*E come si chiama*? What is your name?'
'My name is er, Signore Roger Descartes Jones.'
'*Di cosa si occupa*?'
'What occupies me is that? I am director of a public relations company. *Sono un direttore relazioni publicity*.'
'*Pubbliche relazioni*, the adjective comes first.'
'*Capito. Sono direttore di un compagnia.*'
'*No, agenzia*.'
'*Agenzia di pubbliche relazioni*.'
'*Bravo Signor Descartes Jones. In tutto*. Give me the whole sentence.'
'*Mi chiamo Roger Descartes Jones, e sono direttore di un' agenzia di pubbliche relazioni*. Phew! How about that then Signora!'
'*Bravo. E com'e fisicamente*?'
'Sorry, what? Something about physics?'
'No, what do you look like?'
'*Sono grande*, er, how do you say I'm over six feet tall?'
'*Sono alto piu di due metri.*'
'And eyes, gawd, can't remember now, *occhi. Ho occhi* blue?'
'*Ho gli occhi azzurri*.'
'*Sono alto piu di due metri, e ho gli occhi azzurri*. (*Verde* with lenses.)'
'Cosa!'
'Nothing. *Ho gli occhi azzurri*, like the *Côte d'Azure* isn't it? Though my eyes aren't, at this time of the morning, more like the Thames before they cleaned it up.'
'*Qualcos'altro*? Anything else? *In Italiano per piacere*.'
'Dunno. Oh yes. *Si, sono bellissimo, simpaticissmo* and

molto intelligentissimo. How about that? Always like those issimos.'

'*Sempre modesto Signor Descartes Jones*! Now let's turn to the excercises on page two. I like. *Mi piace, mi piacciono*.'

After the lesson was over, and he had hung up the phone, Richard felt exhilarated. What was he doing! How embarrassing if she ever found out! He'd tell her next lesson. Definitely. He was also exhausted. Didn't know what was worse, taking in the Italian or keeping up his cockney accent. Hadn't used his brain like so much for years. What a girl! She had worked his socks, but did she know her stuff. And it was just like she had said, he could hear her voice repeating the right way to say it, like a tape recording in his head. Those issimos, O.K. definitely corny but she had laughed. Musical laugh.

The phone rang. '*Pronto. Casa Longbridge. Chi parla*?'

'Who's that speaking? Can I just check the number with you please?'

''Tis I, Anne, your bellissimo ex-English husband. Ex-husband that is, I am still distinctly English. Why are you ringing me in the middle of the night?'

'Richard, what are you talking about? And why did you answer the phone in Spanish? Or was it Italian?'

'I've just had my first telephonic Italian lesson, 6 a.m. sharp three times a week for the next three weeks. It's for me Italian futurists innit?'

'Italian lessons on the telephone? How interesting. Richard, I am seriously impressed that you're making such a commitment to widening your knowledge.'

'Thanks to you my darling, showing me the way.' Flattery was always the best way with Anne, and it was worth the £200, to make her sit up. Not Mr Predictable perhaps, after all. Richard suddenly could picture her looking solemnly through the New York telephone directory for telephone French lessons. (Parisian naturally.) Advanced.

'Listen Richard, I'm lying here in my marvellous house which I do not know how much longer I will have, and I can't sleep. I'm worrying about this sale. I was just wondering, have you had any interest yet?'

'Jaakko's ruin you mean. No, I spoke to a couple of

dealers the day I got back, and they said they'd make a few calls, but frankly Anne, your best hope is to get him to withdraw and sell in New York, or put in higher reserves. Failing that, you'll just have to put back your show till next year, when hopefully we'll be out of the doldrums.'

'No, Greenbacher won't do that. And Jaakko's going for broke. He's not interested in reserves. He doesn't care if there's not a soul in the salesroom, as long as everyone hears about it afterwards.'

Richard could hear Guy the Gorilla snoring gently in the background. Really Anne had the oddest taste in men. Nowadays.

'Well, I'd tackle him on the reserves. Make him see he would look a fool if they went for a fiver each. Wouldn't give people confidence in his business acumen in his other operations. Apart from anything else all the impoverished Lloyds names are flogging their stuff at the moment. The salerooms are awash and the prices are so low, it's hardly worth the poor dears printing the catalogues. Try that. But how about your garbage merchants doing a private sale?'

'Don't remind me about them. They came to the gallery show, saw Guy, and Hector Rogers went up to him and said he'd never seen such garbage as his show, and that he should know. Can you imagine? It was awful. His wife was trying to drag him out of the room.'

'Wish I'd been there. Our Hector is a magnificient sight when roused.'

'I'm happy you weren't. Listen, I shall be in London for my own and Jaakko's funeral at Butes, and your Le Feuvre show. Shrewd move Richard, if he can paint as well as win Oscars, the tourists will love him. But will the tourists buy? We're finding they've no money at the moment.'

'I hope to God they have, the Tachistes have been a bloody disaster.'

'Keep this up and we'll both be on Welfare by the Fall. Bye, Richard, I'm going back to sleep.'

'Bye, Anne. Good to hear you. I tell you there's nothing like a telephone lesson with a beautiful girl to make you feel hugely energetic.'

'If she's on the telephone, how do you know she's beautiful?'

'Because I've met her, and I think I'm falling in love with her. And it is one really good way of getting to know her better. She does not however know it's me, she thinks I'm Roger.'

'Let me get this straight. You're pretending to be Roger, but even though you've met her, she can't tell it's you.'

'No, you see I'm putting on a truly superb cockney accent. You know Anne, talking like old Ernie. Doing the Lambeth Walk. Hey!'

There was silence for a minute as Anne absorbed this.

'Richard. Please. When you've finished your Italian lessons, would you do me a favour?'

'What's that Anne?'

'Get some therapy.'

* * *

The church was cool after the summer heat, its ornate interior a great surprise, sandwiched as it was between Marks & Spencers and the delicatessen. And open during the day, a real act of faith. Harriet slipped into the pews, thinking guiltily just how long it was since she'd last seen the inside of a church. 'Mmm deigning to come in now isn't she, now she wants something. Probably spends every Sunday at Car Boot Sales, we know her sort.' Harriet could almost hear words from the small distant figure on the Cross. And who could blame Him?

Ever since Saturday she had felt mixed up. Relieved to have had at last some affection, some outlet for her own need. And let's face it, she'd had a marvellous time. So probably had the rest of the street, she'd made such a noise. But had it been wrong? Laura would say it was pathetic to say so in this day and age. But then she'd never ticked like Laura, never had the nerve. Richard Longbridge zoomed into her imagination. Would she feel like jumping into bed with him too? Everyone else probably did, he'd been far too put out when she'd turned down his dinner invitation.

'Lord, I am confused if I have done wrong: forgive me,

I am very lonely, so often. Show me the way.' Her voice sounded vast in the silence. She looked round suddenly embarrassed in case there was someone there. It sounded so self-pitying and stupid.

Gradually, a generous and unexpected forgiveness washed over her. She walked to the door, pushing two pound coins into the slit in the wall. The widow's mite. Widows had probably been praying about the same thing since Moses. On the quiet.

'Harriet! What are you doing? I never you knew you were Catholic. How exciting. Now confess all!'

As she came out, Georgiana leapt out at her from the doorway of the delicatessen like a spider, and Harriet was swallowed up into the world once more.

* * *

Ow! Was she going to drop it? The plastic cup of scalding coffee hurt her hands as she pushed through the door of the Green Room, the script in her teeth. Half asleep, she felt like death. Orange tweedie chairs and grey carpet. Yuk. No-one there yet but Marjorie, the cast auntie.

'Hello darling.'

Laura put down the coffee and yawned. 'Morning, darling. Good weekend?'

'Not bad. Boys were bloody and there were vast amounts of washing to do, but I've got a reading at Pitlochry for next week.'

'Great. What is it?'

'Hedda G.'

'Should be a bundle of laughs. Nice place if it's not too cold. God help you if it is. Everyone's coming in together look. Hello, Lachlan. Cheer up, Derek. John love, can we go through our scene now. Coffee's foul, powder's gone off over the weekend.' Laura looked at her script. Lots more boardroom battles this week, plus a dreary subplot about a dealers' ring. Yawn.

'Well hello, David.'

David Forsyth mooched in, hair neatly over one eye. He smiled round. 'Hi guys.'

'Sorry to desert you on Saturday night darling, had a date.'

'Didn't matter, your lovely friend Harriet looked after me. Beautifully.'

The way he smiled just for a moment almost made her choke on the plastic coffee. Surely not Harriet!

* * *

Marcus had insisted on coming. Marcus always did insist on coming. Was it out of guilt, compassion, or one-upmanship? Harriet had never been able to work out the relationship between them. Jester Dunne v Marcus Whitehead. A love-hate battle which had continued over forty years, by letter, phone, face-to-face combat, often insulting, often drunk, often storming out of restaurants, but never stagnant.

Throughout her life there had always been these two men, poles apart, yet held in some strange symbiotic relationship. It was well known that Marcus Whitehead who had persuaded Jester Dunne to do the Calvary fresco at St Anne's Cathedral. Yet it was Jester's exhibitions in the late fifties which had first put Marcus in the first division.

One extrovert, gregarious, yet devoted to Ian his partner, a quiet, shadowy figure who had slipped away one week and died in the most unobtrusive way. The other solitary, self-absorbed, yet taking his many women as roughly and as passionately as he painted them. Half-forgotten sounds from countless next-door bedrooms still occasionally filled Harriet's head.

The Willies, as Jester had christened the Willows Residential Home for the Elderly, looked the same as ever, repressed refinement with its gravel path and rhododendrons. Chronic boredom seeping out through the brickwork. Had she brought everything? Grapes, acrylic paints chosen by Marcus in the shop after he'd told her she hadn't a clue, brushes, rags, spirit, easel, palette, knife.

Jester was in the Day Room. 'Good afternoon. Mr Dunne, we've got some visitors. Who's a lucky fellow then?' Jester loathed the Royal 'we'. The nurse who greeted them looked disparagingly at Marcus in his yellow bow tie as if to say, hello sailor, you'll be next. 'Paints. how super for you, Mr D. I've always wanted to be artistic, but what with the kids and the job, there's never been time. Shame really.'

'Barbara Hepworth had triplets and she managed. But then she had talent', Jester growled, turning over the paints. 'No decent greens, Harry. I like at least three greens.'

'You'll have to blame Marcus, he chose them. But I had to call a halt at twelve. Do you know how much paints cost these days?'

'Penny pinching, just like your mother. Never economise on paints, always a mistake. And you should get yourself another husband, Harry, you're becoming an old maid. Too thin.' Jester's speech was clear these days to Marcus and Harriet, a language they had had to learn. Billy who saw him less, found it harder, embarrassed by his own embarrassment.

Yes, Marcus was on good form, with his tales of an art critic, who had just committed suicide, two galleries which had just gone bust, one owing over a million pounds, what a Stanley Spencer had just fetched at Bonhams. A tasteless, obviously suicidal Finnish tycoon about to dump the most ghastly collection of American art at Butes. But Jester did not seem to be listening.

'Harry do you remember Orvieto?'

'Yes, I remember.'

'Do you remember those roofs, those old houses? Looked as if they were about to fall off the edge of the hill. Going to paint them.'

Those years in Orvieto had been among the happiest of her childhood. For once, they had actually stayed put. The smells of the wine, pasta, olive oil. The school children, '*Come ti chiami. Sei Inglese come i Beetles*?' Jester, handsome and muscular, had painted nonstop, when he wasn't swapping stories in the bar, or disappearing off to Florence, leaving her with the *colf, la collaboratrice famigliale*, the family collaborator, Italy's ridiculous new name for its Mrs Mopps. Maria with her crucifixes in every room, and the hairs which grew out from the crevices in her face, like grass on a mountainside.

'Why there?'

'Product of my mind's eye, all I can see.'

'Mmn, that's a good title, could see that as part of the Jester Dunne comeback exhibition.' Marcus scented possiblities. An Italian retrospective, a tieup with the Italian Cultural Institute perhaps?

Jester seemed already exhausted by them. His mind seemd to wander off in his thoughts then he patted her hand. 'You were a good girl you know, Harry, never complained, just came with me. Bloody awful painter of course.'

She minded his getting old, his frailty, his decline into pathos, but most of all she minded that he had never needed her. Even now. This was as good as it was going to get.

In the car Marcus picked up her invitation to the Private View for Alain Le Feuvre, which had arrived in the post that morning.

'Bloody actors thinking they can paint.'

'You can come with me if you want. I can bring a guest.'

'Why would I want to see paintings from a superannuated French sex symbol.'

'Because if you don't, you'll be missing out.'

'Well I shall. We could play hunt-the-sold-stickers. The death throes of a gallery are always instructive.'

Harriet wondered whether she minded when he said that. Was her pirate really on the rocks?

* * *

'*Buon giorno Signora. Comminciamo.* Is that right?'

'*Esatto. Buongiorno Signor Descartes Jones. Come Sta*?'

'*Come sta.* How am I. Full of the joys of spring I am. I love this. *Mi piace le lezioni.*'

'*No, mi piacciono,* I like, plural remember, *queste,* these, *lezioni*. These lessons. *Bene son contenta*.'

'*Mi piacciono queste lezioni*. Oi, are you yawning?'

'No, no.'

'Fibber. Sorry if I'm keeping you up.'

'*Be' son stanca morta stamattina.* Dead tired.'

'Well I was doing my homework at one in the morning.'

'*In Italiano prego*.'

'*Ho fatto i devoirs*, no that's French, *compiti a l'una questo, no questa, mattina*.'

'*Bravo. Adesso facciamo le demande*. You ask me a question.'

'*Signora com'E fisicamente*? What do you look like then?'

'*Io? Ho dei capelli lunghi, long hair, occhi azzuri*, remember the word for blue eyes. E.'

'*Bellissima*.'

'*Signor Descartes Jones continuiamo*, exercises on page 9.'

'Only asking.'

'Then stop laughing.'

* * *

The whining voice came from behind the curtain of the changing room. 'Zip us up Caroline, there's a dear. Well anyway, Charles says that if Rupert doesn't make Colet Court or Westminster Under School, he'll just have to wear tighter trousers and be a chorister!'

There was a ripping sound, and two Fulham ladies swapping size twelve Azzedine Alaia suits dissolved into giggles. The assistant looked at Harriet without expression.

Harriet loved Madame Ada's Dress Agency. Tucked between a bookie and an Asian greengrocer at the wrong end of the Old Brompton Road, it was a secret grotto of goodies for ladies with no money, who liked to wear beautiful clothes. At Madame Ada's the assistants were never pushy. Most were in their sixties and even seventies, mostly ex-theatrical dressers who still survived on fixed rents in West Kensington and memories of Gertrude Lawrence.

Taxis would draw up outside with maids from the embassies, carrying armfuls of designer clothes of which their mistresses had decided they were tired, perhaps after one wearing, and then the ladies of Fulham or, in Harriet's case, W6, would pounce. Where else could one find a Chanel suit for under £200, or a Gucci handbag for £25? Cheap at the price with all the magic of unknown exciting times embedded in the fabric by the previous wealthy owner.

There was too, always that frisson of danger. Marcus had once dragged her to a Private View at Spink & Co in St James's. Lots of society faces, the odd actor, TV personality. An expensive blonde across the room had stared and stared at her. Instantly she had known that it was the previous owner of her Caroline Charles dress (a snip at £50) she had bought just that morning. Funny or embarrassing. Both, and exciting. For a second, Harriet was a little girl again, clattering down the hall in her mother's shoes.

Two women emerged shamefaced from the changing room, explaining that the zip had not been well sewed in. Then they stumbled out into the hot street, still talking schools. Harriet continued to look. She needed a summer dress, something decent to wear to meet Billy in. A jacket maybe? Well, she couldn't keep wearing the same things.

'Would you reserve that for me I'm just going to see if I can match up the bag with some shoes over the road.' A tall rather horsey woman was standing at the counter. 'Yes the name is Descartes-Jones. Veronica.'

Harriet looked up. 'Excuse me, I couldn't help overhearing, Are you related to Roger Descartes-Jones.'

'He's my husband.' She looked suspicious.

'I'm sorry, I should introduce myself. I'm Harriet Gosse. I'm very much enjoying teaching your husband Italian.'

'I'm sorry you must be mistaken. My husband has no ear whatsoever for languages.'

The woman picked up her things and walked quickly out of the shop. Another one bites the dust, thought Harriet. Big mouth. Damn. And she liked him. He was doing so well. But why didn't his wife know? Putting down the clothes she had chosen, Harriet said good bye and walked out into the street. She didn't feel like buying clothes anyway.

She brushed past a red-headed woman dashing into the shop with an armful of clothes. The woman's bright lipstick, stood out in the daylight. She smiled at Harriet, in that way one does when one shares a secret. But then London is a village of half-remembered faces in forgotten contexts. Cremona Kent never tried to remember.

* * *

'It's political art, Le Feuvre is commenting on France today, a confused identity. Yes of course, the images have immense impact. Hope you can come. Yes, yes, ties up with the Curzon.' Richard put down the phone to the art critic at the Glasgow Herald, wondering why these days he felt increasingly like an old tart trying to turn tricks.

Chantal was finishing off the last invitations to the Le Feuvre show and new works fresh from the warehouse were being unloaded off the van outside. Then he noticed the two women, obviously out-of-towners too dressed up, looking at the poor old Puriddu, only two of which had sold. Dead loss.

'What is it all about then dear? '

'This one Madame? Strong isn't it, full of power. It is the representation of the stigmata, it expresses the belief that Sicily had been suffering for centuries from man's sheer – ' Richard suddenly thought of Harriet, her beautiful pale skin, aloof, going with him on sufferance on Saturday, yet when she was teaching on the phone, she was so vivacious. Adorable. Dammit! A tall blonde walked past out on the street, legs up to her armpits, great large breasts leaping up and down, up and down, '– er lust, no, I mean inhumanity.'

'Well make up your mind dear?'

'Well, both.' Richard decided he couldn't for the life of him, remember what it was supposed to represent now, but the Gallerie Lepard had twisted his arm. Puriddu the greatest thing since olive oil. The usual crap.

'For £1,800?'

'Yes Madame. Plus VAT.'

'I'll take it. We had a lovely holiday in Sicily last year, you know.'

The woman went to the desk and wrote out a cheque. Astonished, Richard took it. Midland Bank, Luton. Luton!

* * *

Marcus had gone rather too far this time Harriet thought. Fake Lapis Lazuli round the doors was one thing, but now fake oak panels down the stairs? Ulrike had talked him into it of course. He adored German women, too much Dietrich in his youth.

What a day! Grind, grind, signed off the VAT, signed off the girls' money, done the cash-flow forecasts – not bad, as long as everyone paid reasonably quickly, which of course, they never did. Processed Needs Assessments for twelve chartered surveyors needing German. No chartered surveyors in Germany apparently, so lots of opportunities for the Brits. Then Kirsty-the-Matron's French – non-existent, she would recommend two face-to-face lessons to each telephone session for the first month. Where to start? As for old Roger the Dodger, he hadn't rung up to cancel, so Friday still looked on. Maybe Veronica hadn't told him about their brief encounter.

There were seven girls in the library, ostensibly preparing for the next week's lessons, but judging by the amount of giggling going on, Harriet doubted there was much preparation of any sort. And as their average age was twenty five, she felt like an old school ma'am. Ulrike was singing Tina Turner on the stairs. It was the usual madhouse. 'Would you girls please keep the noise down I can't hear myself think!' she called,

'Bye love, I'm off.' Mrs Mac, always left for her bus on the dot of 5.30. Clatter, clatter. 'For goodness sake Ulrike, would you watch that bucket!' Clatter, clatter. Slam.

Back to work. 'Bye Mireille, Bye Keiko, ciao Graziella. See you tomorrow.' The girls grabbed their work, and their wages and left still giggling. Harriet worked on, not noticing that the evening had arrived, with all its noises of the market closing, the stalls on wheels being trundled away over the cobbles, and the pubs and wine bars opening up for the evening trade. Only when she switched off the computer, did she notice that Danny had come in without her hearing, and was sitting on top of the filing cabinet drawing her. Touched, she noticed he had washed his hands, though there was still a blue smear down his cheek.

'Let's have a look.'

'There you are, the Working Woman. I'll put a bubble coming out of her head, Have I Lost My Sense Of Humour? Honestly Harriet. Would you girls keep the noise down, I can't hear myself think!' Danny put on a high falsetto. Harriet through an apple core at him.

'That's not fair. You try working with all that cackling going on.'

'I was actually. I rather like the noise you lot make. Now are you stopping or not.'

'I'm thinking of going now while I've got the strength to crawl up the hill. Always the same, clearing the deck before Billy comes back.' Harriet stood up and began to tidy her desk. 'Done any good work today?'

'Not bad. Finished the hands I was working on. Got them right at last. Look, will you stop farting around. I've made spag bol you know, it's not bad. Come and eat it.'

'I can smell it. Are you sure, Danny, have you got enough?'

'Look mush, are you saying I can't count spaghettis?'

'No. I'll come right up this minute. I wonder is it possible to run a small business in London and make any money at all? If it weren't for Marcus charging such a low rent, I'd be under water. God knows how other businesses manage.'

'Wouldn't know Harriet, how I keep all my money in my boots, don't trust banks. They're all run by wankers.'

Keys, lock safe, cabinets, unplug lights. Harriet shoved the ferry timetables into her briefcase. As usual she had never got round to booking a holiday, so they would head off in August on adventures in the car and bed-and-breakfast their way round any country Billy cared to choose, as long as it was France, Ireland, or Spain. Or Scotland if they couldn't get a booking.

She always said she worked in a sandwich, Marcus with his stock of new discoveries underneath, Danny a Royal Academy Gold Medal Winner, producing marvellous new work above, while she was the stodgy bread in the middle churning out managers with a smattering of French or German.

Out on the roof – terrace was too grand a name for the flat piece of roofing, with the precarious rail – she never let Billy up here — Harriet slumped, exhausted, on the bean bags, wrapping herself in the blanket and watching the stars come out.

Wonderful warm tomatoey smells wafted out of the tiny kitchen. Danny came up with a large tumbler of wine. The wine was good, even if there was paint on the rim. How nice it was to be looked after, by a man, just for a little while. Who *did* look after her, except Danny who was more like a brother than a possible lover? And Marcus of course.

Thoughts drifted into pictures. David Forsyth appeared in his chocolate commercial, young and passionate, but soft centred, just 100% interested in looking after David Forsyth.

'All men are selfish bastards, Harriet, they can't help it.' Laura's voice broke in. Then her pirate, Richard Longbridge, achingly handsome and tall, strode into her tired mind's eye, wearing a silk dressing gown with a rose between his teeth, ordering caviare, when all she really wanted was a decent cup of tea.

A voice. 'Only asking, *Signora*.' Roger Descartes-Jones. What does he look like? Wears navy-blue pyjamas possibly. Balding maybe, electric toothbrush shining up the most wonderful smile, eager to please. Sounded like the sort of man who would give you a dozen small shiny Christmas presents with expensive wrapping, and then be generous enough to laugh you into a bed, bought off the back of a lorry. How on earth did he ever end up with that snooty wife? And Tom? She could barely see him. And *she* had done all the looking-after there.

Minutes later Danny was feeding her spaghetti, rolled expertly round the fork. Then he let her fall back asleep. He pushed her heavy hair out of her eyes and kissed her forehead, and lay down too. They slept side by side, exhausted babes on the roof, as the nightlife of Portobello carried on beneath.

Chapter Eight

'*Je devrais travailler mais, tant pis, je reste*. Is that right Jean Baptiste?'

'*Parfait Madame*.'

'*Je devrais m'en aller à Harrods, mais, tant pis, je reste ici avec toi, I mean, vous*. I ought not to take such pleasure in talking to you Jean Baptiste, but I do. What did I do before these lessons?'

'Please concentrate Madame, so much to do, but I enjoy you too so much. Madame. Madame!'

* * *

'Clickie Nuggie?' the Chinese girl in the blue peaked cap was asking him, but he just couldn't understand a word. She seemed terribly anxious to help. 'Clickie Nuggie? Clickie Nuggie?'

'And what my darling, are Clickie Nuggie, precisely?' Richard was fumbling for his wallet. Behind him impatient queues of clued-up shoppers muttered and shifted their feet.

'Clickie Nuggie. Clickie. Nuggie.'

'It's no use pointing up to the ceiling, the Good Lord isn't helping at the moment. WHAT ARE CLICKIE NUGGIE? I HAVE NOT EATEN IN THIS RESTAURANT BEFORE. If you can favour this place with such a description.'

'She means chicken nuggets dear', the woman behind him interpreted. 'That's the picture of them above your head look. Chicken balls in batter.'

Richard looked up at the illuminated photograph above his head, and shuddered.

'God no, they look like small timebombs of cholesterol. No clickie nuggie today thank you. Just four Hearty Hamburgers, and chips for four.'

'Dlinks?' The girl was pressing buttons on the till, with one hand, while shovelling a paper traycloth onto the tray with the other.

'Two teas, and two, oh well, two chocolate milk shakes.'

'It is expensive these days for a family to eat here, isn't it love?' said the woman next to him as £7.50p flashed up.

Richard threw open his rack of credit cards. American Express, Diners, Visa Gold Card. A groan went up behind him. 'What? None of them. Cash? Well let's see, 50 dollar note, no that's no good. By the way, do you have any sort of wine list here?'

'What a prat.' Someone muttered behind him. Richard began to sweat.

Billy was sitting just drooling for his first Hearty Burger in months. For once however, Jamie had forgotten his stomach, unable to take his eyes off his father who was trying to manoeuvre the plastic tray over the heads of the crowds, one hand bulging with tomato ketchup sachets. There he was six foot four, sticking out like a sore thumb with his Brookes Brothers' blazer amongst the anoraks. Rich the Dick having to eat fast food! What a miracle worker Billy's mum was.

'I must say Harriet, you have a strange sense of humour, your "special place" turning out to be the home of the Hearty Hamburger in darkest Swindon.'

'Well if you'd had school lunches all term, food like this *is* special. Anyway admit it, there is nothing like sinking your teeth into a juicy Hearty Burger with extra pickle.'

Harriet smiled as Richard shuddered. He was being got at. But, having just read his bank statement this morning, could he complain, when at forty-one he finally met a woman who didn't want the Waldorf as well as the salad? How could that old dear call it expensive?

'It's funny, the end of the year', said Jamie through a mouthful of chips.

'Don't speak with your mouth full', said Richard, himself speaking with his mouth full.

'Why is that Jamie? Do you mean it's because it seems both happy and sad?' Looking at him, Harriet was impressed by the sensitivity of his face, not at all like his father!

'Well it all starts when you go down to the cellar to drag up your trunk, and then Matron comes in with all your kit washed.'

'I know, all the white things the same shade of grey.'

'Yes, and then you have to say good bye to the Prefects. It's really sad. Even Rogers, he was alright really. And Matron, It'll all be different next year.'

'Yes we're going to be Dorm Captains, both of us.' Billy was still exultant. 'Brilliant. Think of the power!'

'Well make sure you don't give the smaller boys as bad a time as you were given last year. I'm not having my son growing up into a bully.'

'O.K. Mum, don't lecture. Do you know three of the boys in our form are going home and they haven't seen their parents all year. They stay with guardians during the holidays. Not real ones, paid ones.'

'Poor little devils, does this mean you appreciate me schlepping down in my Renault 5 for each *exeat*?'

'Of course, stupid. Are you enjoying that, Mr Longbridge?'

'Ask Richard when he's stopped chewing, Billy. And for calling me stupid I'm going to pinch some of your chips.'

'Got too many anyway. You're looking happy today Mum.'

"Mm now you're flattering me!'

'Get off!'

Richard, who now had rabid indigestion, and certain Repetitive Strain Injury from trying to open the tomato ketchup, looked at her. Yes, that blue dress suited her, brought out her blue eyes. She looked wholesome, terrible word, one normally applied to bread, or was that wholemeal? Sexy too. He usually went for women who liked lots of make up, lots of jewellery. One girl had once said he liked over-the-top, vulgar women like his mother, and he had promptly gone off the boil. Harriet wasn't vulgar, she was real. That was it. And he wasn't used to real women. She was positively glowing today, like someone in a shampoo ad, for God's sake. But then he knew she wasn't glowing for him. And

O.K. he was jealous, let's admit it. Of a ten-year-old boy. Face it, Longbridge, you're a prat. But then so what?

Suddenly he decided he would not tell her he was really Roger Descartes bloody Jones, as he had truly been meaning to tell her. But, faced with polite conversation all the way down, he'd never had a chance. But having her teaching him was obviously going to be the only way he was ever going to get her undivided attention. And it would pay her back for all that crap about this being their special place. Billy and Jamie smiled indulgently at him as he tried to close the plastic box which had once contained his Hearty Burger. It skidded onto across the table onto the floor. Super bloody duper.

A happy little family. Handsome parents, nicely behaved boys. Enjoying their burgers and chips. But then the man sitting across the aisle with his ex-children – saw them once a month under the custody agreement, and couldn't think of a thing to say to them, poor little buggers – knew very well that they were not. Richard Longbridge, Cork Street gallery owner rolling in it, they said, though there had been rumours recently. Deb-humper extraordinaire. And the girl, didn't look the Sloaney type, who was she? The filing cabinet of a mind went back. All that hair, funeral. Something to do with reptiles. Yes! The snake man's widow, *Sampson House* somebody Gosse. Love it! All he'd have to do is look it up in the cuts. 'Mrs Gosse!' Yes she looked round. Just testing, look the other way. Well, old Longbridge is coming down in the world a bit. Obviously never eaten fast food in his life – asking for a knife and fork! Plonker. Leaving his children, the man went across the road to ring the *Diary*. Might make a nice short for the London edition, if the lazy bastards weren't out at the pub.

* * *

'We are sorry for the delay. This is due to a person on the line at Hammersmith. We shall be continuing our journey shortly.'

'Another one bites the dust. Have you seen those things they fish suicides out under the track with?'

'No I haven't. I always think it's bloody inconsiderate

though. If you want to kill yourself, why put other people out? That's what I say.'

Stuck in a tunnel on the Piccadilly Line Underground between Earls Court and Barons Court, Kirsty Rogers listened. Someone had felt desperate enough to die, and those two women were talking about it like the weather.

She shifted her seat, fighting claustrophobia. She noticed that the same women were taking in the six Harrods bags. Well if you haven't got it, flaunt it.

She looked at her watch. About now the last stragglers would have left the school, and she would be now sitting in the Laundry Room with the housekeeper having a cup of tea, celebrating. And there would be at least an hour before the first call about little Jeremy's football boots. What had he done to them?

She'd have liked to have finished the term, but then Crouch had found her an embarrassment. Bundled her off like a bad smell. So she had spent the morning at Harrods. Shop till you drop, she'd once seen the words embroidered on a cushion in the window of a gift shop. And she had. A fortune on clothes with labels like fairy tales. Would she ever dare wear a pair of shoes which cost £300? Not out in the street. With a lurch, the train started again.

Further down the carriage, Cremona Kent was writing in her notebook. Get the first three paragraphs done, and then she could knock it off on Monday. 'I have seen the future, and his name is gorgeous blond David Forsyth who will be wielding his gavel in *Auctioneer*, BBC One's forthcoming glossy Sunday-night drama serial. Blah blah, blah. Now Kent, are you exaggerating? Well, he did have a nice tight bum, it had to be said. And a great smile, all his own teeth. He was available and clearly not gay. What more did her readers want? Or her come to that?

Cremona stretched out her expensively stockinged legs, not bad for a member of the gravitationally challenged. Everything sinking like Venice, kept together by willpower and money. 'With a £5 million budget, *Auctioneer* is set to make the Malvern Hills the next TV tourist trail.' The great thing about location reports is that at least you got out of the office, and had a good lunch. Though how those actors coped with all the hanging around, she could not understand. They were like puppy dogs, particularly the forty-plus women, terribly eager to be nice, to have their names mentioned. Let's face it, journalists weren't usually treated so nicely these days.

Why not quit while she could still frame a sentence and write *the* Novel, the blockbuster that would buy her the place in the South of France. Cremona squinted at her notes, quite unable to read her own terrible writing. Far too much like hard work. Better carry on just trying to pay the mortgage on the place she had. God knows she couldn't afford to move, the way property prices were going.

Hammersmith. It was as if nothing had happened—people hanging around looking bored, then Ravenscourt Park, the green bursting in upon the eye, Stamford Brook, Turnham Green. Kirsty got off and walked quickly out of the station, suddenly anxious to get back before Boyd came in. No longer a schoolboy now, starting in the office on Monday, before Gay Paree here we come! But will you still love me now I'm not wearing a badge with Matron on it? Now that we can make love without worrying about one of the boys knocking on the door for a plaster? That, Kirsty said to herself, was the 64,000 dollar question. Well, a wee bit more than that actually.

* * *

'Come in, Harriet. Jamie, Mummy sent the new Robot Exterminator for you. God knows why. It's in your room. Show Billy upstairs. Look, don't wreck the joint, mind the paintwork!' Richard took Harriet's coat as Jamie burst up the stairs with Billy. She could hear their feet going up, and up and up. How many storeys were there?

She caught the eye of the stuffed howler monkey hanging off the tall black halogen lamp in the hall. Looked just like him, a pirate about to swing aboard to capture more doubloons. Ooh Aah Jim lad! And how many doubloons had been paid for that Conroy on the stairs? And the Aston Martin, and the top-of-the-range Volvo she'd been driven about in today come to that? Purrrr. . . .

It was no good denying it. She had been curious to

see how this man lived. Had hardly hesitated when he'd suggested coming in for a drink before running them back to Hammersmith. Now she suddenly realised, she had never once been inside the homes of any of Billy's friends. She was always the one who seemed to do the inviting over in the holidays, and then the mothers would arrive to collect their little dears, take one look at the peeling paint and the obviously cheap carpet, and their eyes would open wide, their smiles tighten, and their voices would go, just that little bit higher, as if they were little girls who had accidentally stumbled into Santa's grotto before the decorators had finished. Harriet thanked God that Billy was a boy, gloriously insensitive to such nuances. There was no way a girl would have missed them — nor escaped the blinding fury.

Walking through the rooms alone, as Richard went downstairs 'to see if Mrs Thing has left anything for us', she thought she had never seen such expensive, artful clutter. Straight out of a design magazine. From an article about a designer who got drunk one night and furnished the same house for two different clients.

Studies of housemaids by Julia Margaret Cameron taken in the gentility of the Isle of Wight hung next to brightly-coloured radiators which were horizontally hung across the windows. Very Russian Constructivist, and clever, presumably when the burglars tried to saw through them they'd get a burst of boiling water. On the ornate Victorian desk there was a lizard desk set, molto Harrods catalogue, Harriet thought, complete with a Phillipe Stark ashtray, a set of Fornasetti coasters, a silver swizzle stick and a green malachite bin. And leaning against a funny sort of lamp, she had once seen in a colour supplement described as a tripod torchère, a teddy bear! Unstuffed, moth-eaten. Best of the lot.

Harriet was about to pick him up for a cuddle, when the phone rang. Somewhere. Phone? There on the Ron Arad chair on a pile of Vintage Car magazines. Where else?

'Hello.'

'Who's that? You're new. He's never fired the housekeeper again. Is my son there.' The thick Dublin accent came as a surprise, its belligerent tone less so.

‘I’m sorry, who do you want? This is, I’m just looking, this is er, 3668.’

‘I know that, the home of Richard Patrick Longbridge. My son. Is he back yet with my grandson?’

‘Oh, Mrs Longbridge, yes he is, this is Harriet Gosse speaking. We’ve just got in.’

‘I’ll be right with you.’

The phone went dead. Harriet winked at the teddy bear, who must know a few secrets about this extraordinary family. How many business men could be rumoured to be on the rocks and yet apparently have such wealth. And Mummy sounded promising. Very Sean O’Casey.

Richard came up with two mugs of tea as the doorbell rang. ‘Damn, who’s that. Hang on a minute Harriet.’

‘I rang on the mobile outside. The new housekeeper said you’d just come in. Is that for me. Yuk, Richard how many times do I have to tell you, three sugars.’

‘Moth-er!’

Small, plump, covered in jewellery, heavy make-up, she had a huge presence, huge hair, and huge perfume, which quickly reeked across the room. Harriet suddenly thought how much her father would have loved to have painted her. Mary Ellen Longbridge was already beckoning to her to come over with a long red nail. ‘Now dear you can take my coat, but it’s good linen mind, so you’ll have to hang it up properly. On a satin coat hanger, no shoving it over the bannister, I know you girls. And they seem to be getting younger every year Richard, this one can’t be more than thirty.’

‘Mother, please let me take it. This is Mrs Harriet Gosse, she is the mother of Jamie’s friend Billy. We’ve just collected them from school.’

‘Together.’

‘Yes I confess, together. And we had a Hearty Hamburger, so that’ll be four “Hail Mary’s” to add to the indigestion.’

‘Don’t blaspheme Richard. So she’s not the one who turned you down for dinner?’

Silence. Harriet felt for Richard, and thought she would break the silence. It would be quite nice to be addressed directly.

'As you can see my mother has never lost her fondness for the stiletto touch', Richard returned from the hall, where he had slung his mother's orange linen coat over the bannisters.

'Nan!' Jamie rushed down the stairs and into his grandmother's arms.

'My, you're so thin, what have they been feeding you on? Bread and scrape?' Harriet was interested to see there was another Mary Ellen, smoothing Jamie's hair back from his forehead, a tenderness which she seemed to have long since ceased to feel for her own son, for whatever reason.

'Go on, come and see my new computer game Mum sent me. Billy's on it, come on.'

'Let's recover in peace.' Richard led the way back into the drawing room, 'I'm sorry you were mistaken for the housekeeper. My mother is exaggerating, I've actually only had three in five years. Not bad for London.'

Harriet's gaze met a wall of pictures. Some fit for graffiti, others fit to die for. How could one man have such different tastes? Mind you, with such a mother, it was a miracle he'd been allowed to develop any taste, let alone so many!

'So are you coming to the Le Feuvre do?'

'Yes I'd love to, I'm most curious to meet him, I remember seeing him in La Tante Italienne when we lived in Lyons. When I was six, I thought he was the most handsome man I had ever seen.'

'Screws everything that moves you know.'

'Does he? Well he was and is a marvellous actor.'

'Did you live in Lyons long?'

'No, only three months. Then we left, for Italy, I think. We travelled all over the place, Italy, France, Spain, Portugal for a year. I just got used to changing schools, picking up and putting down friends.'

'So however did you get into teaching?'

'Well, finally, when I was fifteen, my mother's sisters persuaded Jester to send me to boarding school on the south Coast to get some exams, and I managed to somehow, and scraped into University.'

'Some people would envy you that sort of upbringing. All that sun, and good food.'

'Yes, but a gypsy childhood, you see. Interesting, but

no roots. One never feels one belongs anywhere. I always envy people who have lived in the same house for years and years.'

'In my experience, painters are never easy to live with in any house. But Jester did some marvellous work on his travels. I'd like to meet him you know. Does he paint now?'

'He's just started again, first time in over two years.'

'Shame he can't come to the Le Feuvre bash. Bring a guest though, if you want to.'

'Would you mind if I brought my landlord Marcus Whitehead? '

'Marcus Whitehead? Of course. Whitehead was your father's agent wasn't he? I thought I recognised your office address. I've got a lot of time for him. One of the few gallery people who got out just in time. Took the money and ran. Clever devil. Never had any time for me though, turned my father down flat when he asked him to take me on.'

'Why was that?'

'Sexual orientation may have had something to do with it. No, probably unfair. More likely it was because I was young, arrogant, and thought I knew it all.'

'You're much too hard on yourself. How could you have been expected to know anything much?'

'I don't know. All I know is that then I knew nothing, but thought I did, but now I don't have that comfort. Now I know I know bugger all, ask my accountant. I just act as if I do. Horrible thing hitting middle age. Wrinkled phoneydom!'

'So what'll it be then, Mr Longbridge? Kleenex, gin or a psychotherapist?'

'Gin, every time.'

Ominous tick tack of heels on the Seagrass floor. Mary Ellen had tracked them down. She plonked herself down on a leather day bed, disapprovingly.

'So Mrs, I'm sorry the mind's gone.'

'Gosse.'

'Gosse. Does your husband send you out to work to pay those absurd fees. £1000 a year they were in Richard's day you know.'

'I wish they were still! No, Mrs Longbridge, I'm a widow, and I send myself out to work.'

'Oh a widow? And what work do you do?'

She gave the word widow the same inflection as she might have given to leper, or debtor or sinner. In fact any other two-syllable category of people heading for eternal damnation. Same old unspoken questions. Harriet could have drawn the bubble coming out of his mother's head. Are you after my Son? Why the hostility?

'I run a school teaching business-people languages. Lots of people work in Europe and need to brush up their German or French.'

'And does it pay?'

'It's a living. And it does pay well enough to meet the school fees.'

Mrs Longbridge adjusted her rings. 'Sounds almost as daft as running a gallery for European pianters. I'm suspicious of Europe. Should never have gone in I think. Though Ireland has done O.K. out of it, I suppose.'

She looked directly at Harriet.

'Does your family bail you out from time to time? Like I have to with this good-for-nothing son of mine.'

In the corner of her eye, Harriet could see Richard slumped into his chair. She didn't like to look at him.

'I'm afraid not. My mother is dead, my father had a stroke two years ago and is in a residential home now.'

'Brothers, sisters?'

'My brother died when I was three. My mother died shortly afterwards.' Any more linen you want washing besides that expensively common jacket out in the hall? Harriet did not flinch from the dark assessing eyes. How about a press release? Unexpectedly she began to feel protective to Richard. And yet she'd had enough excitement with the Longbridge family for one day.

'It's very nice to have met you Mrs Longbridge, but we must go now.' Harriet walked to the stairs and called up, 'Billy we've got to go. Now! Come down.' She walked back into the room.

'So do you think my son's worth bothering with then, Mrs Gosse?'

'Oh yes, I'm still hoping he'll take some Italian lessons. I've got some marvellous teachers.'

'That's not what I meant.'

Billy, astonishingly thundered down the stairs to the rescue, without a single prevaricating 'Oh Mum!' Miracle.

'I think he does a good job in a very difficult business. You must be proud of him.'

Mary Ellen Longbridge laughed. It was not a nice sound, but it brought Richard back to life.

'Harriet, let me run you back? Mother if you're staying, would you look after Jamie while I run Harriet and Billy to their house.'

'Sure, you go on, don't mind me. Good bye then, dear. See you soon I'm sure.'

* * *

Robert Gaskell was putting out the empty milk bottles as Richard's Volvo drew into the street. He waved at Harriet, and nodded to Richard. Georgiana must have seen them because she came out too, to deadhead some perfectly blooming geraniums. Gushingly friendly but she had not, quite, been able to meet Harriet in the eye since the night of dinner party.

'Billy! Welcome back dear, had a good term? Florian and Minty can't wait to play with you.'

Billy groaned quietly.

'You remember Richard, Georgiana.'

'How could I forget him, quite made our little party, dashing into the street like James Bond! Good journey, traffic not too vile I hope?'

'Robert, I wonder would you be kind enough to give us a hand with Billy's trunk.'

'Pleasure.'

'Robert, Richard Longbridge. Richard, this is my neighbour Robert Gaskell.'

The men shook hands, and manoeuvred the trunk into Harriet's tiny hall. Robert smiled and left, he seemed a bit embarrassed. It was Richard's turn to stare. So small. Everything so neat and tucked away. He took in the four Jester Dunne's on the living room wall. Their extraordinary power, the very thickness of the paint dwarfed the room. Then the bright pots and pans of Harriet's tiny kitchen beyond, and the bright cushions and all the books and the plants trailing around, and then the carpet and the walls. Serviceable, horrible word that. Harriet deserved better. London was so bloody expensive.

'Mum I'm so glad to be back.' Billy ran up to his room, carrying the cat in his arms.

Richard was still looking around. Harriet was glad she had cleaned up before she left.

'These houses are bijou, aren't they.'

'I suppose so. Locally they're called Alimony Villas, because there are so many professionals here impoverished by wife number-one – our Robert next door being a prime example.'

'Poor man! Looking back, I was very lucky with Anne. This is good, who did this?' Richard was smiling at the cartoon of Harriet as Superwoman, Danny had done one day in the office, when she had been up to her ears in crises.

'Daniel Messenger, he lives over our office. A really good friend. Royal Academy Schools Gold Medal winner you know. I don't have my cartoons done by just any riff raff.'

'He's certainly got your vivacity, the way your nose wrinkles. Look. Would you like to go to an auction with me on Wednesday? At Bute's.'

'Bute, Barnaby & Crieff & Co., to give the full name hardly anyone knows.'

'Is that a Morningside accent? I am impressed. Yes. 6.30. American and Continental Art. My dear ex-wife Anne will be there, but don't worry, she'll be the very model of icy self-control. The client who gave her the dosh to buy the partnership in her gallery after we split up, is off-loading his ghastly Texan paintings this week, in spite of all Anne's pleadings. It's his personal revenge on the art world.'

'Will that affect her that badly?'

'I'll say. She and Henry Lapham her partner were the market makers in this new Texan art. And, but by the grace of God, go all of us, although I told her at the start it was rubbish. So will you come? You're frowning.'

'Something Marcus said. O.K. I'll see you there. You'd better get back to your mother.'

Richard bent down and kissed her on the cheek. 'Bye, Harriet. God, I've got indigestion.'

Harriet laughed, and was blushing as she shut the door.

'Mum!'

'Billy! Why the sudden drama?'

'Do you fancy him, Jamie's Dad?'

'I think he can be very nice yes'

'But he wanted to eat the burgers with a knife and fork.'

'Oh heinous crime. Well you know what they say, the child is the father to the man, so it's up to Jamie to take him in hand.'

'Crouch is always quoting that, but that's not what it means, Mum. Mum, are you listening to me?'

* * *

Maxi Rogers loved Harrods, it was like home, only smaller. But right now, all she wanted was to kick off her shoes under the counter and sink into a cappuccino.

'Hello! My dear! Saw your new daughter-in-law just rushing out, looked as if she had bought half the shop. What big changes for her now!'

Maxi carried on eating, thinking how English voices always manage to carry above background noise. The Food Hall was still full of customers, and yet every goddamn crystal-glass syllable could be heard.

'Mrs Rogers? It is you isn't it? Are you alright? Did you hear me?'

Gulping, Maxi nearly spilt the coffee over her new navy suit.

'I'm sorry Ma'am, were you speaking to me?'

'Jennifer Harman, my son Toby was Prefect of Wolsey house.'

'Oh my. How do you do.'

'Don't know what we're going to do without Matron. So good particularly with the younger boys. The new woman sounded halfwitted when I rang up. But that's it nowadays, you can never keep good people, though I must say a Matron in the family must have been, well, a surprise!'

'We're delighted, now we've got to know her, Mrs Harman, as I am sure you can imagine. She's even learning French ready for when she and Boyd go to run my husband's office in Paris.'

'French, with that accent? How charming.'

Quite suddenly Maxi Rogers felt homesick for Houston and its friendly, easy-going people, who said what they meant. Why had she ever thought an English boarding school was such a great idea?

* * *

'Jaakko? Anne Osborn here. I hope you don't mind me ringing on Saturday like this.'

'No, I don't mind. Why should I?'

'The sale, I'm hoping to be there. We're currently interesting several clients in your pictures. I had Bute's mail their catalogues to them.'

'So you have been busy busy, making waves, doing deals. Good. I am pleased for you.'

'Jaakko. I've been looking at the estimates in the catalogue. May I ask, have you set reserves?'

'Surely that is my business, Anne Osborn.'

'Of course, but there is still time. You could withdraw well, some of them, the mixed media frescoes for instance. I've no doubt we could find a private buyer, given just a little more time. But it's come as a shock, to find you are selling up the whole collection.'

'Mrs Osborn, we sit in offices on different sides of the world, but I can almost smell the fear in your voice. Whereas I, who have had the banks banging on the door for two months now, feel relaxed, at peace. In Denmark the writer Hans Christian Andersen, you know him? He wrote the tale of the King's Clothes.'

'I remember Danny Kaye.'

'You see, I am the King long after the boy has shouted in the crowd. I have learned, just as you will learn now. All those pictures are like those pretend clothes, the King bought from the wicked tailors. And you, Anne Osborn had such fun selling them to me for such Mickey Mouse money. And for you now, the boy is about to shout.'

'Spare me the Scandinavian psychology, Jaakko. Those pieces were fine work, by good artists, whose reputation you're about to wreck on a selfish whim. And I am not some fairytale crook, I've put my whole life and name on the line for this work. Even my own home.'

'Assets are only worth what fools will pay. Ask poor desperate Donald Trump, and those greedy, so well-bred English who trusted their money to the Lloyds. Good bye Anne Osborn.'

Brrrrrrr.

' . . . Fuck you.'

*   *   *

'*Allora, continuiamo, Roger.*'

'*Se, if what . . . vado in citta oggi, arriverò tardi.*'

'*Bravo*. If I go, I will. This is the easiest of the three conditional forms.'

'If I ask you nicely, will we do something else?'

'You got to concentrate, Roger. Now three more.'

'Alright. *Se*, can't think. I'm knackered. Honest.'

'O.K., that's for homework. I'll fax through more examples. Now look at the map. Tell me how to get from the cinema to the cathedral. *Signor, il Duomo per favore*?'

'O.K. O.K., *alla fine della strada, torna a destra e va dritto fino al,* blimey what's the word for bakers?'

'*Panetteria, pasticceria.*'

'Pasticc whatever. Harriet *per favore se* I work hard, can we change the time for the lessons, my brains scrambled.

'Well I was surprised you wanted lessons this early. Most of my clients say their wives would divorce them if they started this early.'

'I'm not married thank goodness! Harriet. Are you there?'

Chapter Nine

The two children were trying to drown each other in the bath, but sitting on the loo seat, reading the *Sunday News* Style section, Georgiana refused to take any notice.

She was a slow reader, with such a busy life, it usually took her till Wednesday night to polish off all ten sections. Not that she was paticularly happy about it this evening, having just discovered that the swags and festoons on her curtains, which she had had done at vast expense, were now as dead as a dodo in the Austere Nineties. Today's look apparently was Hamptons blue-and-white stripes. She gave the ruched Viennese bathroom blind made from cream waterproof brocade a rueful twitch, and went back to the Diary.

. . . to the Home of the Hearty Hamburger in Swindon where our correspondent espied Richard Longbridge – of Cork Street's Europa gallery . . . " 'No!' said Georgiana. "*. . . soon to show Gallic heart-throb and Oscar winner Alain Le Feuvre's latest daubs – trying to eat a Hearty Hamburger without the requested knife and fork. Without success we can report. Heir to a £100 million fortune, held frustratingly in trust, left by property developer father, Ernest Longbridge (whose demolition in '65, of the Nash Seven Crescent NW3, readers will remember had half Hampstead lying before the bulldozers), Mr Longbridge was in the company of Harriet Gosse.*

'Good God! Harriet! Araminta, put him down, no I won't squirt you, I'm reading, . . . *beautiful widow of 'Sampson House, star Thomas Gosse, whose sudden death five years ago, followed the controversial snake-eating hype which almost doubled viewing figures.*

It gave her goose pimples all over, Alain Le Feuvre paintings, and Harriet in the newspaper. How could she take a man like that to a fast-food joint. Incredible. She felt a surge of irritation as she heard Robert's key downstairs in the front door. Damn. Georgiana took her glass of wine off the cistern and drained it off. Only one child in the bath now, God knows where the other one was?

* * *

'See what skills you have to have as a woman. You try painting your toe nails, without blotching all over your foot. Feet OFF the eiderdown Jamie, it's Maine patchwork. Cost me £250 at the General Trading Company, £250. That was the eighties for you!'

Next door, the boys were watching fascinated as Laura slurped on layer after layer of red nail varnish. The smell, combined perfume, face powder and cigarette fumes, and made Laura's bedroom delightfully cosy and feminine.

'I thought H. was never going to go, how many outfits did she try on Billy?'

'Seven I think, or eight.'

'Bad sign. Normally your lovely Mum never gives a stuff what she wears, as long as its second hand, although by the way she makes everyone else feel shabby and overweight. It's called charisma, makes you sick. You've either got or you haven't got style, if you've got it it stands out a mile. Sang that in my first panto dressed as a fifties teddy-boy, winkle-pickers and half-mast trousers. Not that you'd remember the fifties, and I refuse to. No, I think your parents both need careful watching, Something's afoot, my noble lords. That's my Laurence Olivier as Richard the third impression. Please DON'T ask who Laurence Olivier is.'

'Do you think so, Dad and Harriet?' Jamie was horrified, if his father mucked Billy's mum around like he so often did, it would be the worst thing.

Laura noticed. 'Only kidding. So what do I know, as the actress said to the Rabbi. Have a humbug.'

Laura's babysitting was of a unique kind. Her motto: 'No fags, porn, drink or drugs without babysitter's dibs' always won approval, and Jamie, who had arrived earlier by taxi to stay the night, was bowled over. Mud pack on her face, hair screwed up in a bun, grubby dressing gown. His mother never looked like that even in her most off-duty moments. Worst luck.

'Right, you lot, now what are we going to do? Bored with your computer games, I understand that. Nothing on the box, never is in July, so what is it to be? A video, Scrabble, Monopoly, stiff drink or hearing my lines for tomorrow?'

'I just like sitting here. It's nice, our house is so clean.'

'Thank you for that Jamie, I think. O.K., sit up and hear my lines, I've got two copies of this week's scripts for some reason. O.K. Here they are. One of you can be Herr Forster the big swinger from Basel who collects Russian icons, God help us. Who's going to be Hector's wife Oliv–ee–ahh, resident pain in the butt. I think Billy should do her he's got the high voice. DON'T kick me, I'm on the last toe! Just do a take-off of Georgiana.'

* * *

'Lot 42 has been withdrawn. Lot 43 *Niagara Falls* the Gustave Denton, Mixed Media on aluminium, we already have a commission bid of £60,000. Thank you Sir £65,000, £65,000, are you bidding sir, you look as if you are bidding. £65,000, £70,000 thank you Madam, so £70,000 for this Gustave Denton. With you Madam, £70,000. Any advance. All done. Selling at £70,000.'

Down went the hammer, and the Auctioneer smiled a world-weary and rather charming smile at the woman in the green Chanel.

'Lot 45.'

'Showing on your right sir', shouted a porter who looked about twelve, Harriet was pained to note.

'Thank you. *Texas Spring*, Gustave Denton again, acrylic on canvas. Let's start the bidding at £150,000. £150,000 No? £120,000. £120,000. Thank you Sir. Any advance?'

The silence was deafening. In those moments, Harriet held the tableau in her mind. The dealers standing at the back, hooded eyes, and along the side of the room the telephone manned by girls wearing their frilly blouses and light tartan suits with names like Katie, Sophie and Samantha. They always were called Katie, Sophie and Samantha, as if the auction house had christened them the moment they had crossed the portals in their navy Gucci loafers, like some crusty Victorian employer who called all her parlour maids Doris on principle. Or perhaps when one Sophie left, they simply advertised for another?

But no one was on the phones. Katie, Sophie and Samantha smiled winsomely at the auctioneer, so sorry, no cash on the line. And the seven foot splodge was knocked down to a man who looked like a collector. 'Jaakko paid one million two for it in '88', Richard whispered to her, but from the collector there was not a glimmer of triumph at having secured such a bargain.

Butes Barnaby & Crieff, had none of the understated grandeur of Christie's and Sotheby's, it was all chrome, glass, and huge potted plants, Bruton Street and Mayfair versus statelier St James's. As the only auction house in London to sell North American Art, it was always popular with London's American community. It had been founded by three partners, who, it was rumoured, had resigned from the big league having failed to get seats on the Board. The place to go for a bargain, and also the place to offload fast, which was an attraction in the recession for London's hard-pressed upper-middle-classes bankrupted by school fees and large mortgages. Harriet liked its brashness and urgency.

'Lot 49, the Lamb Sea. Henry Greenbacher. Mixed media on canvas. £140,000 Thank you Madam. £150,000. Any advance. £150,000.'

Although the air conditioning was on, the early-evening heat filled the Sale Room, mixing with the warring perfumes of the women, who sat immaculate in Chanel, with earrings the size of boiled eggs. Harriet wanted to wriggle, or read a newspaper, the paintings were so odd, and it seemed inexplicable that anyone would want to sell at one tenth of the price, something which had cost him millions.

Muttering excuses, the couple next to Richard squeezed past Harriet. The lot they had obviously come for, had gone, as the auctioneer had said, for 'only £175,000'. An elegant lady brushed past Harriet, so super-thin she did not need to squeeze. She sat down next to Richard, who was writing rude remarks on his catalogue. Harriet noticed that they kissed on the cheek and she felt the nervous ball in her stomach tighten. Was this what she had been expecting? The woman leaned across to shake hands whispering, 'Hi, I'm Anne Osborn, how are you? I used to be Richard's wife.' No answer to that.

A colourful and familiar bulky shape hovered on the very furthest edge of her vision. Marcus was leaning against the wall wearing the bored expression he cultivated especially for auctions. Crafty old Marcus. In the office, he hadn't said he was coming. Wanting to check Richard out, no doubt. She tried to catch his eye, he looked at her quite deliberately and winked, followed by one of his mock shudders. O.K., Marcus. You don't like the paintings, and Richard is not much better?

Harriet smiled. Richard caught her look, 'Do you actually like it Harriet?' She shook her head thinking what Marcus would make of this new Lot. Give me strength! He had always informed her eye, and taste, telling what was good, and what was bad, taking her to sales and shows with quiet kind Ian, when Jester was busy, which was almost always. After Ian's death, Marcus continued, to do the father bit long after he needed to. For this, unfashionably, she was grateful.

'We have £45,000 on the telephone, thank you Samantha, £45,000. £50,000. How kind Sir, £50,000. £60,000, against you Sir. Sir?'

Bang, another one sold, Harriet couldn't see to whom. But she saw Marcus had disappeared. She was not surprised he disapproved. Even at the height of his fame, Jester's work had never raised more than £40,000. Tops. This so-called New Houston School was Tantrum Art, work which looked as if a two-year-old had thrown up his lunch.

Looking at the profile of Richard's ex-wife, shoulders up to her ears with stress, solemnly writing down the prices with an expensive gold pen, Harriet thought just how much she'd hate to be in such a subjective business. At least German, French and Japanese were real, and relatively unchanging commodities.

* * *

'I don't understand how you could do this to me!' Billy, hands on hips, wearing red lipstick and a feather boa, was discovering his motivation.

'I did it because I love him of course', Laura said. *'I'd do anything to keep him.* I walk over to the filing cabinet at this point.'

'Do I enter here?' Jamie had borrowed Laura's fedora.

'Yes.'

'I am sorry if I am interrupting, but I would like to see the catalogue with the Louvain Nudes.'

'Stop giggling. German accent, come on.'

'The Louvain Nudes. What are they?'

'Three-headed women, who cares? I didn't write this crap.'

'Here you are Herr Forster, Mr Benson is out at the moment.'

'No matter.'

"I'm glad you still intend to do some work in this office." Billy had got Georgiana's upper class whine to perfection.

"I'm a professional, and I don't intend to forget it. Goodbye, Olivia, just get out of this office, and out of my life!" Exit Olivia, close up of me looking determined, please God, I don't get a cold sore before recording day and cut."

The doorbell rang. Laura padded down the stairs in her kimono. It was Georgiana.

'Laura! Is Harriet in?'

'No she's out.'

'Ah, I just wondered.' Georgiana took in the mysterious streaks on Laura's kimono and tried not to shudder, 'I've just cut this out of the paper, I wondered whether or not she'd seen it. Quite an event! You know.'

'Thanks, I'll give it to her.'

'Is she out tonight with him? Is he taking her anywhere nice do you know?'

'Don't know. Bye bye.'

Laura took the paper and shut the door. The words '£100 million' and 'snake' hit her. Oh my God, she's done it this time. Harriet would freak. So would the boys.

Stupid, insensitive cow, as if Harriet would want to be in the newpsapers after last time. Nearly killed her. And Billy. Not everyone can handle it. Although what a turn-up, £100 million, though, thinking about it, Aston Martins don't come cheap. She shoved the cutting in her dressing-gown pocket.

'Who was it?' Billy met her on the landing,

'Only Georgiana wanting to know if you wanted to see Florian tomorrow, I said you were busy.'

'Thanks Laura.'

'O.K. Now can we do the scene in the bank. I keep drying on this bit.'

The doorbell rang, just as she reached the top of the stairs.

'Oh blast, who's that now, I've smudged my toe. If it's Georgiana again, tell her to sod off.'

'I'll go.' Billy took off the boa and went to the door, he'd forgotten about the lipstick, which was unfortunate.

Henry Crouch stood on the doorstep.

* * *

'Harriet have you never heard the story about the woman who sold her husband's limo for ten dollars? Must be the same story in every country and every currency. She sells the car, the buyer can't believe his luck, and just as he's about to drive off, he asks her the question, why? And she says, "because my husband's leaving me and he's told me to sell the car and send him the money."

Harriet watched Anne check that each finger was dry under the hand dryer, then adjust each ring.

'Yes, I suppose I have.'

'Well that is why Jaakko Jokkinen, the Finnish Tormentor, my former client, and I thought, friend, is settling for so far, a tenth of what he paid. The banks are the husband, they are leaving him, in his case, to sink. So he doesn't care what happens tonight; if it's three dollars or three hundred. Nothing matters to him any more.'

Anne Osborn's china blue eyes seemed to be pricing her very bone structure. So controlled, so together, and cool in the circumstances. New Yorkers always make the English feel irrelevant in the nicest way.

'I'm just surprised, knowing the state of the market, that the banks allowed him to sell the collection, particularly in London, when he could get more for it in New York.'

'You're smart. Don't think I haven't asked myself that question, Harriet.' Anne's jewelled powder compact glinted in the strip lighting of the Bute's ladies' cloakroom.

'I think it was just easier, he's here so much, and Bute's sell anything. Before I go back, I would just like to visit your docklands district and see for myself why one of the six richest men in Northern Europe can now be Mr Big Bad Debt.'

'There's not much to see, it's just a building site. Huge, empty office buildings, nowhere near any decent roads. That's the problem. And the light railway is hopeless. The recession has freed up office space in the City, so why should people move out there?'

'Didn't they think of that beforehand?'

'No, I don't think they did, everyone was carried along by the tide. I'm sure it will thrive one day.'

Harriet decided that if she did not notice her laddered tights, no one else would. 'We're all affected. I've lost clients who've either cancelled courses, or been fired, before they could start. Not easy servicing business at the moment.'

She admired the perfect curve of Anne's mouth as she outlined it in red lipstick with a brush.

'It's such a pleasure meeting you, Harriet', said Anne. 'You must tell me more about yourself. What do you do? Do you live here in London.'

'West London, Hammersmith.'

'Oh, I don't know it. Are you and Richard close?'

'We're just friends through our sons, you know.'

'Of course. But let me tell you something. Richard will be the most gorgeous suitable man, just as soon as he's had his mid-life crisis.'

Harriet was going to laugh, until she saw that Anne was serious. 'And when will that be?'

'Every man has to have one. Have you never had Jungian analysis?'

'Er no. I haven't.'

'You should, change your life. Guy, my partner, and I have both been in therapy for years. Jung says every man has to have one for personal growth. It's just part of the male blue print. So let's hope he'll have his soon. It's so boring for everyone when men leave it till later on.'

Feeling she had somehow missed something, Harriet passed out into the hall and saw the back of Richard's dark curly head in the Sale Room.

* * *

'What the HELL are you doing here'

It could have been one of the better lines from *Auctioneer*. The venom in Laura's voice had an electrifying effect on the two boys.

'Term's over, dear. I've been hoping you'd come to visit.'

'How did you get my address. From Nanny I suppose?'

'Yes. I . . .'

'You'd better sit down.'

Jamie and Billy, were looking aghast.

'Good evening boys. I didn't realise.'

It seemed as if he was trying to connect different contexts.

'Don't worry you two. Henry Crouch is my father. We have not met for several years.' Laura's voice was thick. 'Have you been drinking?'

'Just a few on the train, Laura dear, you know.'

'Billy would you put the kettle on, while I change. Jamie you might like to see check out Billy's computer games. Upstairs.

'Did you know Mr Crouch was our Headmaster?' Billy whispered. He had followed Laura up onto the landing, and was now standing there as white as a sheet rubbing off the lipstick.

'No. I did not! He and I haven't set eyes on each other since 1970. He was head of House at Croxley then. I haven't been near him since. My old Nanny gave him my address. Silly cow. I could strangle her!'

The atmosphere in the little house, which had been so jolly just a couple of minutes before, froze over.

*   *   *

£, $, DM, FF, PTS, — the currency board flipped over and over hours seemed to have passed. All the pictures looked alike. Harriet looked up at the board high on the wall. Thousands, more thousands, noughts and yet more noughts like numbers on a bus ticket. Nothing to do with money earned, and put aside to pay bills. As the last lot was announced there was a lull in the collective concentration, Richard seemed asleep, while Anne, who continued to write the prices on the catalogue and add up these endless figures on her neat pocket calculator, now seemed resigned. Not looking at the pictures, which must have seemed the ticket to the big time just a few years before. All passion spent. In some shop or other.

'Milton Heston. acrylic on canvas. entitled *Youth*. I'll start the bidding at £75,000. £75,000 ladies and gentlemen.'

Another black splodge, this time with streaks of red and purple, had been placed on the stand. She could hear the boredom. When would he start the bidding at the right figure? Five quid Ladies and Gentlemen. Youth! Very little to do with any sort of youth, as far as Harriet could see, unless it was to do with some poor soul about to hang himself in a remand centre.

'£80,000 thank you Sir. £90,000 thank you Madam. £90,000 any advance. £100,000 I am bid, £100,000. £120,000 thank YOU sir, £130,000. £140,000. £150,000 there at the back. With you Sir. £150,000. £160,000 thank you Samantha. New bid on the phone. £160,000.'

A few seconds, a few thousands, it was all it took. Shaken awake, the mood in the saleroom was transformed. Richard like an giant cat could smell it, Anne stopped writing and, almost in time, they began to scour the room with narrowed eyes. In that instant Harriet knew why they had married each other – two expensive predatory leopards on the prowl, and on the make.

The board up there with the Mickey Mouse money, clicked and clicked.

'£250,000 I have, £250,000 for this fine Heston. £275,000 thank you Samantha, bid on the phone there, £270,000.

£300,000, thank you Madame, down here at the front. £300,000.'

Sweat appeared above the lip of the young porter standing next to the painting which now had all the allure of money, pulsating from its canvas. Even the title somehow made perfect sense.

£350,000, and people craned their heads to see who was bidding. Silently, dark-suited men glided in from the room behind the auctioneer, partners probably, gazing expressionless up at the currency board, as if trying to divine the will of the Gods.

The cool, beautiful Samantha seemed to melt as she and the auctioneer flirted together with numbers plucked from the ether. Minutes passed, bidders dropped out and it was now combat between the mysterious voice on the phone, who caused Samantha to nod so passionately, and the lady down at the front with the big hair, who never seemed to move a muscle, to whom the auctioneer deferred like a knight at a tournament.

'£375,000, with you Samantha, that's £375,000. £400,000. £400,000. An advance. £400,000!' The word hung in the air, like a curse. The hammer met the desk, and there was a communal gasp, a release of tension as the final figure was analysed with wonder by every mind in the room. As Richard grabbed Anne's calculator, Harriet caught her sudden sob of relief. 'This concludes this evening's sale Ladies & Gentlemen', the auctioneer was saying.

Maxi Rogers got up from her seat, and floated out of the room to pay like the Fairy Godmother on parade. As the crowd gazed at her, she felt in that moment, what it must be like to be Royalty — sheer Heaven — which was nice for her, for not long afterwards she discovered just who had been talking to Samantha from New York.

* * *

'Of course the Headboy and our Matron didn't help.' Henry Crouch was now on whisky, which Laura remembered always made him morose.

'Harriet and I saw them on Paddington station. No big deal. Surprised it doesn't happen more often. So, why are you here?'

Laura's gut ached from shock, her head ached. Unprepared, she did not want this meeting. Horrible, creepy man. He had aged, but he seemed just as arrogant and self-centred. Jamie and Billy had scuttled upstairs like squirrels up an oak tree leaving her alone with him. She just wished Harriet would come back, she was so cool, and God knows her own father had been a right selfish bastard.

'It's the school, you see.' He stared into his glass, turning it round and round. And round. Laura wanted to scream.

'What about the school? I can tell you if, I'd known you were there, Billy wouldn't have gone.'

'Just listen will you? The Governors have accepted a bid from a German company, want to make it co-ed, weekly-boarding, and fill it with German sixth-formers. Offer Japanese, and business studies and God knows what else. Work-shadowing in the City and at the Bourse, can you imagine? All change.'

'Good. We don't have an Empire any more, so boarding schools need changing.' Laura thought how she hated his whining self-pity. How had Mum put up with him all those years? Why had she been so bloody passive – about everything? 'Boarding schools are like zoos, and missionaries. Victorian inventions. Irrelevant, churning out emotionally deprived small boys, who grow up to make their wives' lives hell.'

'It's been people like me who have tried to keep the fees down, and keep up certain standards. But apparently this is bad marketing. You keep the fees up. Anyway I've left. The letter is going to the parents next week.'

'I see. Fired, at last,' Laura was trying hard to keep in control. 'Well, you've had a good innings, lots of fancy houses, tax-free meals, free gardening. I hope you don't expect me to help you.'

'There's the flat in Frinton, I suppose.'

'Good. Goodbye then.'

'Laura.'

'No.'

'You've made a success of your life. Proud of you.'

'Don't start.'

'Why?'

'Look are you going now? I've got lines to learn this evening.'

'Why have you never married?'

'I did. Now are you going?'

'Laura. I'd no idea. Dear, can we....'

'Listen, I may forget, and I might even forgive, given time and amnesia, all blood under the bridge. But don't, Papa dear, start the cosy father bit.'

'Look, I am your father.'

'I don't need reminding. I'd forgotten just what a very convenient memory you have. Nice empty spaces. You were strict, giving your own daughter the cane. Enjoyed seeing her raw bottom did you, you bastard? Turn you on, did it?' Henry Crouch gazed into his glass.

'I am mortified that Billy should have been within twenty miles of you, and I never knew. I just let Harriet get on with it, her decision. It wasn't Croxley, so I never thought to say.' Laura desperately wanted Harriet's key in the lock. Wanted to atone.

'It's after ten, there are no trains.'

'How convenient.'

'Look may I stay here? Please, Laura. Can't you try and forgive me?'

'You took away my childhood, you evil bastard. I hope you rot in hell.'

'It was such a difficult life. Always on show. Your mother, she didn't want..., and I couldn't have my daughter running wild, bad for discipline.'

'I don't want to hear your excuses. Tell your psychiatrist.'

'Please Laura, please understand.'

'Why should I? There's the sofa bed. Don't MOVE off it. And go in the morning.'

'Thank you, dear.'

'Can I make it quite clear that I don't want to see you again.'

'But couldn't we start again, Laura, somehow?'

'Oh, piss off.'

Exhausted, still in shock, Laura went upstairs into Billy's room, he was asleep, calm and beautiful. Fiercely she kissed him. Then she went to the airing cupboard and without explanation threw the sheets and blankets down the stairs, got inside her room and slid the bolt.

* * *

It was probably the first women's magazine Harriet had had time to look at all year. Are you Passive Aggressive, Passive or just Aggressive? Tough it out with our Readers' Quiz! And so, sitting in the waiting room, knowing her dentist had about as much sense of time-keeping as most of her clients, she had done it. Passive. How depressing! Then she had done it for Georgiana. Yes, passive aggressive, getting her own way through her husband's spending power while all the while playing the martyr. Laura was plain, uncompromising aggressive, bless her. Mrs Mac on the other hand was just plain bloody nosey, the way she'd put that *Sunday News Diary* on the desk on Monday morning expecting all the juicy details. They must have been scraping the barrel at the weekend.

Sitting in the Sale Room, watching the crowds leave the room and Anne working them like a pro, as if she hadn't a care in the world, Harriet thought back to that magazine at the dentist's, and whizzed through the Quiz for her. Yes this was aggression in couture. You had to admire it.

Whereas she, standing there, unseen in her lovely, but terribly old pale yellow silk dress, now saw she was horribly passive, always had been thinking about it. Carried along by Jester, Marcus, and Tom when no-one better presented himself. Billy too, had just happened. Then just living for five years without anyone, because it was easy, then letting David Forsyth make love to her, because he was there, like Mount Everest. And now Richard Longbridge had asked her, along for the ride on this odd roller coaster, and she, apparently willing, but still unable to assert herself enough to ask where this relationship was going, had become. Just turning down his dinner invitation had practically given her the vapours.

Yet could she really be passive? The way she went after clients, and new business? Looking at Anne, Harriet knew the answer before asking the question. Aggressive only as a mother to buy the best education she could for Billy, the very best frame of reference. To give him a home, warm and paid for. Not assertive for herself, not her own person at all really, like Roger Descartes Jones, who couldn't even admit he was married.

And that puzzled her, his acting out some kind of role, where a wife didn't fit. Though, such role-playing had happened a dozen times before – all those teachers' weddings to prove it.

'Mrs Gosse!' Maxi Rogers, flushed with success, came up to her. 'How lovely to see you here! Michelle is talking great French already. Loves it! Thank you so much. So? Do you like it?'

'Oh the painting. Yes of course, it's very Texan, very illuminating.'

'Oh come ON you don't mean that. Hector's going to cry! No I bought it for the St Anthony's art collection, to thank them for all they did for Boyd.'

Harriet knew she would never understand Americans.

Richard had lost Harriet. Now Anne's hair was at least six inches high, so he could never lose her, even when he wanted to. Though she had annoyed every person in every theatre she had ever sat in front of. Not that she ever thought about it.

At today's exchange rates, Jaakko had taken a 80% hit, or his banks had. But it could have been worse. And with that bit of madness by the headboy's Mummy, the total was not quite annihilation. Though it didn't make sense why she'd bought it, particularly as Hector had taken against Guy the Gorilla. But then you never knew why people buy art, look at Luton Lil who had carried off the Purriddu, for which relief much thanks. He saw Anne heavy in conversation. Oozing positive thinking. She was so exhausting. Harriet, where the fuck are you I'm starving.

* * *

'Good God, Mr Crouch.'

Harriet stood by the light switch. Chinese food always made her thought processes slow. What was Billy's headmaster doing sleeping in the living room?

'Oh. Good evening, I hope you don't mind.' Henry Crouch

groped about for his glasses. 'Mrs Gosse, how do you do. My daughter said you wouldn't mind. I'm leaving first thing.'

Harriet sat down and just stared at him. He was just an old man, balding, red faced, without his gown and his power.

'Your daughter. Laura?'

'Laura. Yes.'

'Laura is your daughter?'

'Yes, you see, well, we rather lost touch you know. I hope you don't mind this.'

'Not, no not at all, Mr Crouch. Please, don't get up.'

'Good God, Henry Crouch.' Richard walked in, having given up trying to park in a straight line. 'Just the fellow. Nice pyjamas. Didn't know you and Harriet were that friendly.'

'Mr Crouch is, it turns out, Laura my lodger's father. Excuse me, I'm just going up to take off my jacket.'

Cold, Harriet could barely make it up the stairs. It had taken years, and a lot of love, before Laura had been able to talk about her childhood, and seek help. She suddenly felt sick. Why had Laura invited this man to spend the night under her roof? Perhaps she had been in shock too? Perhaps she had been worried about him taking it out on Billy. Both Laura and Billy's doors were locked, not a sound coming from either room, not even a snore. Downstairs Richard was laughing, gloriously uninvolved with anyone else on the planet.

Chapter Ten

6.10 a.m. Thursday. Furtive and trapped, Richard lay in bed, listening to the farming programme, and wondering why those farmers always had to whine, and what the hell he was going to do about Harriet.

Jamie adored her and would kill him if he put a foot wrong. Kill him anyway probably. How could he get through to him? It seemed as if there were a block of bricks between them. Perhaps he ought to take him to the Science Museum? Wasn't that what fathers did? Already he was ten. Soon he would be a young man, bringing home girls who would think of him as, an older man. Richard groaned feeling inadequate, as he usually did whenever he thought of his son.

The taste of last night's noodles was still in his mouth, better than clickie nuggie he supposed. But the memory of Swindon's Hearty Hamburgers came back to him, making him smile, how she had enjoyed it, and the boys. Glad he hadn't mentioned that wretched diary piece, might have bothered her. Though frankly they must be scraping the barrel if they thought he was that interesting, and pegging it on poor Thomas Gosse was pathetic. What must she have gone through with all the hoo-ha at the time? He couldn't begin to imagine.

And now, Italian in just.... twenty minutes' time, another thing he didn't know what to do about. So stupid, childish pretending to be Roger. Why had he done it? Apart from making Roger jealous – he was always so good at feeding the straight lines – and for getting his own back on Harriet for turning down his dinner invitation. Stupid. She'd come willingly enough to Mr Wong's last night. He'd probably just come on a bit strong. Girls of Harriet's sort didn't tick like the Annunziata Tarrants of this world. Worst luck.

So, should he confess that he was really Roger the Dodger, and that his friend had lent him his identity for two inordinately expensive tickets to last week's fight? Or should he carry on, and end the course as decently as he could?

She was such a good teacher. He was already reading Oggi in the bath, and he'd actually tried out some Italian on the phone and that bastard Respighi had complimented him. Not that you ever knew with Italians, they'd sell their granny for a thousand lira.

So what to do? Harriet was real. She had integrity, humour, charm, she managed things without being bossy, she was a good mother, and beautiful. And yet she made him feel trapped into the beginnings of a relationship he wasn't ready for. And now she seemed more interested he was rapidly going off the whole idea.

Anyway it had sounded last night as if she hadn't had a boyfriend for five years. Anne was so good at twenty questions. Could she possibly have done without sex for five years? Weird. Five days was bad enough. And then Anne had said, 'Language lessons by phone, how interesting', and had looked meaningfully across the table at him. He could have strangled her. She hadn't even tried to look jealous, the bitch.

And he hadn't had any sex for days which was making him tetchy. Victoria had just sent him a 'Goodbye I've got a job in Bermuda' card. But at least she knew the ropes and just thought about bonking like good exercise.

Richard rolled out of bed, and down the stairs to the cappuccino machine. No Jamie. He was still in W6, with old Crouch on the sofa bed. Odd, Harriet had looked as if she had been about to faint. Might have been the prawns. He'd offered to wake Jamie up and take him home, but she'd wouldn't hear of it. He would keep Billy company she said. The lodger seemed nuts as well, coming down to make cocoa, like Lady Macbeth, shooing him out. Bloody madhouse.

So early. Whizz, bubble bubble. The coffee helped Richard

to think. Future conditional. What was that. I would have thought. *Avrei pensato*. What? God knows. He went upstairs to his desk to make the call, knowing before she answered, that her voice would come over the line, fresh as a daisy, full of laughter and he would be back as Roger the cockney charmer flirting with her over the vocab as soon as you could say *gigolo*. What a berk.

Dimly he knew that this was not just an act, that in this situation he was free of all pressure and expectation. And self invention. Which left him where? Confused of Belgravia that's where.

* * *

'I'm glad you still intend to do some work in this office!'

Oh God, bloody Fenella give me a break, Laura thought. Overacting again. How does she get away with it? As if she didn't know, the reason was sitting three yards away, scratching his crotch.

'I'm a professional and I don't intend to forget it.' Move to the desk, pick up report. '*Goodbye Olivia, just get out of my office and out of my life.*'

'And cut!' The crotch scratcher, alias the Director 'Andy' I'm-terribly-democratic-if-you-do-exactly-as-I-say Turpin jumped up. 'Nice work, Laura love. Make Up could you give her a bit of colour for the next scene. Bit Ophelia today aren't we.'

'Sorry, Andy', Laura said: 'Cretin!', she thought.

'You've used up me blusher budget dear', the make-up girl (a euphemism if ever there was one) advanced with the blusher brush. Laura got a congratulatory hug from Fenella, a sure sign she probably was going to be written out. Smile, Laura, a morning for wearing a mask. Eyes and teeth, show must go on, all that crap. How she wished she could go back to bed.

'Quiet on the floor, please. I want Wilson, Mrs Grant, Herr Forster. Scene Three. Quickly please. Quiet on the floor!'

Why do floor managers have to bawl? Laura picked up her script and went into the Green Room. Might be able to scrounge a fag off David.

She met the Production Secretary coming along the corridor.

'These just arrived, Laura love, do you want them now or shall I have them put in your dressing room?' She handed Laura a small bouquet of white flowers.

'For me? Oh no, I'll take them now.' Feeling suddenly cheerful Laura read the card. 'Love you lots. Don't cry and don't dry! Harriet and Billy.' Freesias, their smell restored Laura a little. How sweet. She had left so early, goodness knows what Harriet must have thought last night. And Richard Longbridge. She wasn't sure about him.

'God, Laura, you look awful.'

David Forsyth however did not. They'd got him all togged up in Armani, this morning. Molto unstructured, Laura thought.

She sank into the chair.

'Don't David. Had a bad night last night. Terrible. My father turned up like Banquo on the doorstep and insisted on sleeping on the sofa. Didn't sleep a wink. Anyway he's gone now. Thank God. Spare a ciggy for us?'

'Go on. Here.'

'Even complained it was lumpy, ungrateful old sod. Is it?'

'What? Keep still, Laura, I've only got one match.'

'Sofa bed, lumpy?'

'Wouldn't know.'

'I keep asking Harriet to replace it, her constant pleading poverty drives me mad.'

'Didn't sleep there, act-u-ally', he said with a wicked leer.

It took at least ten seconds.

'Oh God, David. You didn't.' Her head felt it was about to burst.

'Well, I shouldn't say. Modesty forbids.'

'You didn't promise anything or lead her on? David, you can be such a thoughtless bastard.'

'Now that's nice after I've given you my very last fag.'

'I'm sorry, but you know.'

'Laurakins, if I were you I'd start looking after Number One, you look bloody awful this morning.'

'I just don't want her hurt.'

'Yes, and who buggered off for the evening? Look don't

worry about Harriet. It was a one-night, thoroughly happy, fulfilling, consenting bonk. End of screenplay.'

'I'm not interested.'

'Oh aren't you? Sounds like jealousy to me. She was happy, I was happy.'

'Thank you. Between you, I now feel a complete fool.'

'I'm sorry you feel like that, but you did ask. And she's hardly fourteen. Laura, just let go and, you might land yourself a man worth one hundred million. I can join up the big words in the *Sunday News*, you know.'

'This sounds a good scene. When are you two doing this?' Fenella Frost came into the room right on cue. 'Laura, Andy wants you, your bit's next.'

Shock, jealousy, rage, kick-the-cat frustration, the feeling that she didn't know her best friend at all, the little girl howling, it was all there underneath the next load of lines. A migraine hovered just on the outskirts of Laura's brain, as she walked out into the corridor. 'Please God, help me through this morning', she muttered into the flowers.

That was the second time she'd prayed that morning. Things must be bad.

Later, the thought that the worst might be over, and that meeting Dad again had been a scene she had been waiting to play for years, came pushing into her head. Perhaps she could get on with her life now, with the past, suitably labelled, back on its shelf high out of the way? A call from her agent later with news of a telly for STV was just further proof that God was on her side.

* * *

It was the game they always played. Trying to rush up Kensington Park Road before the bus sailed past. The sun was beating down, bouncing off the stucco of the newly done-up houses.

'Come on Mum, you're slacking. Come on.'

At Westbourne Grove they stopped, watching a group of Japanese down the road, guidebooks in hand heading for Portobello market.

'Don't those books tell them to go on Saturday? It's OUR market the rest of the week!'

'Don't be like that, Mum. Now don't you feel better? Five minutes of school fees saved.'

Billy hugged his mother, yet not quite old enough to feel embarrassed about it.

'Come on you, I mustn't be late.' Harriet ruffled his hair, certain he was the best thing in her life, marvelling at his ability to make things right.

'Mum, do you have to teach so early?'

'No, only this one client, he's just paid for ten lessons.'

'How many school-fee minutes is that?'

'About a week's worth.'

'You were laughing so loudly. You woke me up.'

'Sorry. This one's a real Cockney, lovely sense of humour. He makes me laugh, though I don't think we're covering the ground we should be. Did I really wake you?'

'Not really. Jamie and I peed in the wastepaper-basket so we didn't have to go out to the loo, and meet Crouch.

'Oh thanks!'

'It was awful, Laura really hates him, you could see. What'd it be like having him for a father?'

Harriet wondered just how much he had overheard, Laura could be so irresponsible.

'Anyway I needn't have worried, I peeked out at seven o'clock and Laura had already left for the studio and taken him with her. And he didn't leave his blankets all folded, like we have to!'

'No, he's a difficult man. But he won't come here again, don't worry.'

Harriet started to get the office key out of her bag: already the street was buzzing.

'Laura and her father haven't been in touch for years, but really it's none of our business. I sent her some flowers though, from us both to cheer her up. Anyway the good news is that he's leaving St Anthony's apparently, all the parents are getting a letter about it.

'Brill!'

'Do you hate him that much? '

'He's just mean, he wouldn't even let Matron finish the term.'

'Come off it, Billy, members of staff shouldn't have *affaires* with the boys.'

'You can only have *affaires* if you're married, Timothy's father told me. He's a divorce barrister. And they weren't.'

'What are you doing talking about *affaires* to Timothy's father? Anyway it's a question of responsibility.'

'I still don't see why she had to be bundled off like a criminal. Boyd stayed.'

'Look, I wouldn't worry about old Matron. I saw her mother-in-law last night; she bought a hideous picture for the school, really ghastly. For four hundred thousand, imagine that. Anyway she said to me afterwards Kirsty was fine, and Mireille's teaching her French.'

More Japanese appeared round the corner. 'You know you don't have to stay at St Anthony's if you don't want to, I've always said that. Though the new people who have bought the school are going to update everything, and introduce lots of languages, so you might enjoy it a bit more.'

'I do enjoy it.'

'Look, Billy. Look at me, stop walking for five seconds. You Don't Have To Stay. Just tell me and I'll write tomorrow.'

'No I like St Ants. I've got used to it. And Jamie's there.'

'O.K. Put away the guilt, Harriet. Look, there's Marcus buying grapes over there, go and say hello.'

* * *

Dear Richard,

Thank you for this week's letter. I can't say I was surprised to receive it, rumours that your gallery has been running on hot air have even reached my ears.

You can't carry on like this, can you? You've already had £500,000 from your Fund towards your business in the past two years, each time with the promise from you that you would sort yourself and the business out, but nothing seems to be getting any better.

Thanks to Dad, you will be a wealthy man, but I'm not dead yet, and I still feel, late in the day thought it is, you might, just might, grow up.

Dad thought small, he built up the business gradually,

and as far as possible never went near banks, unless he knew he could pay them back quickly and save interest. He hated them, said they were thieving bastards, you know that. And he was right, ahead of his time, just read the papers these days.

But you – and Anne come to that – don't think I haven't heard about her rotten mess as well – you two are babes in the wood, still living like the Hooray Henrys before Black Monday. Borrow big, and then worry about the business. You've both got Gold Cards on the brain, funding a life you can't afford, with a business that can't stand on its own two feet.

We're now in recession, and I for one, don't think we'll get out of it quickly. The Government keeps saying the recovery is just around the corner, because they're scared, but it's rubbish. You are too soft to know what that's like – but your little friend does. The one I met on Saturday. I could tell. I bet her business is run on a shoestring, and she makes a profit.

So because I love you, I'm not going to let you have any more money from your Fund. Get the books looked at, by someone who knows what he is doing. Sell the lease, and start working from your front room. Like your father and I did. It won't kill you. But if you carry on like this, I might.

Your loving mother,
Mary Ellen Longbridge.

* * *

She had never written to him like this. Humiliating. And he knew she had probably had the spelling checked at the secretarial centre where she had had it typed up. And the punctuation. Bloody mother. Bloody Harriet, held up as an example of business acumen. It was crap about his father not being in hock with the banks. Borrow big. He and Onassis invented the concept. He just stared at the letter. Now what was he to do? Had to find money from somewhere. All the costs were upfront, printers, insurance, photographs, rent due, VAT, tax, salaries. He was even his own technician these days, hanging the bloody pictures. And how long was it going to take him to put up Le Feuvre's stuff?

'Richard, I'm glad one of us is giving our child some quality time!' Anne had marched into the office, Jamie in tow.

'Sorry? Hello Anne darling. Hello Jamie.'

'We're getting the boat from Chelsea Wharf, won't that be fantastic when all the shops are occupied? Then down the river to Greenwich, lunch at the theatre, and then the Royal Observatory.'

'Great. Jamie, here's a fiver for drinks. Did you and Billy have a good time last night?'

'I must meet this Billy, his mother is charming.'

'Yes she is. Me and Billy had fun with Laura their lodger, going over her lines, she's an actress, and then. . . .'

'I know, and then Crouch turned up.'

'Dad, he's her father!'

'Even the nicest people can have shitty fathers, and mothers come to that. I hope neither of us will ever write to you like Granny just has, when you want a loan.'

Jamie shrugged.

'O.K. Got the message. Granny's right. I'm sorry for the word shitty Anne. I promise Jamie you and I will have a day out this holiday. I'm just having a bad morning, Alain Le Feuvre's agent talked down the phone at me for half an hour, and then this letter from Mother. She says we're two babes in the wood Anne, living in debt with gold cards on the brain.'

'And she's right. American Express will be clothing Jamie this visit. Just when did you buy him any clothes, Richard? His trousers are up to his knees!'

Later, Chantal came in with the new catalogue. 'The transparencies have arrived, the black-and-white prints are coming round this afternoon. Here's the list of names for the Press View and the revised Private with the new names we're adding. Do you want to check them?'

'Yes I'll go through them now, we'll have to get them out today, the Press ones should have gone out yesterday.'

Richard looked at the catalogue. *Lifetime in Relief*. New work by Alain Le Feuvre. 20 pages of glossy A4. Introduction written by the art bod at the *Telegraph*. Just the feel of the paper, and the pictures made him feel better.

The gallery business, couldn't give it up.

'How much are you going to sell it for this time Richard?'

'Oh, £10 after we've had the View, and a few autographed by the great man himself at £50 each.'

'And that's all for the charity?'

'Yes, after covering our costs. I suppose somebody will have heard of the Anglo-French Foundation for Aids Research, I haven't. Can't imagine the English and the French co-operating on anything, let alone Aids. Nice cover isn't it. Still, miracles happen, old Liz Taylor might pop up at the Press lunch for a photo call. Aids seems to be her new career.'

'Is Alain... you know? '

'No of course he's not, my child. But I should think he's lost a lot of friends thanks to AIDS. Haven't we all? Don't look at me like that Chantal, we're in art, not the bloody Civil Service.'

'Don't swear at me Richard. I know you know Daddy was a Permanent Secretary. And there's a literal on Page one, expressive with three Ss.'

'Bugger.'

* * *

Coffee at the new Colombian Cafe in the Museum of Mankind, followed by shopping in the Arcade, lunch at the Royal Academy, quick look at the pictures, and then back in time for the school run. Georgiana had worked it all out.

She pushed open the door of the Europa Gallery, it gleamed at her, just the sort of gallery Georgiana thought she would visit, if Robert liked modern art.

'Can I help you?' The girl behind the desk was looking her up and down.

'Oh Good morning, I was wondering if Mr Long..., Richard was in today. Just passing, you know.' Stupid to get flustered, it was just she wasn't used to this sort of place.

'I'll ring through to him in his office. May I have your name?'

'Georgiana Gaskell. If he doesn't remember me, just

say Harriet's next-door neighbour. We met at our street party.'

'Oh. How delightful.'

Feeling a fool, Georgiana nervously peeked at a couple of pictures in the side gallery. Not very relaxing, all swirls and whirls, she preferred nice quiet landscapes ... or that Elizabeth Whatsername, who did the flower paintings. . . .

'Hello Georgiana, rather busy this morning getting invitations out for the next show. What can I do for you?' He was coming towards her. Such *élan!*

'Good morning Richard, I was just wondering.' Georgiana started to speak, and then looking up at him, didn't quite know how to go on. 'Alain Le Feuvre, I wanted to buy one of his works. Great admirer of his films you see, I've seen all them, and I just wondered, if. . . ?'

What an ass she was making of herself! She was sure that girl was laughing at her.

'Chantal, give Mrs Gaskell a catalogue and an invitation to the Private View. The catalogues are £10. They're all hugely good value, you know, and a percentage is going to one of his charities. You could come with Harriet, if she's coming.'

'Oh of course, I imagine she will of course be coming! Thank you so much. Here you are, sorry the note's so crumpled. I did see that bit in the Diary, wretched reporters, still, good bye.' Clutching the catalogue and invitation like a little girl who had just visited her first Father Christmas, Georgiana stumbled out onto the sunny street. What a charming man. In a few days she'd be meeting Alain Le Feuvre! In the distance, Burlington Arcade twinkled invitingly.

* * *

Sitting in her office swatting flies, Harriet decided the silly season had officially arrived. No one was in their offices, all 'away on holiday for the next two weeks, Mrs Gosse'. London was too hot, too smelly, full of tourists, and unbearable. But then on the other hand she could perhaps start taking the odd day off before disapearing herself for two weeks. The VAT had been sent off, the end-of-year accounts had been agreed with the accountants, a 22% increase of business in the last year, not bad in a recession, and a £155,000 turnover. Not the same as profit – Marcus had taught her that – but not bad.

And she'd made two useful new business calls this morning. When the people lower down the ladder were all in Marbella, you could sometimes get through to the M.D. And she had marked Roger Dodger's homework before faxing it back. Why did he always write in block capitals?

She decided to mooch downstairs to see what Marcus was doing. Danny had taken Billy swimming at the Kensington New Pools, so she was free to do nothing very much. What luxury.

'You O.K., Marcus?'

'Aha. At a loose end aren't you Harriet? I know that "haven't any big contracts on and I've nothing to do" look. Come and give us a hand then.'

She stood there while Marcus hung the collage on the rails. He had always prided himself on his hanging system, no-one else's gallery ever had the same look, of pictures hanging there as an experiment, as if they could be moved somewhere else just as easily, which they very often were, into the back of cars double-parked on the corner.

'There that's it. Just check it's straight will you? My astigmatism's getting worse with everything else. Fine. Good, that's it for this morning. I'm just rearranging the house stock, no new stuff till September. So. You looked a cosy threesome last night?' Marcus always had a habit of slipping things in.

'You could have joined us.'

'Never sit down at auctions, you can't see what's going on, the dynamics. No I thought the work was interesting but unformed, immature. A Jasper Johns or a Pollock would knock them out of the room and yet there would not be much in it with the prices, that's the terrible thing. The boyfriend looked bored.'

'Marcus! I'm not rising to that one.'

'Oh come off it, Harriet, I may be a half-dead old Queen but I have eyes in my head. I actually thought he'd improved with age. He obviously thought that the paintings were crap and you were first-class material. But that wife of his, the original iceberg. She used to come into to see me in Bruton Street years ago. Terribly earnest, Long Island old money, always wanting to learn things. Exhausting woman.'

'It was an exhausting evening actually. There was no dressing it up, prices were a tenth of what they fetched three years ago. Anne kept describing herself as a market maker. She made the paintings sound like a commodity like oil or pork bellies.'

'Depressing result of the eighties I'm afraid. But it is a commodity like anything else these days. There! Now what do you think of this!' Marcus held up a nude, full length, paint put on with a palette knife, rough, exciting, 'Not unlike Jester's when he was young and callow, good though. What with the Japanese, and corporate collections sprouting up, art is just a commodity. But should we complain? Gallery owners are just as greedy as the man selling fish fingers. We all want to make our pile, spend it, flaunt it. Though, years ago I always felt that the pictures were at the centre of things, buying something because you liked it, not just as an investment.'

He put another picture up against the wall, his head on one side as he always did, looking Harriet always thought, like the Owl in *Winnie The Pooh*. A couple came in carrying their fruit and veg from the market, had a look, and wandered out. No clue to their thoughts on the paintings which dominated the gallery.

'Now backing a young artist is like training a horse or a greyhound. Make him too visible too early and everyone asks is he the next Lucien Freud? I've seen it happen. The pressure can completely screw up a young painter.'

'Let me hold it while you fix it up. I hope that won't happen to Danny.'

'No, I won't let that happen. Slowly, slowly building it up, that's what he wants to do. But he'll be as big as Lucien or Frances, just you wait.

'Are you O.K., Marcus? You look very pale.'

'Don't like this heat. Be careful with that Longbridge fellow. He's beautiful, and terribly charming but wouldn't he suit Laura better than you? Couldn't you pass him on?

You're too fragile. Jester always said that. Posh barrow boy, without his Dad's nouse.'

'Marcus I'm not a figurine, you know, and I do know what I'm doing, well most of the time.'

'Of course you do. Come on, let's go and get some fish and chips. Did I tell you I knew his mother years ago, when I lived in Great Titchfield Street? Had a fling with old Harold Maitland, greatest knight the theatre never had. Everyone knew except Ernie of course, terribly discreet.'

'You know, I've never ever seen your place Marcus. That's so odd.'

'Well why should you want to? My gallery is where I live, always has been.'

'I met her on Saturday, very Edna O'Brien I thought.'

Still talking, they locked up and stuck a note on the door for Danny and Billy to join them. Why is it, on a hot day, there is nothing quite like fish and chips?

* * *

Jester was painting, very slowly, applying the paint precisely in spite of his shaking hand. To Billy who was watching him, the colours on the palette seemed just indistinguishable shades of sludge. Yet to Jester they each had a role to play on the canvas. Even with the shaking, feebleness of old age, there was power and fierce passion. For a while, Billy watched, fascinated, then feeling cold, wriggled, waiting for his mother to come back. It was all very well, but leaving them alone for some 'quality time' – Jamie was very funny when he impersonated his mother – but how long was she going to be? He wriggled again, accidentally nudging Jester.

'Sorry.'

'Are you bored? I'd be bloody bored watching me trying to do first-year stuff.'

'No I'm not bored really Grandad, I just was wondering where Mum had got to.'

'Liar. You're bored.'

'Are those the vines down the hill.'

'Yes, wonderful place. Your mum was a little girl there, all long brown legs, rushing about, no shoes half the time, losing them.'

Jester went back to one corner, painting for some moments as if he was alone. Billy decided to try and count up to a thousand in French and not wriggle.

'Make any money at school?'

'Sorry, did you say money?'

'Yes money selling fags and dirty postcards?'

Billy was shocked.

'Well you would if you had sense, only way you get any decent grub. We used to send the Smalls down to the village.'

'Were you at boarding school, Grandad? Mum never said.'

'Scholarship, then ran away to join up, said I wanted to be a war artist, and they sent me to Yorkshire cleaning latrines. rotten buggers. So, did you?'

'What?'

'Make money this term?'

'Yes, my friend Jamie and I made over thirty quid, Benson & Hedges and a Penthouse. We don't have postcards these days.'

Jester grunted.

Billy carried on counting, *sept cents quarante-deux, sept cents quarante-trois . . . sept cents quar . . .* the pace of old people made him so impatient, everything they did was so slow! And yet Jester was so fierce, even now.

'Come here.' The old man was trying to get into a leather pouch. Very slowly, he took out a roll of notes and gave them to Billy. Ten-pound notes! There must be more than £100!

'No Grandad, I couldn't really.'

'Shut up. Buy more pictures and make a real profit this time. Get a decent bike.'

Billy looked amazed and the old man's twisted face creased into a smile.

'Don't save it Billy, spend the lot. Don't be sensible, you will have long enough being that.'

Through the window in the distance, they saw Harriet walking in the grounds, talking on her mobile phone. The old man and the boy looked at each other, and laughed.

'Buy her something. Poor girl needs a man. Get her some perfume. Now, piss off and let me get back to work.'

Jester was back in Umbria, toiling on the hillside with his brush before Billy had even shut the door behind him.

'So how was it? Was he OK?'

Harriet reversed, and was soon back on the A5 heading into town.

'It was alright, I understood him better this time. He even gave me some money.'

'That was kind.'

'Told me to spend it.'

'Go ahead why not? You must get fed up with me. I'm thoroughly sick of being economical.'

'Are you?'

'Of course! Do you know, I would love to go into a shop and buy clothes which were not second-hand. Imagine how wonderful that would be. Perhaps I will when I've paid the accountants. Or to be able to go into Harrods food hall, say, and buy as much smoked salmon and chocolate croissants as you wanted. Imagine!'

Billy wondered what she would say if she knew that he had £140. £140 in his pocket, enough for all that! And what would Jamie say?

That took the edge off a bit. Jamie would think nothing of it, his parents gave him that just to get him to pick up the phone. He watched his mother carefully edging into the right-hand lane to turn off into Maida Vale. Jamie's dad had possibilities if Jamie would just stop bullying him.

Georgiana was obviously out, and for once there was space to park outside the house. Feeling rather weary, Harriet went in, kicking off her shoes onto the stairs. The answer machine was winking on the hall table. Wink, wink, wink, wink, wink.

'Five messages, we're popular!'

'Mum, can I have some lemonade?'

'Help yourself darling. Stick the kettle on will you?'

'Bleeeeep. Hi Harriet and Billy. Thank you so much for the flowers, they're beautiful! Made my day, you shouldn't have! Got through today really well in spite of a small bone I have to pick with you young H. Don't worry about pater, he's gone for good. See you whenever, Marjorie's putting me up so I don't have to schlepp out to Denham tomorrow. Byeee'.

Bleeep. 'Billy, it's Jamie, Mum wants to take us both out tomorrow before she goes back. Do you want to ring me?'

Bleeep. 'Harriet, it's Georgiana, just a thought, would Billy like to come with us to Seaworld on Friday?'

'No I don't! Mum, tell her no.'

'You don't have to do anything. Just be quiet I can't hear.'

'Ring me byeee. By the way I went into Richard's gallery and he's invited me to the Le Feuvre show. Can't think *what* to wear. Let's talk soon.'

'Clothes, Georgiana.'

'Now be quiet Mother. I can't hear.'

'Stop imitating me, do you mind?'

Bleeep. 'Harriet. Marcus. Don't feel 100%. Hate these infernal machines. Lost your mobile number. Could you come round, bring the boy. Of course you don't know. 45 Russell Mansions, Elgin Avenue, Maida V. Where the old tarts live. Can't laugh, feel rotten, please come. Press the buzzer when you get. . . .'

Something bothered her about it. 'Billy, we'd better go. I don't like the sound of Marcus at all. He sounds really slurry.'

Bleeep. 'Harriet, hello. it's Roger here. Sorry love, but got to cut the lessons now. Just got too much on just at the moment. Sorry. Thanks a bundle for all you've done. *Ciao*.'

'Why was Richard talking in that phoney cockney accent?'

'It's not Richard, Billy, it's that client I teach early. He was doing so well? Why did he want to finish?'

'Cause he's got that French film star's show, Monday week.'

'Stop being silly, just take the keys and get in the car. Now I'll have to go back into town, and God knows what the traffic will be like.'

Feeling a headache coming on, Harriet, switched the machine back on and wiped the tape.

Chapter Eleven

Europa Gallery
Cork St.
W1

Dear Mother,

Thank you for your recent letter. I am sorry you think I am such a wastrel. £200,000 isn't such a great deal. As you say, times are hard, and I am very keen to stay in business, but if that makes me a babe in the wood, then Cork Street must have relocated. Ask Wolfgang Fischer, Kasmin, even old Leslie W., life is not easy at the moment. For a start, we're all probably carrying too much stock, and the sale-room prices are falling, so people think they can pick and choose. Anne's sale last week was a case in point. Decimation. On the stock front anyway, I intend to offload as much as poss at F.I.A.C. – that's in Paris – and Cologne, if I'm careful, I'll be able to do those two for under £50,000.

Richard was sure he could find just the right tone of injured innocence and wit, and could make her realise just how close he was to closing. Such a lot to do. He had ordered the champagne and the buffet for the Press, who always eat as if they've never seen food before. Dorothea's Kitchen prices weren't getting any cheaper either. Then canapes and Cava for 130 for the Private View. He needed people with real money, unaffected by this recession, just like old Maxi Rogers.

Only £200,000! What on earth was the point of being in line to inherit millions if it was all in trust till your mother's death? She had no intention of popping off for another thirty years — outlive him probably at this rate. It was such a joke being interviewed as an eligible bachelor, when in fact everyone saw him coming and charged him double, and he was up to his neck in debt.

I shall be making further cuts. So please Mother give us a chance to make it work. You are right, Harriet Gosse does run a business at a profit — she has an economical look about her doesn't she? But then she only pays about £1500 quid a year rent to a friend, and languages are rather more in demand than pictures, now we're all panicking about the Single Market. Her main costs are labour — teachers who then apparently run off with the clients — at least pictures don't give me emotional problems!

Would that produce a thin smile?

He didn't know why he was bothering to let her wind him up about Harriet. She hadn't even bothered to be civil to her. No. Time to sell some pictures, the ones he had been keeping at home for his old age, not that he'd get twenty grand for them in Bute's, Christie's would be better, but it was either that or legging down to the pawnbrokers. He'd probably have to do both before the banks had finished with him. Rotten bastards, inviting you to cocktail parties one minute, cutting your balls off the next.

He could still picture that bank manager, when he'd gone to get his first bit of plastic at the new bank. '£10,000 limit Mr Longbridge, for ordinary customers, of course, not for you.'

'But how could people repay that sort of money Mr Crabbe?'

The man had smirked, 'Oh they can't, that's when they come to us for a remortgage.' Bastard! Harriet had said something about that artist above her office keeping his money in his socks, red socks for gas bills, blue for phone, green for food. Wisest fool in W11.

'I do really need this money, no repeats. Your loving son Richard.'

He finished off the letter and shoved it into the envelope. He had a feeling he'd put the last sentence into a previous letter to her, but if the gallery went to the wall, she could just feel guilty as hell. The old had been murdered for less.

The phone rang at his elbow.
'*Sunday News* for you Richard.'
At least Chantal was awake.
'Mr Longbridge, Cremona Kent. Good morning. Just thought I'd let you know we're running your interview this weekend, section three, the hook will be the Le Feuvre show, as we're giving a readership ticket offer for *Les Aventures* when it goes on general release.'
'That's great, thanks for letting me know.'
'I'm afraid it's been cut a bit, because Features are doing an interview with Le Feuvre himself, but every bit helps.'
'Since I can't remember what I said to you, Cremona, the less you've put in the better, bit jet-lagged that day. My excuse.'
'Don't worry, the editor was thrilled, she's a fan of yours.'
'Really? That's gratifying.'
'Anyway being nosey, I was wondering, was the actor's widow the one who turned down dinner?'
'Er, no comment.'
'What an odd girl to prefer a Hearty Heartburner.'
Richard laughed. 'Good name for it! See you at the Press View next week. Bring your editor I'll need all the fans I can get.'
'Bye then. Don't want you going under do we? How many has it been now in Cork Street this year? Three?'
'Don't.'
Nice woman, if cheeky. Going under? As if! Why is it so many women journalists end up with those gorgeously raddled and sexy faces that only alcohol, and too many cigarettes, and late nights can provide?
He'd felt much better leaving that message on Harriet's phone last week. Silly idea, now she could just go into her box as Jamie's friend's Mum, much the best thing. Not his sort. He hadn't replied to that nice letter she'd sent to 'Roger D.J.' Lovely girl, but far too much like hard work. So full of integrity, so grown up and reasonable, when frankly all he wanted was freedom to do exactly what he liked, without complications.
So why was he picking up the phone, yet again, and dialling

her office? Perhaps she and Billy would like to come out with them? Jamie was bored rigid with Mrs Thing, Anne was threatening to spirit him away to the Hamptons, after the View. She seemed to have recovered, staying in economical Scottish splendour at the Caledonian Club in Halkin Street, descending on Jamie like a Valkyrie most days, to punish him with more quality time.

Today it was going to be the Canalettos up at Woburn Abbey, poor little bugger. And she obviously wasn't worried over money at the moment. Perhaps old Lapham had kept the banks sweet somehow, donated a couple of Hockneys to their corporate collection perhaps? A quiet word to the Chairman at some charity committee, you never knew. And now she was raving about Canadian Indian work.

Jamie? What was he supposed to do with him on his Jamie days? Harriet might have a suggestion, though she was sounding on another planet at the moment. Sort of girl who'd actually like doing the British Museum all morning – shudder. 'Hello? Good morning is Harriet there, please? A Scots voice informed him the office was closed until 9am tomorrow. Bloody great.

* * *

Always an outsider, always the new girl. Never fitting in. Except with Marcus, who was outside society himself in some ways, and Tom. Now both dead. As dodos. Far away. The very worst moment of any funeral is when the coffin is carried past you. The punch in the stomach, the realization that the person won't be coming back. Even to haunt you.

Bleak. The priest didn't know him, but obviously had a very clear idea where Marcus would be heading for. And she hadn't even known he was Catholic, until the solicitor had rung to ask her to come in. All the instructions had been drawn up beforehand, everything organized, typical Marcus. The whole thing prepaid for, even. That was Marcus.

She thrust her hands into her coat pocket, the day was so cold and grey, like winter although it was July, so she'd felt like wearing a winter coat. Her fingers touched the detritus of life lived last winter. Old bus tickets, a comb she thought she had lost, a toffee in crinkly paper, a ticket to a show at the National that was a big treat. She'd gone with Laura and Marcus, and they had trooped backstage afterwards to see one of Laura's friends. Enormous chap. He'd joined them at that Italian place near Waterloo station. He and Marcus had had them howling with laughter all evening, playing who'd had whom. Wicked – and almost all news to her!

Now behind her sat a *Who's Who* of the Art world, well-kept faces, collectors with whom he'd worked over the years. But although she had known him all her life, or thought she had, she didn't know a lot of the other people. Who were they? Friends of Marcus in the other areas in his life. And that, too, was typical Marcus, apparently open and on view, and yet really just showing you part of the picture. What an exhausting double life it must have been for gay people of his generation?

She felt Billy's hand, as up in the gallery a counter tenor sang Ave Maria. Who was he for instance? What had he to do with Marcus? Jester coughed. He really wasn't well enough to be here, he was so stubborn when he wanted to be.

It hadn't taken too long to get to Maida Vale that night, she'd gone the back way through W11 and W10. Something telling her to hurry, and she had even driven through a nearly red light at the top of Ladbroke Grove.

And then getting there, and no answer. No one in the other flats to help them when he didn't answer. Like a black, frustration comedy, running up and down different stairwells, a nightmare. She would never forget that marvellous young man. Musician, in jingles, banging on the door. She had called for the police on her mobile. They thought it odd that she'd never been to the flat before although she said he was an old friend known since childhood. 'He's a very private person, I work in his building. He lives a very private sort of life.'

She had never felt easy with his homosexuality, to be frank it had made her skin crawl when she was younger. As she had got older and had seen Marcus and Ian together, very much a couple, she had tried to understand if not accept.

It was not a life she would wish for anyone. The loneliness, the separation from the mainstream ordinarinesses of family life.

Marcus had been just sitting there in his chair, and had seemed asleep. Like Tom, it had been the peace and the babyish pink of his skin that had struck her as so amazing. Death took years off you! Obviously natural causes, the police said. Nothing she could do. Billy had been very shocked. She hadn't wanted him to see, but he had been very grown up, taking care of her! The doctor had come, he had not been able to give a death certificate without a post mortem because he wasn't sure of the cause. Heart attack probably. How old was he? 75-ish she'd said.

Harriet wriggled in her seat. Someone was playing the violin now and the priest was coming down giving people a wafer. The Catholics didn't make such a big deal of the Eucharist did they? Not like Anglicans, queueing up for their nice slug of red wine. The priest was so thin lipped, not much milk of human kindness there. Love the sinner, not the sin. What a conundrum it was! Would Marcus be languishing in some politically incorrect Hell this morning, while they were all sitting here in W11 praying for him? There has to be a Hell otherwise how could there be a Heaven? And yet let him who is without sin cast the first stone. How many thousands of priests Catholic, and Anglican come to that, were as bent as ten-bob notes? Hiding their secret life behind their avuncular vicar act? When they weren't knocking off their choirboys, or bitching about women priests.

Back again her mind went. She had made everyone tea in the immaculate kitchen, original tiles. Marcus had such good taste. It was only then, walking back down the long narrow corridor all those mansion flats have that she suddenly noticed the pictures and had almost dropped the tray. Not a flat, but a treasure store, no wonder he had never wanted visitors. She remembered gazing around astonished, carrying all those porcelain mugs. Cadells, Fergussons, Lucien Freuds, Francis Bacons, Hockneys, Picassos! A small Chagall above the front door, others she knew the style of, but wasn't quite sure. Unbelievable! Never seen them before! A squirrelling of a century's art, bought probably, knowing Marcus, when the of life lived last winter. Old bus tickets, a comb she thought paintings. How could he have left them here unprotected!

The police sent for a locksmith, who came quite quickly, not even bothering to move his tools from the doorway as the body was slowly carried out on its way to the morgue. She said she would ring his secretary who would know who his solicitor was. Marcus had never spoken about dying. He had always thought of himself as twenty-five maximum. Did he have any family? No? No-one at all? Should speed things up. She was barely able to impress on them all how very valuable these pictures were. How they ought to be stored in a vault not left in an empty flat.

Why could she have not reached him in time? The days had passed in a blackness. Richard Longbridge had rung up and she had explained about Marcus. 'Harriet, I'm so sorry, you won't get a rent like that anywhere else.' Money, always money with pirates, poor things knowing the price of everything but never the value. But a small bunch of white roses from Pulbrook & Gould had appeared in the office the next day with a card, sending Mrs Mac and the girls into transports of gossip.

She had organised days out for Billy, what a rotten way to spend his holidays. Georgiana had stepped into the breach, and he had gone off to the cinema at Whiteleys, reasonably uncomplaining. Anne Osborn had arrived too, with Jamie, to bear him off to the ice rink, ice-blue eyes sweeping round the room. While she was there, Marcus's girl had rung up with the results of the post mortem. Heart attack. Could have happened at any time. Laura had rung every day too. She had stayed away at her friend Marjorie's. It was much easier to get to the studios she'd said, but Harriet would have loved her to have come home. How wonderful the way she'd dashed into the church just now, wearing the most over-the-top blue hat.

The priest was now giving a final blessing, in that hurried way which made her think he probably had a wedding in twenty minutes and wanted a sit-down, while his flock now had the struggle through the rain and the traffic over the river to Mortlake crematoriaum. How Marcus would have hated the suburbanness of that.

Everyone shuffled out, huddling under umbrellas on the pavement outside. As there was no family, there was no focal point. Jester, Danny, Harriet, Billy, Laura all stood together. And Ulrike, who had begged to come. Marcus had encouraged her so much with her decorating in the last few weeks. And her whole personality had changed. No, Marcus would not be making any more 'discoveries'. Harriet felt the tears creeping back. A few people from another time came up and shook Jester by the hand, but she wasn't sure if he knew who they were. It was all rather an ordeal for him. A sudden wind blew down the road, a few leaves scurrying in the shower under the traffic wheels.

'Do you know', Laura suddenly said, 'I can feel winter in the air. How extraordinary. I haven't even had my summer hols yet.'

* * *

It was after three when Harriet and Billy got back to the office. Jester had complained all the way back to Edgware, hadn't wanted to leave the restaurant, they'd done it very nicely, but then the traffic, with the non-stop rain, had been dire. Harriet's French plait, which had been done too quickly, in too big a state in the morning, was now descending, and Billy was being fractious like a five-year-old. Going into the hallway, they didn't like to look into the gallery, so dark, and closed-up, no life left, and they went on up the stairs into the office.

'Hello, come in you two, Harriet you look done-in. Billy dear, sit down, you look absolutly shattered. I'll make some tea. I've bought some cream slices from the shop, sweet things, that's what you need.' Mrs Mac was in there filing. Oh God, I've got to pay her this Friday... with what? Harriet suddenly felt her whole life was unravelling as fast as her stupid hair.

'I think Marcus would have liked it. It was nice to see so many people. Anyone phone?'

'Richard Longbridge, Again! Told him you were out. Sounded disappointed.'

'Anyone else?'

'Mirielle to say she's got flu. Which is not the end of

the world because she's no lessons till Wednesday, someone selling office furniture and Mr Hudd about the Japanese course.'

'I'll get back to him. Billy do you want to go up and ask Danny if he'd like a cake, he might have already started work though. Did Ulrike come back?'

'Yes, she's collected next week's work, and done the Assessment on Mr Knightley at the bank.'

'Good, at least some business has been done. I'd better get on.'

She felt as if she was swimming through black treacle, seeing everyone through a fog. Work was probably the best antidote if she didn't throw up.

'What will happen about the office Harriet? Will we be able to stay?'

'Don't know Mrs Mac. Really. And I can't think about that. Not now. Let's open the second post shall we?'

* * *

Richard ringing again at five fifteen was told that Mrs Gosse had not been feeling well, and had left for the day. Chantal said she didn't think he was looking a happy bunny, and could he please sign off the invoices to the warehouse. And the decorators wanted to know if any other bits of paint work needed touching-up before they knocked off.

* * *

Twenty-four hours had made no difference, but even in her numb and zombie-like state the list meant took her breath away. As the man said, an A–Z of British Art. She had been brought up with these people, taken round to galleries by Marcus, and Jester and Ian, spending hours looking at them. Nasmyth, Henry Raeburn, Joseph Nicholls, Thomas Lawrence, Serres, Frances Wheatley, Jospeh Mallord William Turner. Turner! Two! Rossetti, George Leslie Hunter, Cadell, Fergusson, Lawrence Lowry, Burne-Jones, William Morris, Stanley Spencer... William Orpen, Matthew Smith, Gwen John, Edward Wadsworth. Mind-blowing! Auerbach, Bacon, Freud, Hockney, Dunne. How marvellous, Conroy, Watt and it went on. Nearly two-hundred paintings that had covered every inch of the flat. A treasure trove.

'An important collection, you will agree Mrs Gosse, hugely exciting', he was saying to her. Marcus's solicitor was looking at her as if she must be half-cut. Did he need to sound quite so condescending? She cleared her throat. 'It certainly is.'

'It will need to be valued of course, and the paintings have been moved, into secure accommodation for the moment. The collection will be given to you free of tax, Mrs Gosse, the residuary estate should cover the revenue's pound of flesh. Ha! Thanks to the nice Tories. But if it does not, then some may have to be sold, with your agreement as to which, Mrs Gosse. Probate should take six to nine months if we're lucky. Then you'll be a wealthy woman. You should take advice about storage, and insurance, you might want to sell some to rationalise the collection. The Tate might be interested in a loan.'

Oh such a smart outfit. Hickstead Parsons of Lincoln Square. Harriet just looked at him. Now he was talking about the sale room prices, how she ought to hang on till the recovery came.

Here was another public-school pirate thinking of art just in terms of money. Yet they were paintings to take your breath away. Works of art, sweated over, creativity bursting from the canvas. Look at Jester's. How pleased she was to have those. Marcus always knew which were the best. And she had known what agonies had gone into their creation! But in this plush office they were just items on a balance sheet. The bottom line of her worth and their creators. Poor fools, the painters who didn't go out and train to be nice, safe solicitors. And what a poor opinion of her this sensible man would have, if she said a word.

'I'll get my chum from Christie's down to value them' he was saying. 'The Revenue may or may not take our word for it. Might send their own chap down. Should be on the three-to-four-million-pound mark. Even in a recession. Remarkable man Marcus, terrific eye and a nose for a good buy.'

Harriet felt she was staring at the man like a goldfish.

'I must say I thought it odd you weren't made an executor, but there you are, when I suggested it he said he wanted you to have a surprise. "Like Christmas" were his exact words. I'd no idea of course exactly what he meant by that. A one-off. He'll be much missed.'

'Would you tell me please about the gallery premises. My business operates from them, and obviously I shall need to make new arrangements.' Harriet dreaded the reply.

'You may of course discuss these with the new owner. The terms of the will are that Mr Daniel Messenger receives the flat in Elgin Avenue and the gallery premises in Portobello Road. The residuary estate, after revenues have been paid, will be given to the Contemporary Arts Society to encourage new painters in a new annual competition.'

Danny, the man of money in his socks was now her landlord. Even more amazing.

She got up to leave. 'Thank you Mr Hickstead. I am still dumbfounded. It won't bring Marcus back, but it was so kind of him.' She tried to smile, but not wishing to embarrass this rather uptight man with the emotions which would inevitably follow. Out in Reception, Danny was sitting on the edge of his seat, in his one and only suit.

'Harriet, how was it? What did he say? I'm shit scared.'

'Don't be, Danny.' She kissed him. 'See you later.'

'What d'you mean? Can't you stay? I hate lawyers.'

'I can't Danny, I need to think.'

Out in the square she felt lost, disorientated, and for the first time in her life she hailed a cab which she would pay for herself.

* * *

A coach party had just left, and it was cool and deserted in the basement. Harriet stood there looking at Van Gogh's chair, what subtlety of colours. Marcus had loved paintings, what pleasure he must have got looking at them each evening. They had been his children.

Looking at pictures had always helped her think more clearly. So much was going on outside her control. Like that odd little moment when Billy said Roger Descartes-Jones had been Richard. Stupid of him, but the man had disappeared out of her life as soon as he had come into it. He had not answered her letter. But as everything was paid up, there was no further account needed to be given for their friendship. But could it be Richard? No, he would never do all that homework. And what about him, ringing up, sending her flowers, and then being very see-you-around when she had spoken to him, completely taken up with his latest show, with that French actor.

And Laura, who had been acted really strangely at the funeral. She and Marcus had never really hit it off – both in competition in a funny way. She'd bolted back to the studios straight after the church. Harriet suddenly felt in the eye of some unseen, unknown storm. And she was so very, very tired.

'Great painting isn't it?'

A voice at her elbow made her stiffen, Oh God, she thought, a pick-up in the National Gallery.

'It is marvellous isn't it?' She replied politely before moving on. It was several seconds before she recognised him. 'Oh, Mr Rogers!'

'Excuse me!' The plump man in the perfectly cut suit, she could see it was Savile Row even in this light, was obviously surprised, 'Do I know you Ma'am?'

'Harriet Gosse, Mr Rogers.' It obviously didn't mean anything to him. 'I don't think we've been introduced, but my son Billy, is at St Anthony's, Junior House. One of my staff is teaching Matr. . ., Kirsty, French. I run a language school you see. I saw you and your wife at the Speech Day.'

'O.K. I get you. Well how do you do Mrs Gosse, I beg your pardon for startling you. You were just looking so intently. Know about this I expect. Art.'

'A bit, my father was a painter.'

'So was mine. A house painter!' Hector Rogers, laughed, a deep rich southern chuckle, 'Still, I have my artistic pretensions!'

'Everyone should!' Harriet laughed, and they moved on to the next room.

They looked at the pictures in silence. Harriet thought the Impressionists were always soothing on fevered brains, and this man, with his gold Rolex and white shirt, had a stillness, and power, she found quite comforting. He didn't chatter, he knew the value of silence.

'Are they happy?'

'Who?'

'Your son and, and... Kirsty. Are they enjoying married life?'

'Yeh, real happy. He's working in our London office right now until the Fall. And do you know what? I'm coming round to thinking she might be right for him. She's no bimbo, she's tough!'

'Oh I am pleased, I always thought she was lovely with the boys.'

'It's the working of the Lord, and you don't mess with it. She's doing a good job, making him grow up. She was brought up on the wrong side of town, municipal housing. Not what his mother hoped for, of course. Nor I.'

'I actually saw your wife last week at an auction at Bute's. She bought a painting for the school.'

'Don't remind me. Do you know who she was bidding against?'

'Oh dear!' Harriet tried to hide a smile.

'Yeh, real dumb. There I was in New York, bidding to some cut glass English lady and all the time Maxi was there, sticking up her hand. I sort of laughed, when I found out. But don't tell Maxi I said that. Gave her hell!'

His laugh was rich, infectious. 'Do you come here often. That's a cliché I guess, Mrs. Gosse?'

'Not really, I come here when I can. I've just lost a very dear friend, and I needed some time out of the office. You know.'

'I know. So do I quite often. To nourish that inward eye which is the bliss of solitude?'

'Is Wordsworth popular in Texas?'

'You'd be surprised by what Texans know, young lady.'

'I didn't mean to sound patronising'

'No, I know, but we fit a sort of caricature over here. We're all JRs! Hick hustlers in cowboy hats.'

'God forbid! May I ask, why are you giving the school the picture? It'll be very modern, for them.'

'Oh, well, the New Houston School might seem nothing to you, with Van Goghs hanging all over town, but we wanted our State and our city Houston to be counted in that school. Boyd did do a lot there, he's not just the boy who ran off with the nurse. I hope he made them think a little less like the people in *Upstairs Downstairs*.'

Harriet laughed, 'If he did that, it was an achievement. I think you're right. Painting isn't just about money, it's making a statement. The title was *Youth* after all.'

'Right. Not just money, though the price of this statement... hurt somewhat. You're a nice lady, Mrs Gosse.'

It was the solidity of him, not just the obvious wealth. The man was real, on this earth, trustworthy. What she'd heard called 'bottom' – you couldn't say the word integrity nowadays, it had been used to death in the eighties by politicians and City crooks. Looking at him, the stale, sour aftertaste of bereavement began to fade, for the first time in days. God, or the Lord, as he would say, had sent her this unlikely angel all the way from Houston, Texas. A fifteen-stone garbage recycling multi-millionaire who could talk to her and ease the pain.

'Mr Rogers would you like to come to tea with me now? I've just spent the morning at solicitors and I'll have to head back to the office soon, but, please would you join me... as my guest? And please call me Harriet'

He seemed struck by her request. He was the same height, and his eyes creased when he smiled. He had a gold tooth which winked at her from the back of his mouth. 'Well, Harriet, that's real nice of you. I'm old-fashioned, I'm not used to not paying! But I'm enjoying our conversation.' He bowed, 'I accept your offer.'

She took his arm and they wandered towards the Strand, and a patisserie she knew he would like. In her experience, middle-aged men always loved waitresses in frilly caps and aprons and creamy, fussy cakes, with little teapots. Marcus had taken her there a couple of times, and Jester, years ago. And she suddenly realised that now there would be Marcus as well as Tom, sitting up there on their clouds, knocking back the booze and watching over her and Billy. Not alone then, after all, Harriet, she said to herself. It was a needed feeling.

* * *

Slam! 'Would you shut that bloody door, Chantal?' Late July rains and the wind beat in to the gallery, sending price sheets scattering over the floor. Prices he'd almost killed Le Feuvre and his bloody agent for, before they'd agreed. But for him, the Anglo-French Aids people would have got exactly zilch. He had had to sit both those French bastards down and teach them something new – marketing – a revelation to the Gallic mind. Lesson one, rich Oscar-winning actors going public for the first time as painters, had to be seen to be donating to charity, otherwise far from being attracted by the novelty value, the press would go for the goolies, no-one would want to know, and everyone would lose money. *Comprendez*?

Richard could feel the little knots at the back of his neck, knotting themselves up even tighter just thinking about that day. Calma, calma. What you need is a drink, old son. He locked the door after Chantal, who must have left in a huff, she hadn't taken the post with her. Not that it mattered, as tomorrow was Sunday. He went into his office. The good claret, where was it?

The twelve large Le Feuvre works were neatly stacked againt the wall with the 25 finished studies next to them. Quite a night, should take about three hours if he was on good form. The roars of a motorbike made him look out at the door, a pizza delivery boy with a peaked cap ran up the step. 'American pizza with extra anchovies for Longbridge', he was shouting outside. Richard paid him, and locked the door again. He would catch the early-evening news on the telly, then set to work. Where the hell had she put the mirror plates?

* * *

'Is that him? He doesn't look like me, does he?'

'No darling, he doesn't. You take after my side, good Dublin blood. Drink up now, don't spill it.'

'What's he standing next to?'

'Can't see. I've put down my reading glasses somewhere, oh yes, here we are. Oh, it's a corn dolly. You see Jamie, now farmers do square bales with machines, but years ago, it was all tied into long rolls with a tie in the middle, they looked like dolls from the road, rows of them. That was taken in Somerset when we were staying with your Auntie Eileen. Great Auntie I should say.'

'How old was he there?'

'I remember this one! This was him at about, well ten or eleven, he'd made a Dougall from a washing liquid bottle, do you still get *Blue Peter?*'

'Don't know, don't watch children's TV much, not with videos. At school they don't let us watch any.'

'Well, it was his favourite programme. Everything they made had sticky-back plastic all over it, and all Richard wanted, was a *Blue Peter* badge to take to school. Wrote off all the time. Until finally he got one for doing a competition. Sold it for ten bob. Fifty pence. Yes that was Richard all over!'

The housekeeper was laying the table in the next room, sausages, baked beans, chips and summer pudding, Jamie's favourite. But in here, in the huge sitting room, there was the same furniture he had always known, the same pictures the old rocking horse, and books of photographs everywhere, all over the floor, perfect. He loved photographs, old ones, and any sort.

'I want to be a photographer when I leave school, Nan.'

'Just don't try and run a gallery, Jamie, that's all I ask.'

'Dad said you wouldn't give him any more money.'

'Did he? Well he shouldn't discuss it really, but no it's time he sorted things out himself. Like you do when you're at school. I'm saving up for your first photographic exhibition, let's invite the Queen shall we, and the Queen Mum!'

'She'll be dead by then.'

'She'll be going strong, don't you worry, and so will I!'

'I like this one, when they got married, what colour was your hat?'

'The woman in Harrods called it Magenta, but it was more puce, awful! Anne's mother thought it was hideous, I could tell, and when we were getting merry after they'd gone off on honeymoon, I had to tell her I agreed with her. She was so embarrassed!'

'Did you enjoy the wedding?'

'Oh your Mum looked lovely, stick thin and emaciated of course, but lovely and your father, well he was blotto, but it was good, the reception was kneedeep in flowers, you know how Americans do things, the last word. Your grandfather made a very funny speech, it was a marvellous day really.'

'Yes, they looked really happy.' He tried to turn the sigh into a yawn, 'Would you like him to marry again, not to Mum, but someone else?'

Mary Ellen took off her glasses, and shoved them into the gold case. She began to tidy up, out of habit, not because there weren't staff coming out of her ears.

'I don't know about Richard any more. Mothers have to let go. He's a grown man, he'll have to sort himself out. As best he can. Your mum too. They're very alike you know, not bad people, not lazy, just unthinking. And it's easier to be unthinking, that's the trouble.'

'I'm not going to be unthinking, Nan'

'No you're going to be fanjamietastic. Eat your heart out, Norman Parkinson! Hang on, that's your tummy rumbling. Look Karen, is that meal ready yet, my grandson dying of starvation, so he is!'

* * *

Just putting them up was making him feel excited. Making things happen, who said his gallery was on its uppers? O.K. everyone, but where there's life... What he needed, please God if You're up there, was some nice red spots for the press. Hopefully his Blue list would do the trick before the lunch. Three said they'd come, all still rolling in it, still collecting, and they knew the stock markets would soar when the Chancellor cut interest rates. £15,000 a picture wouldn't be much for them, not from a living Hollywood legend.

All up, twelve in the main space, twenty-six finished studies in the studio. Looked good. 12 x £15,000, 26 x £1,200 = ... if they all sold. What? A stay of execution. He took the spray and carefully wiped the glass, no thumbprints, thank you. The men had touched-up the paint quite well. They were big pieces, heavy, six feet by five. He could have done with a hand, even Jamie would have been better than nothing, but he'd gone beetling off to Fitzroy Square as fast as his little legs would carry him. That boy caught taxis like buses, he'd probably enjoy New York more this summer.

Still two days to go, crazy doing it on a Monday probably, crazy doing it in July come to that, but that was just the way the cookie had crumbled. Lef was hardly Schwarzenegger. But there was quite a bit of interest, people ringing up, press wanting sneak previews, and interviews. Thank goodness the press office at the film company had taken a lot of that off his hands, Chantal couldn't have coped. Lucky to have got that plug on Barry Norman.

By eleven the rain had stopped outside and Richard had finished. It had taken far longer than usual, but after a while, he couldn't see straight, astigmatism at the best of times. He kicked the bubble pack into the corner, he could clear up tomorrow. Chantal had volunteered to come in to help with the labelling, she'd have to check the press packs and put in the Lef's biog. There was still the lettering on the window to do, and the window cleaner had been promised first thing on Monday. The visitor's book would have to be sorted out, new gold pen. Make a list Richard, otherwise you'll forget the lot. Wearily he pulled down the security grille, set the alarm and locked up. Loads of keys, the insurance companies were so touchy these days.

The wind had dropped, and the air was full of London smells after the rain. He suddenly remembered how he'd run barefoot up to the lamp post to catch Harriet. It seemed weeks ago. With her little briefcase, looking up at him. He decided to wander down to the Ritz and see if the men would be out there yet with the Sunday papers. Cremona's piece on eligible bachelors would be in.

Chapter Twelve

'*Eh bien, maintenant même,* even, *par exemple. Il prend du vin rouge même avec du poisson*, he even drinks the red wine with his fish.'

'Jean Baptiste how vulgar whoever 'he' is, he must live south of the river.'

'No, it is just an example *madame, alors*, can you give me one?'

'I'd love to! Oh I don't know, *il demande même un chambre sans chauffage centrale.* How about that?'

'*Très bien, il demande même UNE chambre sans chauffage centrale.*'

'*Une*. Now, that would be typical of my husband, terribly mean and he'd demand a discount unless it was a freebie of course, in which case the radiators would all be pumping out full blast. Jean Baptiste, I've been meaning to tell you something. Tomorrow I am going to meet Alain Le Feuvre.'

'Le film star? Magnifique!'

'*Mai oui, et demain, er, je vais pour acheter une belle petite robe noir* — a little black number! I intend to be terribly charming to him, and buy one of his pictures!'

'Madame, how exciting. Now, we must finish, enjoy yourself with him, *en Francais*! I shall now fax your homework to you as usual.'

'Merci Jean Baptiste, though it seems to be getting more difficult every week!'

'*Pas du tout madame*. You always improve. And I am sure you will be the most beautiful woman there tomorrow.'

'Oh, you make me feel a million dollars. Francs rather! *A mercredi alors, je m'impatiente. Merci Jean Baptiste, merci.'*

'De rien Madame. Au revoir.'

* * *

'Jet lag is sexy. It must be, because gallery owner Richard Longbridge tells me he suffers from it regularly, and he most certainly is. He arrived late for our interview glamorously apologetic, roaring up into Cork Street in a shiny Aston Martin, pleading jet lag from a New York round trip and, more strangely, lateness due to a visit to a Hammersmith street party.

'Is this extraordinarily handsome man a born liar, or just blessed with imagination? Grimy and pretentious W6 is not your usual street party territory, nor the terrain where one would expect to find one London's most handsome and eligible bachelors. I didn't like to point out that you don't get jet lag in Concorde.'

'What a bloody nerve calling us grimy and pretentious. Who wrote this? Cremona Kent. Well we all know what the subs must call you, ducks! Can you hear me H.?'

'Yes Laura, go on.' Harriet was in the bedroom doing press-ups.

Laura shifted in the bath, and ran more hot water onto her toes.

A distant church bell rang out in the distance, a Sunday reminder.

'O.K. Lord, I promise to watch *Songs of Praise* this evening. Guide's Honour. I quite enjoy it actually, even if those well scrubbed women could all use a decent lipstick.'

'Go on Laura, are you talking to yourself, or reading the article? Twenty-three, twenty-four.'

'Oh yes, so it goes on. *Dark, handsome and six foot four, he is best known to the general public for his pithy contributions to the Pictures series on Channel Four this Spring*. I didn't know he'd done that. Did you?'

'No I didn't, he never said. Twenty six.'

'Richard Longbridge has been a well known face round

in the London clubs for years, a regular at Annebelle's, and favourite escort to London's best with the crests, most notably Lady Annunziata Tarrant, who last month wed Lachlan, Marquis of Lore. Blimey, you're consorting with the great and the bad, Harriet. *"This week sees his Europa gallery launch French heart throb Alain Le Feuvre as a serious painter, coinciding with his latest film (see Film Offer section 5 p. 24).* Blah, blah. Are you still going to that H?'

'Yes, think I'll take Danny. Cheer him up.'

'Oh charming!'

'Oh go on Laura, you said you'd babysit!'

'I know, but Billy'll have to hear my lines, got forty-three pages to learn this week! What else, dear oh dear, he was born in Leyton. That's not very Belgravia is it, only child, father was Eastender made good Ernest Bridge, who took his mother's name, why did he do that? Well so did I come to that, Laura Crouch yuk! *Now left a multi million pound inheritance, a house in Belgravia, and a house in Ireland.* Good God, did you know his ex-wife was an Osborn, as in Osborn Fidelity? Serious mooleronis?'

'No, but it explains how come she's so thin.'

'Harriet, are you up to all this? Oh I keep forgetting you're an heiress now, any day fortune hunters will be chasing you!'

'Laura, I'm not up to anything. It's just a rather odd friendship. And we live in different worlds, Marcus's paintings won't make any difference. You should have seen his face when he came in here. And I can't play the little games he is obviously used to, even if I wanted to. They must give these girls lessons in Chelsea somewhere, as part of finishing them off. Though, I think he finds me a bit attractive, novelty value I think.'

'You don't send schoolfriends' mothers flowers when they lose a friend, Harriet.'

'No, but I think he was just being nice, Jamie has practically lived here this holiday, poor child. Richard and his wife don't know him at all.'

'Have you stopped those press-ups, I didn't hear you get up to forty!'

'Now I'm circling my ankles to improve circulation.'
'What are you going to wear?'
'Don't know, hadn't thought.'
'Harriet for once, do us a favour and buy something new. Now shut up and listen. Where was I?... *only child. Mother lives in Fitzroy Square, Irish, trustee on the Board of the Kilburn Theatre*, rabbit, rabbit. Nice picture of him, standing by a fireplace, very Jermyn Street and Establishment. Looks as if he's never been pushed in a pram up Leyton High Street in his life.'

* * *

Spot the literals, and of course there they were on page two of his c.v. Felini, and Jose Penas spelt with an i. Great.

Hadn't realised Le Feuvre's mother was a Gibraltarian, which was why he'd had the English to crack Hollywood in the late sixties. And what a lot of stuff he'd done... what a life. A French Sean Connery.

'Richard, stop worrying, only start if Lef calls off. Here's some coffee.'

'Thanks, Chantal. Got the labels done yet?'

'Yes, they're there for you to put up. I'll redo the biog, only the second page needs doing, and that's it.'

When he wasn't snapping at everyone, Richard enjoyed being in the gallery setting up a show on Sunday mornings; the anticipation, the feeling that came with working whilst eveyone else was in bed was rather nice. The phone rang.

'Europa Gallery. Richard Longbridge.'

'Ah Richard, Antonio Respighi. There was no-one at your house. About the pictures in September. And I wondered if I could come tomorrow?'

Five minutes later he put the phone down, 'What's the matter, Chantal. Seen a ghost?'

'You were talking in Italian. Sounded marvellous, really native!'

'I've been taking lessons from a wonderful and hugely beautiful teacher, and I now a spika de Italiano as befits one of London's most eligible bachelors. Don't snort, Chantal, it's not ladylike, didn't they teach you that at Bedales?'

'Sign these cheques, would you Richard? And letsa hopa they wonta bounca!'

* * *

Harvey Nicholls took one's breath away even on a Monday morning, even when the sales were on. She just wasn't used to such places, but Laura had dragged her.

'You've got to look stunning, and you don't have anything to wear for evening. All suits, and frilly dreses. Nothing remotely sophisticated.'

'I don't want to go. I've no money, yet. And I still don't feel up to it. Anyway can't I go to Madame Ada's. Blast it's Monday, it's shut.'

'Exactly. So get your butt through that door, they won't eat you.'

'How come you're not rehearsing this morning? '

'Because they're doing other people's cutaways which they forgot, can you imagine, to do last week. Weren't in the shooting script, and someone is being sacked as I speak. Oh hurry up, it's like taking a four-year-old shopping!'

'I hate shopping.'

'You hate spending money, you mean. Pathological you are. But just think how much Marcus liked you putting on the razzle! Oh God — Harriet, — please, don't cry I'm sorry.'

'It's all right Laura, I just, it comes creeping up, I miss him.'

'I'm sorry, H. I'm just stupid and insensitive.'

'No you're not.'

'No I'm not, you're right, I'm trying to cheer you up, Harriet, I think tonight is going to be fun. Seeing Richard Longbridge in his habitat, whether it's a friendship or it isn't. And Alain Le Feuvre, you saw all his French films without subtitles, and how many people there will be able to say that. And you love looking at paintings, so enjoy!'

'Yes.'

'Then come on then!'

* * *

The gallery owner who once said that the sight of that

first red spot going up was better than sex, had been exaggerating, Richard thought. But only just! It was the sheer relief. And old Costas had done the biz bless him, No. 12, *View in Provence*. Nothing to write home about, but livable with, for a nice round £15,000, which meant that his costs were already some way to being covered, though 60% of the first £10,000 and 50% thereafter wasn't much, considering everything he'd had to pay upfront.

Would they be meeting Monsieur Le Feuvre? Unfortunately he wouldn't be coming until later, to the Press View, but perhaps we could arrange something.

The door opened and a short grey figure entered, Richard, who had been putting off having his eyes tested for months now, on principle, called over, 'Chantal, tell the gentleman we're closed will you? Sir, the show opens tomorrow.'

He turned back to his three wise men, who hopefully would be bearing gifts in the shape of large cheques over to the desk any moment, De Burgh seemed to like the Boulevard collage. Who was he to question why?

'Richard, don't you want to sell anything?'

'Good God. I didn't think you'd be interested, today is just for, well, you know.'

'Favoured collectors.'

'Exactly.'

Jaakko Jokinnen took out his glasses and started to look at the pictures. He'd aged a lot since '88, but then hadn't everyone? 'Don't worry Richard I would like to make a private purchase. Didn't you know I put finance into *Les Aventures*?'

'No I did not. I knew the producer had raised the money privately. Hope you get your money back on it, wouldn't want you having as many sleepless nights as poor Anne has had to put up with lately.

'Life is hard. Now, I think I'd like a little souvenir. where are the studies? Over there?'

'Er, yes, they go from £1200. Finished studies of course. Though I don't know if I feel like selling you one.'

'Longbridge, don't kid yourself.'

Anne stay away. I do not need a scene. Richard had the feeling it was a day when everything was up for grabs.

'You know Richard, you must never believe everything you read in the papers. I don't. I'm not finished yet, just as you are not yet an eligible bachelor!'

* * *

Size eight, must be the fiftieth thing she'd tried on. Nothing. She was going to starve as soon as she got home. Everything bulged. 'That's why they're in the sale, Harriet, most people are sizes 10 to 12. This is Knightsbridge, not in Marks & Sparks land.'

'Look this is a complete waste of time. Laura, I've got to get into the office.'

'Just a minute, what about those black satin trousers, over there? Beautifully cut. Marese too! And £60 reduced from £300!. Harriet you must try them on.'

'I look terrible in trousers.'

'No you don't, it's just in your head. Just shut up and try them on. Be adventurous for a change!'

'What would I wear them with?'

'Your antique lace blouse, and... I could lend you my purple sash. There! You've got a tiny waist, it would look very dramatic.'

'Oh alright.'

Harriet sighed and headed for the changing room just as Lady Madeleine Humble burst out.

'Mrs Gosse!'

'Oh good morning, Lady Humble. How nice. May I introduce you to Laura Marchant? Laura this is Lady Humble.'

'Good morning.'

'You're an actress, aren't you?'

'Er yes.'

'I loved you in — what was it? — *Sampson House*. My daughter and I were so sorry when you were written out!'

'Er, thanks, are you shopping?'

'Yes, trying to find a few things. Going to a View tonight to see Le Feuvre's paintings. Alain Le Feuvre. I am so looking forward to meeting him. I've always thought he was one of the great stars. Up there with Omar Sharif, and O'Toole!'

'I'll look forward to hearing your French then, Lady

Humble', said Harriet. 'I've been invited too – if I can find something to wear!'

'Oh yes, how nice. Yes. Er. Goodbye, Mrs Gosse.'

Laura and Harriet looked after her as she hurried away.

'Below the salt, Harriet. Snobby old bitch.'

'She's alright really, I don't know why she was like that.'

'Is she the one that got pissed at the School Speech day?'

'Extremely, gave Billy the *Victor Ludorum'*

'What a scream! How's her French?

'Comme çi comme ça I just provide her with a French teacher with an Yves Montand voice.'

'Oh, she's one for your Chelsea bats who get the hots over the phone!'

'Well, I wouldn't put it quite like that, but she is one of my well connected clients, who learn French purely for fun. Which, I suppose, is the same thing. Stop laughing it's not funny.'

'Sex is always funny Harriet. Imagine, getting turned on doing your French exercises. Courtesy of BT. Give me more subjunctives, Pierre chéri.'

'Jean Baptiste actually. Keep your voice down, the assistants are staring!'

'Love it. Nice Catholic name. Oh Harriet, it's hysterical. While her hubby's boring the pants off his fellow Members, she's doing Jean Baptiste! *Je viens, tu viens, il vaaaaa*!'

Even two women hanging on to each other howling with laughter, could not lower the tone at Harvey Nicholls.

* * *

Twelve journalists turned up in the end, with twin bubbles coming out of their heads. 'FEED ME' said one, and 'IMPRESS ME' said the other. But was he glad to see them! Clive Sawston, Neill Lambourn, all the nationals, some of the trade press, and the *Evening Standard*, best of all. And the AIDS lady to give them the charity line. It was all going well, so far. They all seemed to like the food and drink, which was vital. Less taken by the paintings, but hopefully well fed and watered, they wouldn't say anything too nasty.

'Richard, *Kaleidoscope* have turned up, they want to interview you and Alain.' Chantal was in her element, even the way she said Alain, had a certain — *élan*. Richard began to weave his way through. The TV would be turning up at two o'clock. Please God.

It was quite a crush. Cremona's editor had turned up late, and was now monopolising Le Feuvre, who was being terribly charming. All a big act, hope he kept it up for the evening performance. Catherine someone, all cleavage, and shoulder pads, could barely get through the door, I thought they were going out now shoulder pads! Like soaps.

Richard suddenly thought of Harriet's dead husband, Thomas. Big chap. But then thoughts of Harriet had been popping up like white rabbits all morning. Perhaps he should give her a ring, once he'd done the interview, check she was coming? Old Whitehead's death was a turn-up, poor old bugger. Once he'd heard a rumour that the old boy had put together an amazing personal collection. Bet *he* hadn't left it tied up in a trust.

* * *

'He's some old French actor who's done some paintings at his holiday home, he's ancient. Fifty, sixty. At least.' Jamie was in his room, playing Ranch Hero on his new computer. Billy had just lasered Scumball for 150.

'Why can't you stay over at our house? Laura wants us to hear more lines. She's always forgetting them, I think she must have bits of cardboard with them on, behind the camera.'

'You mean prompt cards.'

'How do you know that?'

'Just do. Can't come, Mrs Thing's looking after me. She's called the cab, by the way.'

'Has she? Bother. Why do you call her Mrs Thing? Is that her name?'

'No, Dad 's never bothered to find out her real name, it's Wishnizzi or something, Polish.'

'Oh. My mum's going.'

'What, to this actor's do?'

'Yeh.'

'So's mine. Would you like them to be friends?'
'Your mum and my mum?'
'No stupid. Your mum and my dad. Would you mind if they, you know bonked?'
'Jamie!'
'Well it wouldn't bother me. I like your mum. Might make him clean up his act.'
'I don't know. You are funny, you don't talk about him like he's your father.'
'No, well, he's just terribly immature, you see. Pass us the crisps. I'm going to zap Scumball into cyber-atoms!'

* * *

It was a fine evening. The fact that Georgiana's bathroom window was open, and the street was thick with the smells of enough aromatherapy oils to stock a health farm for a year, told Danny and Harriet that it was going to be a Big Night. Kissing Billy and Laura silent goodbyes, they slid into the car.
'You look great', mouthed Laura, making faces up at Georgiana's windows.
'Stop it,' Harriet mouthed back. And they managed to get in the car, and three-hundred yards down the road before Georgiana still in curlers, stuck her head out of the window. It was probably mean not to give her a lift, but everything she did, even sitting in a passenger seat for twenty minutes, was so stressful. And Danny and Harriet did not need stress. They were still treating each other like eggshells people, reading all the guff from the solicitors together, very very slowly. 'Joining up the big words', Danny called it. And neither felt any less impoverished.
'You're looking nice, Harriet, Laura had a go, did she?'
'Well, our Laura is a frustrated BBC make-up girl, which is why I look like a fairy godmother with knobs on. How she got my hair this curly I don't know, there's enough lacquer, if I fall over it'll crack.'
'It's good, pre-raphaelite I'd have said. Make-up's good, too very ethereal.'
'It was very nice of her to take the trouble, she's trying

to make me feel better. When do these lights change? But it's all going to be a bit of an effort, Danny. Let's not stay, if it gets too much.'

'Shall we have a signal?'

'Why not scratch your head when you've had enough?'

'Then everyone will think I've got fleas.'

'Yes, but then you'll be on the way out of the door, so it won't matter.'

'Agreed, unless I meet Miss Right. In which case, I'll pull my right ear lobe!'

'Danny, you are a dope.'

'I'm not! Miracles happen.'

'I know, I want to change lanes, let me in someone!'

'And what will you do Harriet, when you meet Mr Right?'

'That's the 100-million-pound question, Danny. No, I think now my Mr Right died in Charlotte Street, whatever his faults. Two Mr Rights would make a Right Royal Wrong.'

* * *

She was instantly wrapped in a bear hug. 'Harriet my dear friend, I'm going to be a grandpop!' Hector Rogers had seemed to have put on three stone with happiness, his face pulsated it, and Harriet, while trying to think of something to say was passed on like a much loved parcel into Maxi's embrace, 'Oh Mrs Gosse, Harriet. The baby due in January. Very premature!' She winked in happy conspiracy.

'Mother!'

'If it's a boy, we'll put him down for St Anthony's at birth!' Hector roared with laughter, 'And Harriet, how are you? Feeling a bit better about your friend?'

'Oh, I, you know?' What was she supposed to say? No I'm bloody not.

Boyd had grown up unbelievably, in the last few weeks, taller than ever, the proud husband. Now far too discreet in his blazer and grey flannels, ever to have had hot kisses on Paddington station. Kirsty stood next to him, petite and modest in pearls and Yves St Laurent. Smiling, like the Scots cat who got the Burns supper.

'Did you have to leave Billy behind?'

'I don't think this is his scene, Kirsty. Congratulations.' Harriet kissed her.

What a crush. TV lights made the gallery so hot. There were well kept faces she vaguely knew, people talking, holding drinks being terribly knowledgeable and valid, that awful meaningless word. Noise, laughter, shouts from the camera crew coming in after interviewing a man on the pavement. Of course Alain Le Feuvre himself! Distinguished, beautifully dressed in that way only Continental older men achieve. The oofle dust of fame and glamour separated him from the rest of London, which jostled and barked. Why were they not all in Chiantishire by now? She took a drink and a glacéed fig from the waiter. That's the recession for you.

'H., which one's Richard Longbridge?'

Danny was looking round, in awe.

'Oh, where is he? Yes, look, over there, tall, curly head.'

The tall curly, head was looking down at someone laughing, head thrown back.

'More Cava, Madam?'

'No thank you. I'll take one this slowly.'

'I'm going to look at the paintings, Harriet. See you.'

'Good luck Danny, but I don't think you'll be able to in this crush.' She was undecided whether to go and say hello to Richard first, but he would have far more important people to see. Should she look at the pictures? Or go back to the Rogers – could do – they were very friendly. How she missed Marcus, he would have taken her by the elbow, and steered her round, to the best pictures, and the most interesting people, and then, just as the evening began to dip, would spirit her off to North Soho, for a cheap Italian meal, lots of red wine and funny, bitchy asides. Bless him. Oh, bless him. Don't panic.

'Mrs Gosse.' Lady Madeleine Humble was waving at her full of friendliness. Very chic in black. And sober.

'Mrs Gosse how nice to see you. What do you think of his work? Isn't it marvellous? I've just bought the still life over there.'

'I haven't had much of a chance to look yet.'

‘Now may I introduce you to friends of Richard Longbridge?’

‘How do you do.’

‘They’ve driven in from Oxfordshire. Lovely drive in this weather, I always think.’

‘Really? I’m sorry I didn’t catch.’

‘Now I must go and talk to Clive Sawston over there, Eric’s on the Arts Committee.’

Dumping operation completed, Lady Humble shimmered away. Harriet took a sip of the champange, and smiled. . . . ‘I’m sorry I didn’t quite catch your name.’ She recognised the woman. From?

‘Roger and Veronica Descartes Jones.’

* * *

Richard was in his element. Andrew Lloyd Webber had bought one of the Nice scenes. The best one. Hooray! Seven biggies sold, and seventeen studies. Richard, you clever bastard.

‘Richard congratulations.’ ‘Richard come and meet. . .’, people wanting him, for once. People with cheque books, people who had been writing him off weeks before. He was losing his voice he’d given so many interviews with Alain. He was beginning to quite like the man, what a pro.

‘Madeleine good evening.’ Good God, she was drinking orange juice.

‘Richard dear, good evening. I bought the still life.’

‘Very good investment, super painting, I’m sure you’ll get a lot of enjoyment.’

‘Do you? So do I. Do you think I could meet Monsieur Le Feuvre? He won’t even need to speak in English. I’ve been having telephone French lessons for months now. On the phone would you believe! I’m a different woman.’

‘Have you? Who with?’

‘Oh the Gosse School, I notice she’s here, do you know her?’

‘Yes. Is she here, where? Our sons, um, anyway, Alain allow me to introduce you to Lady Madeleine Humble, her husband is the Minister, hoping he’ll get away from the House later.’

‘*Enchanté Madame*.’ Alain Le Feuvre kissed her hand.

Richard thought that you had to admire the way he turned it on, when he must be pushing mid-sixties if not more. The old girl was practically having a hot flush. Where was Harriet? Just look for the hair.

There! Good gracious. A Rossetti creation tonight. What a girl! Fantastic! Never seen anyone in his life so unconsciously and incredibly sexy. And who was she talking to? Old Rog. Oh, Christ.

'Richard it's going well, I think, you might be able to keep your head above water till Christmas.'

His mother, a vision in Oscar de la Renta, was prodding him in the stomach.

'Thank you Mother. Will you please keep your voice down.'

'I'm pleased for you that's all, lots of people. Now, when are you going to introduce me to the big man. I'm thinking of buying that little study. Number 44.'

'Good. Hang on, I must. . . .'

Next he was hauled away by a collector to meet his new boyfriend the concert pianist. So liked the nudes, etc. etc. Harriet! Stop talking to them, he wanted to shout. Let me explain, it was no big deal, just a joke to get know you better. He could tell she had found out, something about her shoulders. And she seemed to have shrunk. Had he even invited Roger? What a mess. Couldn't remember. Or was he on the shortlist of regulars Chantal had just gone ahead and sent out?

'Richard!' 'Richard!' 'Richard!' Everyone wanted him. He noticed everything and he noticed nothing. That journalist, Cremona, just come in with another girl, looked quite alike, all hair and hopefulness, bright blousy colours like peonies, or some flower or other, not that he knew. Who was it? Harriet's neighbour Georgina someone. Could be sisters, except one had lived, and the other clearly wanted to.

'Richard! Chantal has just told me Jaakko came in today. I can't believe you actually sold him a picture!'

'Anne, hello, darling, you look super. Could you give me one minute.'

'How much did he pay? And how did he back this film? What with?'

'I don't know. Apparently he knows Alain's second wife, Ulla, who lives near him, or something. Look St John's just arrived, I must go.'

'I see. O.K., I'll swallow it Richard. Sufficient unto the day is the evil thereof. Don't look so worried, Richard. Sermon on the Mount.'

'Is it? Well, Jesus was right.'

It was impossible. He was waylaid, and waylaid. More drinks. More canapes. He was swirled around, between backs and shoulders. What would the bottom line be for all this? Where had Harriet gone! Just as well it was Cava, not the real thing. He saw Chantal putting up another spot. Good. He saw the Rogers, grouped together, by the door playing happy families. Who'd have thought? Maxi would be knitting bootees next.

The room was so crowded, no air to breathe. Wonderful. Terrifying. Someone open the doors! The pictures on the wall remained the same, either sold and unsold, but the pictures before him changed constantly. That girl Georgiana was now talking to Alain. He knew that look. Alain had just found his bed for the night. Georgiana, she was flirting like a little girl. Madeleine was flashing it about too, young man. Very shabby, who on earth did he come with? Why was he pulling his earlobe so frantically like that? Odd. And by the door.

'Harriet. Harriet!' he yelled. People turned and stared. Was he cracking? Was she a critic? Bodies, in front of him, for yards, couldn't get through, bloody fireplace in the way.

'Excuse me. Excuse me St John. Harriet don't leave yet!'

Still ten yards to go. He felt like Dr bloody Zhivago. Then he saw her turn, unreachable. So pretty. And then looking terribly alone, she began to walk down the road.

But not half as much as he felt as he turned to face the party. Cremona was at his elbow, with a bottle in her hand pouring a drink. She smiled up at him.

'This is for you Richard. She had to go for a quarterpounder.'

Chapter Thirteen

'Have another, Harriet.'

'Laura, I'm already sloshed, really!'

'Doesn't matter. Sometimes getting sloshed does you good.'

'Should you be drinking, if you're working tomorrow?'

'With my liver? No, I'm not called till eleven.'

They were wrapped up in blankets in the garden looking up at the stars. It was quiet, even the traffic from the Goldhawk Road had faded, and the orange lights in the sky from the flyover met the stars half-way. Laura opened the other bottle.

'No more Laura, honestly. Oh well. That's enough. Did Billy get to bed alright? '

'Fine, he's so good these days, really grown up. Didn't argue at all.'

'Yes, he'll be wanting to have his own life in a few years. Oh God Laura! I feel so stupid!'

'Harriet, come on don't be like this, please.' Laura thought she had never seen her in such a state, she had come home, beside herself.

'Why, was it so terrible? He might have been just trying to get to know you better. Prince climbing Rapunzel's tower sort of stuff. Have it out with him if you must, or just forget about it.'

'It was exploitative, and horrid. I feel used and stupid and cheated and oh, everything.'

'Oh, don't exaggerate. He paid you, so what's the problem?'

'I put myself into those lessons, Laura. I liked Roger, or who I thought was Roger. He was different. Oh I don't know, on the phone you build up a mental picture of someone.'

'Did you find him attractive?'

'I did, yes. It seemed safe, laughing, O.K. flirting with a man on the phone.'

'Well take it as a compliment. I imagine he did it to get back at you, after you turned down his date.'

'Don't be silly, a very expensive revenge.'

'He can afford it. Anyway, if you feel a fool! At least you know how I feel?'

'Meaning?'

'Oh, it doesn't matter.'

'It does, what do you mean?'

'David. He told me, well, it just slipped out. Perhaps I'll rephrase that?'

'Oh. What did he say? He didn't brag? Oh he didn't!'

'No, it emerged because I asked if', Laura began to laugh. 'if the sofa bed was lumpy, and he said he had no idea.'

'Oh Laura.'

'Is that a giggle? I told you you needed to get sloshed.'

'I didn't tell you Laura because. . . .'

'It doesn't matter, none of my business, but there was I plotting to stop you being West London's first Vestal Virgin, and all the time. . . . He was very discreet by the way, though he obviously hadn't been bored.'

'It just happened, I was surprised as you. And God knows how much Georgiana heard, she was having a dinner party.'

'Love it! Orgiastic screams with the avocados, how funny, must have woken the guests up.'

'She must have heard, she's been very odd towards me since. Tonight I left her half wrapped round Le Feuvre.'

'You didn't! I thought she was frigid!'

'Well she didn't look frigid to me, there was steam coming out of her Donna Karan earrings.'

'Good God, what will our Robert say? But isn't she turning Catholic to get Araminta into the Sacred Virgin High?'

'Oh I don't know, but it'll be six "Hail Mary"s! And

Danny I left chatting up Lady H., the one who scooted out of Harvey Nicks. She'll eat him for breakfast!'

They fell silent, Laura tried to picture Georgiana wrapped round Alain Le Feuvre, and Danny with Madeleine Humble, but even with her imagination it was an effort.

'Oh I've just been rather silly with Richard, I was flattered, who wouldn't be? Not at first but when we went to collect the boys, and then there was the auction, and the white flowers. I was taken by his glamour, thought we could be friends, with the kids, perhaps have a few trips together. But to him, I was just a low ticket joke. Well, he's a rotten father and a selfish bastard.'

'Don't beat yourself up like this, Harriet.'

'The way those Descartes people looked at me, and I'm supposed to have a good ear. Billy noticed it was Richard instantly, and I told him not to be silly.'

'Sure you didn't know subconsciously? '

'He was a client, full stop. Although I know one does half-acknowledge things subconsciously. Like I always knew deep down Tom wasn't perfect. I sometimes wonder if we'd be together now if he'd lived.'

'Who can say? But no one's perfect, Harriet, you seem to spend your life on a pedestal above the rest of us. Tom felt that, and he was just a man like any other.'

'Laura. What does that mean?'

'It doesn't matter, shut up Laura, let's go to bed.'

'Are you saying — what are you saying? Are we going to make this confession time? Did he have *affaires*?'

'Look, it doesn't matter.'

Harriet was standing looking at her, very still, yet Laura had the idea that pieces were crashing and locking together in her mind.

'Did he?'

'Yes.'

'And did you? Please?'

'I think I'm about to make myself homeless. Yes I did Harriet.'

'I see.'

'No you don't. It was just a one night stand, remember when the Sampsons went to Holland, yonks ago, I'd only just joined the show, those Dutch TV people had put money in, and there had to be some tulips and windmills to keep them happy. It was two weeks' filming, and we were there in a godawful hotel, bored rigid having to eat plastic cheese for breakfast. I didn't know he was married even, we were just colleagues, it was just a one-night . . .'

'. . . bonk.'

'Put it like that if you want. It meant . . . nothing. And after, I felt badly when I met you. But it went to the back of my mind and much later after the funeral, when you said if I'd like to stay, I thought you'd never need know. It was nothing, really.'

'To you. And for him?'

'No man, however much he loves his wife would turn down sex if it's available with no comebacks, and Tom was just like every other man. But he adored you.'

'You're right. It doesn't matter.'

'Harriet, please don't be angry, but you don't have to write yourself off and just work all the time, I told you because Richard has fallen from grace but he's human, a normal man playing little boys' games, not growing up. And Tom was just the same, and worse because he was an actor and by definition, we never get real. You have, but somehow you bypass real life. Stop wasting time. It's a waste of your life being the little widow keeping his memory green.'

'It is Laura? Thank you for telling me.'

As Harriet came up to her, Laura thought she was going to hit her, but to her surprise, Harriet suddenly bent down and kissed her full on the lips.

'Harriet. Are you O.K.?'

Harriet folded away her chair,

'Livid and liberated Laura. I don't think he was ever on that cloud over West London.'

She did not have a clue what Harriet meant. Should she have told what she had? The stars winking at her weren't giving anything away. Laura thought of Tom's muscular body in that hotel room, the morning he died. She had just lied, and life was a bitch.

* * *

Harriet! His head exploded, and then Richard thought of her, standing there alone in the road. Had he screamed it aloud, or was it just in his head? He lay on her, limp, so tired he could sleep for a year. Soft, white skin was probably all these women had in common. She was like a pillow, soft, suprisingly firm under all that armourlike underwear.

She was stroking the base of his spine, nice. But he could tell she was fumbling with the other arm for something. A cigarette. Of course.

'Richard. Get off there's a dear. Like a fag?'

'Thanks,' he rolled off, and looked at her. The large white breasts were now partly covered by the sheet, her neck was wrinkled but she was looking at him pleased with herself. Comely, an old fashioned word.

'Well, Private Views obviously agree with you.'

'I don't know they're exhausting. It went well though, didn't it?'

'It went very well. And so', she pinched his bottom, 'so did you.'

'Good. I aim to please. It's only two thirty, shall we go to sleep now?'

'No more play? I thought Richard Longbridge was famous for all night swinging from the chandeliers.'

'Not tonight, Josephine. I've had it.'

'So have I!' Cremona rolled over and went to sleep. He lay turned away from her, his body satiated, but his mind making decisions before sleep threw them out of the window.

He awoke about seven. What? Tuesday morning. Head splitting, he should never mix wine with whisky. Oh my God, who is this? He remembered, dimly, Harriet going like that. Having to be on parade for, what seemed like hours, a great success everyone said, innovative show. Well done, Richard. Then everyone had gone, even, finally, Alain Le Feuvre – carried into the taxi, promising himself a new career. Most of the pictures sold, another series for Channel 4. Lots of ideas, promises, plans, discussed, and probably forgotten, but all useful capital in bullshit.

He looked at the woman next to him. What was her name. He felt like death. Cremona Kent. Oh God. She had been lying in wait for him, in his office when he'd gone to turn out the lights. He had been high on life, and wanting, needing Harriet. It had just come to him, just looking at her there, that he did need Harriet. What she was, what she represented, the sensible gypsy.

And then this woman had been there, inviting, knowing like Wilde he could resist anything but temptation. Making love on the floor, and then on a canvas, nothing special, some art student or other had sent it in. She had somehow gone home with him. Clothes everywhere. Had to get her out before Jamie got up. Or Anne would give him hell.

He flung on his dressing gown, his head reeling, balls aching, felt awful, 'Cremona, Cremona. Let me make you something to drink, but I'm sorry, you'll have to go. My son, well, I don't really want him to, well see us?' Gallantry would be wasted on this man-eating spider. Just an older version of all the other women he'd taken to bed. How was it that somehow they always ended up screwing him?

'Cremona.'

She suddenly turned, what a mess, eye shadow down on her chin. He couldn't go on like this. Too old for it. Quickly he got downstairs and made some coffee, instant, came up and began picking up her clothes. What if she met Mrs Thing on the way out?

'Cremona?'

'I'm going Richard, I've only just woken up, you don't have to make it quite so obvious.'

'I'm sorry.'

'And I was right. You are a spoilt little boy. Well this discarded teddy bear needs at least ten minutes. Capisc?'

'Yes it's just that my son...'

'Bugger your son. He probably knows more about women than you do. Now fuck off, let me get up.'

So he did, camping out on the landing, his head on fire, restless to get on and do, well, he didn't know what. Something had to change. Slam, he heard the front door go. Here we go, Mrs Thing arriving to look down her nose with all that chip-on-the-shoulder disapproval the Poles specialise in. He looked out of the window, and surprised, saw that she and Jamie were walking hand in hand, about to cross the Square. She had been going out? What a star! Where were they going? Harrods food hall for croissants that was it, she'd promised. He looked over the bannisters, and noticed Cremona's coat had been neatly folded over the hall chair. Good, old, discreet Mrs Thing. Take it back about the Poles.

'Right I'm going. Goodbye.' Cremona came out, she looked sulky, defensive. He would pay for this, he knew.

'Look Cremona, forgive me for hurrying you, I'm sorry.'

'It's alright Longbridge, I'm a big girl, stop acting.'

There was a sourness about her mouth, that made her look a-hundred-and-five, vicious too, he didn't dare go near her. Ungallant, wrong-footed. The dark thinlipped figure of his mother's priest shifted into his mind like a cardboard puppet. You're a sinner, Richard. Why had Anne quoted from the Bible last night?

Slam! For the second time. Cremona was walking across the Square, hailing a cab with a wolf whistle, and getting in. The taxi wheeled round and headed back east. He didn't even know where she lived; or if it was her real name. He was just thankful the city had gobbled her up.

Richard stood there for some moments on the landing. Quite still, undecided what he was to do. Waiting to find out.

And then he ran down the stairs, nearly banging his head on the low stair ceiling, and into the kitchen. Where did she keep them? He pulled out drawers, opened cupboards. Hopeless, no logic. Finally he found them, a neatly rolled pack of fifty black bin bags, bought from Sainsbury's on the Cromwell Road. He grabbed her apron hanging on the back of the door as he ran, it had a child blowing bubbles on it. Well he wasn't going to be doing that any more.

Standing in the hall with the roll tucked under his arm, he didn't know where to start, he just knew that he hated everything in his house, everything.

Hated this stupid fucking silk dressing gown for instance. He tore it off, and slung it into a bag, and standing there naked, he put on the apron, which reached to his knees, and then went into the drawing room. He looked at the sculpture with Jamie's freezer label. 'What inheritance dickhead?' And what was he giving to Jamie other than cynicism and inattention?

He swept the Philippe Stark ashtray and the Fornasetti coasters into the bag, they were quite light, his marbled paperweights – didn't like them, and the stainless steel knick-knacks he had picked up in Milan. Didn't like them either. And the hand-tufted Eileen Grey rugs, and the malachite waste bins, two of them. Both out! Someone at Oxfam could use them for ball practice. The opaque glass pyramid, he didn't need it any more. All these things. Crowding him out of his own home, weighing him down with their demands. Eating up money that was not to be his for years.

Next, the library, a pretentious name, he never opened a book unless it had pictures in it. The swag table hit him on the knee. Out! Too big to bag – it fell broken by the front door. The Aubusson. He would send it to Butes. Out. Too fussy, too valuable. And he couldn't afford the insurance. He stopped at the 1930 lamps. So beautiful, he loved them, O.K., they could stay, and his teddy bear.

Now books! Every *How To* book ever published, bought at every airport from Osaka to J.F.K., didn't need any of them. And if he never made another cent, he was not going to be a debt junkie any more. Though God alone knew how he was ever going to get into the black, even with Le Feuvre churning out the stuff for the next decade. He ran upstairs and found his nail scissors and cut up his credit cards. Ouch! That hurt, but then was he going to buy anything ever again? From now on, it was going to be Gosseconomics. He was going to be like Harriet. Not that she would ever speak to him again, but he would write to her and explain. He *was* going to change.

Exhausting work. After half an hour, the house was Beirut. The halogen lights were in the hall, absurdly out of place. The rhodonite and crystal table lamps he'd paid £35,000 for, were in the Bute's pile. Buffalo-skin bridge set, obscene! Into the Oxfam bag. Along with green lizard desk set and the howler monkey. 'Sneered at me for the last time, you bastard!'

Richard stood panting, but free in the hall surveying the wreckage. It was a big house, but before there had never been any space, Jamie had never been able to bring toys to play with downstairs because there was no room for him. And his father never had the time. Richard headed on up the stairs with his bin bags under his arm.

* * *

She felt quite cool, and calm. She was going to hit him in the groin, have him doubled up, and then she would hit him again. For Tom. And then she would walk out. A reasonable course of action in the circumstances. She no longer cared what he thought, or what he said. And she was not going to be passive any longer.

She left a note on the table, 'Laura, please could you send Billy to Georgiana before you leave?' And if he didn't like it, and rowed with Florian all morning *tant pis*! She was sick of being the perfect suffering bloody mother.

She sloshed water on her face, and stuck on the nearest lipstick. It gave her a slashed appearance, against the white freckled skin. She dragged the comb through her hair. How liberating not to give a fig how one looked. She flung on a tracksuit, and glanced at her watch. She'd be back by half eight, in the office by half nine, at a pinch. Honour satisfied. And then she was going to go on holiday and forget about London. Maybe they could move out altogether, did she need to be here at all? London was getting so dirty and smelly and expensive. The house had too much emotion studded into the brickwork. And why could she not start up a school in Bath, or darkest Cornwall? Edinburgh? No reason whatsoever.

She ran out slamming the door. Laura's curtains were still closed, Georgiana's were half open, as if she had only got up grudgingly, because her family were making demands. Poor old Georgiana, breaking out for one night, seen Paree and was now back on the farm.

She was soon at the Shepherds Bush roundabout heading up Holland Park Avenue. He wouldn't have left yet. Still drinking cappuccino in his jacuzzi, probably, eating *pain au chocolate* on Limoges and brushing the crumbs onto the carpet for some other poor sod to clear up.

She reached Belgrave Square in fifteen minutes, London in the summer light was perfect, no school runs to clog up the arteries. Sweeping round into Eaton Place, Sandringham Square was ahead of her in its stucco splendour. He hadn't got a clue how the rest of the world had to live.

She parked outside, and getting out of the car, nearly fell over a black bin bag on the pavement. Then she noticed that there were black bin bags everywhere, all over the pavement and up the wide steps, looking as if they had been hurled out on the street at random. How many were there? Twenty, thirty? All tied with big firm knots. What could they contain? Not normal rubbish surely?

Suddenly she felt a fool. Why lose the high ground, and lose his good opinion, if he had one, by storming in and screaming like a fishwife. It was so unprofessional. but she was so *angry*! And tired of being sweetness and light. And anyway why should she take it now. She was rich too!

From inside she could hear china breaking; the door was suddenly flung open and a black bag came at her head. She ducked, and it went crashing onto the pavement behind her. She pushed open the door and stood there. Richard was looking down at her, his fists clenched, just staring at her. And then she went up the steps and hit him. Just as she said she would. And fell over a bin bag into the hall.

It was then, lying there, feeling ridiculous, that she noticed that he was naked, except for the apron, and he hadn't shaved, that he looked very Irish. She'd never noticed that before.

He bent over to help her up, silently. But she shrugged him off. Then she noticed the chaos. Everywhere. Hundreds of pounds' worth of books, furniture, china, glass, lying all over the carpet.

'Richard, what are you doing?'

'I'm throwing things out, Harriet.'

'I see. Spring cleaning after your grand success? So why do it? Why pretend to be him?'

'I'm sorry. Childish wasn't it? I just felt peeved, wasn't used to someone not wanting to go out with me that's all. And each lesson I meant to tell you, and somehow, I felt it would then be work, you would change. You're very forbidding Harriet, in a way.'

'I see.'

'Don't glower like that.'

'I want to bloody glower. I feel you made me a complete fool of me. Why are you doing all this anyway?'

'I want to live differently. Jamie calls me a dickhead. He's right. And I don't need any of this junk, so it's going out.' He bent down and another bin bag flew over her head.

He sounded breathless, contrite, but Harriet successfully fought her natural urge to apologise for being so unladylike. 'Don't make me laugh, you're just making room for the next fad, the latest piece of crappy, flashy art work to flog at your next dinner party.'

'No Harriet. I'll never get the hang of the Italian subjunctive, but swear if I had met you ten years ago, I would not have made such a cock-up of my business and my life.'

There was silence between them. Out in the street a taxi drew up near the kerb and they could hear the door open and muffled curses as someone fell over.

Harriet got up, and looked at him carefully. *Impasse.* Then she walked up to him, and reaching up to his face with her hands, brought his head down to her height, and kissed him fiercely on the lips.

'Then you'd better marry me now, Richard Roger Dodger. I can afford it.'

'Marcus?'

'Marcus.'

She kissed him again. For Richard, it was Christmas in July.